"I hate being treated like an invalid!"

"You won't be one, honey," Rand said gently. "I spoke to your doctor. He said you're going to be just fine. Relax and enjoy yourself."

Dani couldn't relax, but the excitement of the airport crowded out some of her apprehension. She was actually going to Europe! In spite of the trauma connected with the trip, it was undeniably glamorous.

"What is there to see in Monte Carlo?"

"There are nightclubs and museums and fancy shops. I'll take you to see everything. I have a feeling you're going to be my first priority for the next few weeks."

"Isn't there anyone with a prior claim on your time?"

Rand was amused. "Are you referring to your grandfather or my love life?"

"I was trying to find out if you're married. I'm allergic to other people's husbands."

"You can put away your antihistamine pills. I'm free as an eagle."

And just a ⬛⬛⬛ *thought.*

Dear Reader,

Spellbinder! That's what we're striving for. The editors at Silhouette are determined to capture your imagination and win your heart with every single book we publish. Each month, six Special Editions are chosen with *you* in mind.

Our authors are our inspiration. Writers such as Nora Roberts, Tracy Sinclair, Kathleen Eagle, Carole Halston and Linda Howard—to name but a few—are masters at creating endearing characters and heartrending love stories. Their characters are everyday people—just like you and me—whose lives have been touched by love, whose dreams and desires suddenly come true!

So find a cozy, quiet place to read, and create your own special moment with a Silhouette Special Edition.

Sincerely,

The Editors
SILHOUETTE BOOKS

SE-RL-3R

TRACY SINCLAIR
Forgive and Forget

Silhouette Special Edition

Published by Silhouette Books New York

America's Publisher of Contemporary Romance

SILHOUETTE BOOKS
300 East 42nd St., New York, N.Y. 10017

ISBN: 0-373-09355-1

First Silhouette Books printing January 1987

America's Publisher of Contemporary Romance

Printed in the U.S.A.

TRACY SINCLAIR

has worked extensively as a photojournalist. She's traveled throughout North America as well as parts of the Caribbean, South America and Europe. Her name is very familiar in both Silhouette Romances and Silhouette Special Editions.

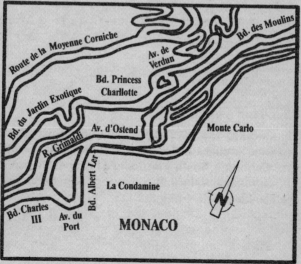

Chapter One

Cleve Barringer skimmed through the short article in the overseas edition of the *Herald Tribune*, then went back for a closer look.

It was an upbeat story, in contrast to some of the grimmer ones that predominated. The brief account gave only the pertinent details:

Dani Zanetelle, one of three survivors in the mountaintop crash of an airliner on January 26, is scheduled to be released from the hospital tomorrow. Miss Zanetelle sustained only minor injuries to her right leg. She was the least injured of the trio, who were all suffering from exposure to freezing temperatures when a search party located them after two days.

"Zanetelle," Cleve murmured. "It couldn't be." His

eyes narrowed as he reread the article. "*Dani* Zanetelle? It *has* to be!"

He got up from his desk and walked over to the big picture window that gave a breathtaking view of Monte Carlo's fabled harbor. The blue water was filled with expensive yachts, and the beach was studded with bikini-clad beauties. It was a sight to distract even an older man like Cleve, but his mind was elsewhere. He was looking into the past, at events that had happened twenty-five years ago.

There was sadness in his eyes as he turned back to his desk after long reflection, but there was excitement, too. He summoned his secretary and handed her the newspaper.

"Find out everything you can about this Dani Zanetelle. I especially want to know how old she is, and what she looks like."

The view from Dani's New York hospital room was bleak. A tree outside the window was only a black skeleton with soot-flecked snow on its bare branches. The slate gray sky threatened to dump more snow, but Dani's room looked like spring. It was filled with flowers.

"Everyone's been so kind," she told the young doctor who stood by her bedside. "I'll almost be sorry to leave here. *Almost*," she stressed, laughing.

"We'll be sorry to see you go," he assured her, gazing appreciatively at her glowing red hair and green eyes. "We don't get that many heroines in this hospital."

"I wish the newspapers hadn't called me that," she protested. "I didn't really do anything."

"That's not the way I heard it. You were the one who gathered branches and made a fire so the search plane could find you before you all died of exposure."

"I was the lucky one. The others had broken bones."

Dani's expression sobered as she relived the horror of those two days. The weight she'd lost made her eyes seem enormous in her heart-shaped face, and her pallor accentuated the vivid color of her long auburn hair. She looked fragile, and hauntingly beautiful.

"It's all over now," the doctor said gently. "You'll be fine as long as you stay off that leg for a month."

"I'll be able to go back to work after that, won't I?" she asked anxiously.

"Probably."

"But you said—! I can't afford any more time than that. I have to earn a living!"

"You're not going to earn it as an aerobics teacher unless you let those torn ligaments heal," he warned. "Just keep a good thought and try to be patient."

After the doctor left, Dani got out of bed. A streak of pain shot up her right leg when she tried to put her weight on it. The physical therapist had told her to expect that in the beginning, but it was frightening, nonetheless. Suppose the ligaments didn't heal properly? Or what if it took a lot longer than a month? She had a savings account, but it wouldn't last long. And there was no family to fall back on. What was going to happen to her? Dani felt slightly panicky as she faced an uncertain future.

Cleve Barringer frowned at the younger man lounging on a couch in the den that served as Cleve's office at home. "You took your sweet time about getting here. Didn't I leave word that I wanted you back immediately?"

The chilling tone had reduced many of his employees to quivering wrecks, but it had no effect on his second in command, Rand Stryker. It would be hard to intimidate a man who was over six feet of solid bone and muscle.

If Rand had chosen acting instead of international business, Hollywood would have cast him as an intrepid big-game hunter, or a dark, swashbuckling pirate. He had the reckless air of a man who worked hard and played hard, a man who had known and enjoyed many women and given as much pleasure as he'd received.

His unusual topaz eyes were gleaming with amusement now as he said, "Singapore isn't exactly around the corner. What's got your feathers so ruffled?"

There were few people who could be that flippant with the fabled industrialist and get away with it. Cleve tolerated it from Rand because they had almost a father-son relationship.

"I want you to go to New York," the older man said.

Rand frowned. "What about the merger with Kral Industries? They're expecting me back in Singapore."

"It can wait."

"You must be joking! The people at Kral are as skittish as a middle-aged virgin. If we don't rush them to the altar while they're in the mood, they might reconsider."

Cleve shrugged. "You win a few, you lose a few."

Rand's eyes narrowed. This wasn't the man he knew. When Cleveland J. Barringer wanted something, he went after it with no holds barred. It was a trait they shared. This new assignment must be very important.

"What do I do when I get to New York?" he asked quietly.

"I want you to find a certain girl and bring her back here." There was a small pause before Cleve added, "She's my granddaughter."

Rand didn't allow his surprise to show, although it was a shock. Which wife was responsible, he wondered.

Cleve's only child, a son, had been married three times before he wrapped his Italian sports car around a tree and killed himself and the next Mrs. Daniel Barringer.

Danny had always been a wild kid, a rich man's son in the worst sense of the word. His mother had died when he was in his early teens, and Cleve had never remarried. Would it have made a difference? Rand didn't think so. Danny was a classic example of a bad seed.

Cleve hadn't been overindulgent, nor had he been too strict. He tried to make Danny face responsibility, yet he couldn't resist getting him out of scrapes. Ultimately, Danny got himself into one fix that even his father couldn't get him out of.

Why hadn't Cleve known about his grandchild before? If it really was Danny's daughter, that is. There was a lot of money at stake here. It could very well be an elaborate hoax. Cleve would be so overjoyed to discover a long-lost grandchild that he might not want to ask questions.

Rand's generous mouth set grimly. If someone was trying to take advantage of the old man, he'd put a stop to it immediately!

"This is rather unexpected, Chief," Rand said casually. "Why didn't you know about the little girl sooner? And which wife is the mother? Danny was married three times."

"Four, actually. The first marriage took place when he was twenty. It was annulled."

"I see," Rand murmured, doing mental arithmetic. They weren't talking about a little girl, then.

"It isn't a story I'm proud of, but you'd better know the facts." The lines in Cleve's strong face deepened as he began. "When Danny was in college, I had a bout with pneumonia that almost did me in. The doctors even called him to come home. After I left the hospital I was confined to the house for a long time with a nurse to take care of me. She was a beautiful young girl named Elizabeth Zanetelle. It was one of her first nursing jobs."

Rand thought he knew what was coming. "Danny stuck around while you were convalescing?"

Cleve nodded. "It was winter break by then, or some such thing." His eyes grew even bleaker. "I suppose I should have recognized the signs, but I had been through a bad time. Besides, Elizabeth was two years older than Danny, and she seemed like a levelheaded girl. I underestimated my son," he said grimly.

"They fell in love?"

"Elizabeth did," Cleve replied tersely.

"Danny must have, too. I mean, if they got married..."

"I'd always known Danny was spoiled, but it was the first time I realized how far he'd go to get what he wanted. Part of the story is conjecture, because I had only Danny's word for it, but I can imagine what happened. Elizabeth had never met anyone like my son. The old-fashioned expression is that he swept her off her feet. But she was a girl with high moral standards. I suppose she refused to sleep with him. Danny wouldn't have been above promising marriage—and going through with it when promises weren't enough."

"It's possible he really loved her." Rand didn't believe it, but that would lessen the older man's pain.

"Hear me out," Cleve said stoically. "After he got what he wanted, Danny lost interest. He came to me and confessed what he'd done. He said he realized almost immediately that it was a terrible mistake, and he wanted the marriage annulled. When I asked if Elizabeth felt the same way, he said yes."

"They were young." Rand shrugged. "It happens."

"That's what I thought. It seemed the best thing for both of them would be to wipe the slate clean. Danny went back to college right after we talked, which also seemed like a good idea. I didn't find out until after he left that he hadn't mentioned the annulment to Elizabeth. She was blissfully happy."

Rand made a disgusted sound he tried to cover with a cough.

"When I told her Danny wanted the marriage dissolved, she didn't believe me. She was convinced I was trying to break them up because I didn't consider her good enough for my son." Cleve gave a bitter laugh. "It was the biggest favor anyone ever did for her."

"She must have found out the truth when she got in touch with Danny. She wouldn't have taken your word for it that he wanted out."

"Danny left his mess for me to clean up. He wouldn't even talk to her on the phone."

"That must have given her a clue!"

Cleve shook his head. "She merely thought I'd turned him against her. I tried to soften the blow without coming right out and admitting my son had acted like a swine. She wouldn't have believed me, anyway." He sighed heavily. "Elizabeth couldn't have known then that she was pregnant. When she found out, she never contacted me. It's taken twenty-five years to find out I'm a grandfather."

"What makes you think so?"

Cleve handed Rand the newspaper article. "Zanetelle is an unusual name. But the clincher is the girl's first name, *Dani*. Elizabeth named her after her father."

"You don't know that," Rand protested. "Maybe it was out of nostalgia for her first love."

"I had a hurried dossier assembled, with a photo sent by wire service. Everything fits. Dani is twenty-five years old. If Elizabeth married again, it would have to have been almost immediately, and her daughter would bear that husband's last name."

"Couldn't Elizabeth have taken back her maiden name?"

"Possibly," Cleve conceded. "But nobody except Danny could have fathered that child. She's the living image of my son. You'll see for yourself when you get to New York."

"Is that really necessary? Why don't you just send her a ticket?"

"I don't know how much Elizabeth told her. Suppose she made up some story—that Dani's father was a dead war hero, or some such thing. It would be cruel for the girl to find out this way. There's another reason, too. If Elizabeth told her the truth, she wouldn't come. Dani would hate me, as her mother probably has all these years."

"In that case, you want me to tell her the true story?"

"No!" Cleve's denial was explosive. "It's too late to make it up to Elizabeth, but I won't have my granddaughter's illusions destroyed. Danny is dead now. Let her remember him the way her mother described him."

"How am I supposed to get her here, then?" Rand demanded.

"You'll figure out a way. You've never let me down yet." The eyes of the two men met. "I'm sure you know how important this is to me."

Rand sighed. "Okay, I'll see what I can do."

He was filled with misgivings as he packed a suitcase. Rand wasn't worried about his ability to deliver Dani to Monte Carlo. Once she discovered her grandfather was a multimillionaire there would be no problem, he thought cynically. What bothered Rand were the possible consequences. If Cleve's story checked out and Dani really was his granddaughter, suppose she was like her father in more than just appearance?

Rand had been a silent witness to the suffering Danny had caused his father during his lifetime. Cleve was tough as nails in business, but he was very vulnerable in his personal life. He was really a lonely man. The only family Cleve had in the world were his flighty sister, Lulu, and her adopted son, Keith, who was as worthless as Danny had been.

Rand smiled grimly. This latest wrinkle would really put the fox among the chickens. Lulu had squandered her personal funds on three fortune-hunting husbands. She and Keith were dependent on Cleve, who supported them handsomely. But that didn't satisfy either of them.

As he was the only logical heir, Lulu expected Keith to inherit Cleve's money. Dani's appearance on the scene would change all that. It would almost be worth it to see their faces when they found out.

Almost. Rand's eyes turned as hard as the topaz they resembled. If Dani Zanetelle was anything like her father, they were all in for a rough time.

Dani was unaware of the change about to take place in her life. Her problems at the moment were worry and boredom.

"I'm so glad you came over," she told the friend who was visiting. "I'm going bananas stuck in this little apartment all day long."

Enid Thompson looked around the flower-filled room. "The phone's rung three times in the half hour I've been here, and those aren't backyard blossoms. I don't see that you have much to complain about."

Dani's discontented frown vanished. "You're right. I should be counting my blessings. It's being this inactive that drives me wild. All I can do is think about the bills piling up."

"Will you stop worrying? The exercise studio will take you back as soon as you're able to get around. Maybe they'd put you on the reception desk."

Dani's eyes darkened to jade. "You don't think I'll be able to take over my classes again, do you?"

"Of course I do! I only mentioned it as a stopgap so you'd have some money coming in."

"It's a little scary when there's no one but yourself to depend on," Dani said soberly.

Enid studied her friend's lovely face. "You could always get married. If I looked like you, I'd hook some rich guy and make a career out of buying things without looking at the price tags."

"No, you wouldn't. Besides, a husband is the *last* person in the world you can depend on."

"I've never known why you were so down on men. Would you like to enlighten me?"

"I'm not necessarily against men, just marriage."

"It's getting popular again. Women are even having babies."

"They've been doing it since time began. You don't need a husband for that," Dani said tersely.

The doorbell rang before Enid could answer. "I'll get it." She was speechless when she opened the door and saw the tall, rugged man looming in the hall.

Rand had decided against telephoning first. His mission was too delicate to explain over the phone, and he didn't want to risk the remote chance that Dani might refuse to see him. As he stared into Enid's dazzled eyes, Rand's face was impassive. It was wishful thinking, as he suspected. This was the woman Cleve thought looked like his son?

"You're Miss Zanetelle?"

"No," Enid admitted regretfully. She opened the door wider, gesturing toward Dani.

Rand stared at the woman on the couch, feeling excitement leap through his veins. He didn't know if it was because Cleve was right, or because she was the most exquisite woman he'd ever seen.

Dani was used to a lot of attention from men. It usually left her unmoved, but something about the way this man was looking at her made the tiny golden hairs on her arms prickle. His clothes were expertly tailored to his big body, and the thin gold wristwatch looked expensive. Everything about him spelled respectability. It should have been reassuring, but there was an underlying, primitive quality that couldn't be disguised by custom clothing or expert barbers. This man wouldn't play by the rules.

Rand walked slowly toward her without taking his eyes off her lovely face. "I'd like to talk to you, Miss Zanetelle."

His deep, slightly husky voice broke the spell. Dani realized she was being fanciful. "I suppose you're another reporter." She struggled to get up.

Enid rushed over to push her back on the cushions. "The doctor said you're not to be on your feet any more than necessary. He can do his interview while you're lying down."

"Do stay where you are," Rand urged. "I'm not a reporter, though."

Dani smiled. "If you're a salesman, you came to the wrong place. I couldn't afford even a tiny piece of the rock, and I have all the brushes I need."

"I'm not a salesman, either."

Her smile vanished. "I think you'd better tell me what you're doing here."

He hesitated, glancing at Enid. "My business is rather personal."

"You can talk in front of my friend," Dani assured him.

"If that's the way you want it. My name is Rand Stryker. I work for Cleve Barringer." He paused to see if it Would ring a bell.

Enid responded first. "Is that Cleveland J. Barringer, the fabulous millionaire who got a write-up in *Personalities* magazine?" she asked eagerly.

"That's the one," Rand said quietly. "Although it was an unauthorized article."

"I think you'd better leave," Dani said coldly. "We have nothing to discuss."

"Are you crazy?" Enid demanded. "Listen to what the man has to say. Don't you know who Cleveland Barringer is?"

"Yes, I know," Dani answered tautly.

"Your grandfather would like to see you, Miss Zanetelle." Rand's voice was very soft.

"Grandfather!" Enid exclaimed.

Dani's face was pale. "He might consider himself that. I don't."

Rand chose his words carefully. "I can understand how you feel, but there are things you don't know."

"I know he—" Dani stopped abruptly, aware of having an audience. She turned to her avidly listening friend.

"Would you mind leaving us alone, Enid? There are some things I'd like to say to Mr. Stryker privately."

Enid looked doubtfully at Rand's imposing physique. "Will you be all right?"

"I can assure you I didn't come here to harm her." He turned the full power of his smile on both women. It hit only one target.

Dani wasn't impressed. "I'll be fine," she stated grimly.

"Well, all right." Enid moved reluctantly toward the door. "I'll call you later," she said, with a last look at Rand.

Dani waited until they were alone before turning on him angrily. "You're wasting your time, Mr. Stryker. I don't have a grandfather."

"You can't deny his existence," Rand said calmly.

"I have for the past twenty-five years."

"Don't you think that's long enough to carry a grudge?"

"Is that what you call it?" Dani's eyes sparkled with green fire. "That's a pretty mild term for what I feel toward your employer. You obviously don't know what he did to my mother."

"I know the story you were told."

"And what story were *you* told? The truth is that he ruined my mother's life! My father was the only man she ever loved, and Cleve Barringer canceled her marriage as though it were a rained-out ball game!"

Rand cursed the restrictions Cleve had placed on him. "No human relationships are ever that simple. Perhaps he thought he was doing the best thing for both of them."

"Do you know how difficult it was to be an unwed mother twenty-five years ago? While Mr. Barringer was patting himself on the back for a good deed well done, my mother was putting up with insults and working twelve hours a day to support me.''

''He never knew about you! If your mother had contacted Cleve when she found out she was pregnant, everything would have been different.''

''You bet it would! He would have taken *me* away from her, too. That's why she dropped out of sight and raised me in a small town. How did he find me after all this time?''

''The plane crash. It received wide coverage, and yours is an unusual name.''

''Well, you can go back and tell Mr. Barringer that I'm doing fine—without any help from him.''

''Your grandfather is a very wealthy man, Miss Zanetelle,'' Rand said impassively. ''I'd advise you not to make any snap judgments.''

''I wouldn't take a penny from him if I were starving!''

''Perhaps your mother might feel differently after all these years. Don't you think you should discuss it with her?''

''My mother is dead, Mr. Stryker.''

''I'm sorry.'' Rand's stern face softened. Poor Elizabeth. But maybe it was better that she had never known the truth.

''You might tell my father she never stopped loving him,'' Dani said bitterly. ''I don't suppose he's interested, but it's something he should know.''

''Your father is dead, too,'' Rand said quietly.

''Oh . . . I . . . that never occurred to me.''

Rand's expression was compassionate as he looked at her stricken face. Now that it was too late, was she regretting the fact that she'd never known him? It was the one thing Rand found to be grateful for in this whole affair.

"You and your grandfather are the only ones left," he said gently. "He wants you to come and live with him."

"Never in a million years!"

Dani sprang to her feet, forgetting about her injured leg. It buckled under her, but Rand caught her before she fell. In the long instant that she was cradled against him, Dani was aware of every rippling muscle in his long body. He held her tightly in a close embrace that acquainted her intimately with his taut stomach and powerful thighs. The man was almost indecently masculine!

Dani's cheeks flamed as she struggled to free herself. "Let go of me," she muttered.

Rand lowered her gently to the couch and squatted in front of her, keeping his hands at her waist. She felt so fragile that he was afraid he'd injured her.

"Are you all right?" His deep voice revealed concern.

"I'm fine." Dani gritted her teeth. She wasn't about to be taken in by phony sympathy. "I'd like you to leave now."

Rand straightened up and looked down at her with enigmatic eyes. "Aren't you even a little bit curious about your grandfather?"

"I know the important things—that he's a cruel, ruthless man."

"Do you think it's fair to judge someone without ever meeting him?"

"I don't have to. I'm living proof of his callousness."

Rand's well-shaped mouth thinned to a straight line. "You're wrong, Miss Zanetelle. Cleve Barringer is the finest man I've ever known."

Dani smiled cynically. "He must pay you very well."

"He does, but that has nothing to do with it. If you'd just see him, you'd know what I'm talking about. Come for a visit," he urged. "You don't have to commit yourself beyond that."

"I'm sure that's what the snake said when he offered Eve the first bite of the apple," Dani remarked dryly.

Rand's white teeth gleamed in his tanned face. "Do I look like a snake?"

He looked every bit as dangerous, Dani thought. In a far different way. Although he was smiling, she sensed the steel lurking under his relaxed manner. This man would use any means to get what he wanted. His imperiousness hadn't bothered Dani, but her nerves went on red alert when he switched to charm.

"I'm not trying to have you cast out of Eden, Dani." His voice was as smooth as melted honey. "Quite the opposite. Have you ever been to Monte Carlo?"

"Is that where he lives? You want me to go to Monte Carlo?" she exclaimed incredulously.

"It's beautiful," he said seductively. "The hillsides are covered with villas that face the Mediterranean. You can look down and see your grandfather's yacht moored in the harbor."

"Stop it!" Dani said angrily. "Do you think I can be bought like the rest of his possessions? Why didn't you just offer me a check?"

"That could be arranged, too," he said unemotionally.

"You're insufferable! How can I convince you I don't want anything to do with him?"

Like a giant cat's, Rand's topaz eyes watched her. "Cleve sent me to bring you back, and that's what I intend to do."

"You'll have to kidnap me," she flared.

"It's an option," he answered calmly.

"You must be out of your mind," Dani gasped.

"No, just determined."

She set her jaw stubbornly. "It won't get you any-where."

Rand bent over her with the fluid grace of a jungle an-imal making its move. He cupped her chin in his hand and held her eyes hypnotically. She was immobilized as much by the force of his personality as she was by his re-straining hand.

"You're coming with me, one way or another," he said softly. "It would be easier if you gave in now, but I'm willing to do it the hard way if you insist. Just remember this—every person has a weak point, and I intend to find yours. Before this is over I'll know everything about you." He smiled slightly. "Perhaps even what you have for breakfast."

A cold chill raced up Dani's spine. She felt very small and vulnerable, all too aware of her human failings. But Rand didn't seem to have any. Could she hold out against such cold implacability?

Dani moistened her lips nervously. "I'm not trying to be difficult. Can't you understand my reason for refus-ing?"

"Which is? That you won't see him because you want revenge?"

"Is that so unreasonable?" she asked defensively. "After all, I'm only human."

"So is your grandfather, my dear," Rand said softly.

Dani stared at him, startled. She had grown up think-ing of Cleve Barringer as synonymous with the devil. He was never a real person to her, only a distant evil. What he had done was unforgivable, but he had suffered for it, too. He was an old man without children or grandchildren—except for her. Didn't she have a right to refuse his overtures? Wasn't it a fitting punishment? Instead of feeling triumphant, Dani felt only confused.

"Tell me about him," she said in a low voice.

"I think you'd like him if you let yourself. He's a tough old bird in business, but he's very charming socially."

"You said we're the last ones left. It's strange that he never remarried. He was only in his forties when mother nursed him through an illness."

"Perhaps he should have," Rand said somberly. "Danny was his only child."

"What was my father like?"

"You'll have to ask your grandfather that." Rand's voice was expressionless.

"I haven't said I'd come," she protested.

His slow smile warmed Dani's blood. "Are you going to make me earn my salary?"

"What do you do?" she asked curiously. "Tracking me down isn't exactly a full-time job."

"No, this was a bonus." His eyes gleamed as he looked at her delicate features. "Normally I convince people to do things they don't want to do—sell their companies, or reorganize more efficiently, things like that."

"Mr. Barringer must depend on you a great deal."

"It's mutual."

The deep feeling in his quiet words made Dani realize how devoted Rand was to her grandfather.

"Can you be ready to leave soon?" he asked.

"I . . . I have to think about it."

"Could you think fast? Cleve pulled me out of Singapore to come for you, and I really should get back."

"You wouldn't be going with me to Monte Carlo?" she asked anxiously.

His voice deepened. "Do you want me to?"

"Well, I . . . It might make it easier. I've never met my grandfather."

"Nobody could be more welcome. You'll see," Rand said gently. "I'll make all the arrangements." He glanced around the small living room. "Do you have a lease here?"

"What difference does it make?" Dani asked sharply. "I only agreed to go for a visit. I have to be back at work in a month."

"Whatever you say." Rand's voice was deceptively mild. "Suppose we plan on leaving tomorrow afternoon."

"You must be joking!" she gasped. "I can't possibly!"

"Why not?"

Everything was happening too fast for Dani. How had he maneuvered her into going to Monte Carlo? An hour ago she hadn't known of Rand Stryker's existence, and suddenly he was taking charge of her life. She tried desperately to regain control.

"I need more time," she said firmly. "I have a million things to do first."

"Tell me what they are and I'll do them for you," he offered.

"I scarcely think you could change my nail polish or shampoo my hair."

His slow smile was seductive. "I don't know how good I'd be at finger painting, but I'm sure I could wash your hair satisfactorily."

"That won't be necessary," Dani answered sharply.

There was no doubt that he spoke from experience. A vivid mental picture arose of Rand in the shower with some woman. He would have worn that same expression as the warm water rained down on their bare bodies while his long fingers massaged her scalp sensuously.

Rand didn't press the point. "What else do you have to do?"

She really couldn't think of anything. "I have to pack," she said helplessly.

"That shouldn't take more than an hour. You needn't bring too much. There are great shops in Monte Carlo."

"I can't afford to buy anything. And I don't intend to let my grandfather outfit me either," she added before Rand could suggest it. "Maybe we can put the past behind us—I really hope so, although I can't guarantee it. But I still don't want anything from him."

Rand gazed at her firmly set little chin. "I wish I'd known your mother," he said softly. "You must take after her. I think Cleve finally lucked out."

"Mother always told me I looked like my father," Dani said uncertainly.

"You got the best of both of them," he answered huskily. "I can't wait to get you to Monte Carlo! Are you sure you can't make it tomorrow? The plane doesn't leave until four."

"Well . . . I suppose I could be ready."

"Great!" He took both of her hands in his big, capable ones. "I'll pick you up at two-thirty. If there's anything you want or need, call me at the Plaza."

Dani remained on the couch for a long time after Rand had left, trying to sort out her feelings. What was she letting herself in for? How could she have agreed to fly to a foreign country with a virtual stranger? It was odd that Rand didn't seem like a stranger, though. She had found out a great deal about him in the short time they'd spent together.

He was capable of great loyalty. He was resourceful—talking her into this trip proved that! He was impatient, but he could be very gentle. It was strange to know a person's traits without really knowing anything about him.

Was he married, for instance? It didn't seem possible, given some of the suggestive things he'd said, but you never could tell. Maybe Rand's loyalty was reserved for her grandfather. Whatever his marital status was presently, it was a sure bet that he'd given pleasure to a lot of women.

Dani's skin tingled as she remembered the brief moment his rugged body had absorbed the full weight of hers. She had a sensory memory of his broad, tapering chest and muscular thighs. The accidental contact had aroused totally unexpected emotions. It warned Dani how vulnerable she would be if Rand chose to make her a target.

The sudden jangling of the telephone startled Dani out of her troubled reverie.

"Is he still there?" Enid asked breathlessly.

"No, he's gone."

"I didn't like to leave you alone with him. My God, what a macho man! What's this all about, Dani?"

Dani sighed. "It's a long story."

"Why didn't you ever tell anyone Cleveland Barringer is your grandfather? And who was that gorgeous man?"

"He works for my... for Mr. Barringer."

"Did he come to give you a million dollars, like on that television show?" Enid asked eagerly.

"No, he wants me to go to Monte Carlo."

"You're going, aren't you?"

"I guess so."

"You *guess* so!" Enid exclaimed. "I wish someone would make *me* an offer like that—preferably someone like Rand Stryker. This is the answer to all your problems."

"Or the beginning of them," Dani murmured.

Chapter Two

Dani was a bundle of nerves by the time Rand came to pick her up the next day. She had spent a sleepless night wondering if she was doing the right thing. Rand's appearance made her realize she hadn't really had a choice. From the moment he'd walked into her life, he had been in charge. Dani's overwrought nerves seemed to sense a trap snapping shut, though the hunter was smiling.

"You did a good job without my help," he remarked approvingly.

"What do you mean?"

He wound a shining lock of auburn hair around a long forefinger. "It looks beautiful."

She drew back. "Just so we understand each other, let me make something clear. You've bullied me into this trip, but that's as far as my cooperation goes."

He chuckled. "Do you think I'd seduce my employer's granddaughter?"

"I don't think you have a lot of scruples when it comes to women," she said bluntly.

"Do you always judge men so harshly?"

"I'm not as trusting as my mother was," she answered evenly.

Rand's laughter died. "I can see she'd be a good example, but I'm not like—" He stopped abruptly. "I have a taxi waiting downstairs. Are your suitcases ready to go?"

"They're in the bedroom."

While Rand went to get them, Dani limped over to the couch and picked up her purse and the cane that the doctor had instructed her to use during the first weeks of her convalescence.

When Rand returned and saw the cane he said, "Sit down while I put these in the cab. I'll come back for you."

"It's all right. I can make it if you don't walk too fast."

"Stay here," he ordered.

Dani had no intention of having her arm held like a little old lady's. After he'd gone she checked to make sure she hadn't forgotten anything, then went out to the elevator.

Rand was waiting to come back up when the doors opened at the ground floor. He gave her an annoyed look. "Didn't I tell you to wait for me?"

"I'm not used to being told what to do," she answered calmly.

"Not even when it makes sense?" He swung her into his arms.

"You don't have to carry me," she protested.

"I won't have you spending your first weeks in Monte Carlo in bed." A mischievous grin replaced his irritation. "Especially since you've made it clear that we're not going to share it."

"I'm glad you got *that* straight, anyway," she remarked crossly.

The short walk to the waiting taxi seemed endless. Dani was very aware of the shifting shoulder muscles under her arm and the hard wall of Rand's chest pressing against her breast. A body that powerful was slightly intimidating. She breathed a sigh of relief when he slid her carefully onto the leather seat of the cab.

"You're not to carry me into the airport," she warned.

He smiled. "I'll get a wheelchair if my services aren't satisfactory."

"I don't need that, either. I *hate* being treated like an invalid!" Some of Dani's secret fear crept into her voice.

"You won't be one, honey," he said gently. "I spoke to your doctor. He says you're going to be just fine."

"You talked to Dr. Campbell? Why?"

"I needed to get your records."

"But I'll be back in a few weeks at the most. You shouldn't have done that!"

He patted her hand. "Why don't you just relax and enjoy yourself?"

Dani couldn't relax, but the excitement of the airport crowded out some of her apprehension. It suddenly occurred to her that she was actually going to Europe for the very first time! In spite of the trauma connected with the trip, it was undeniably glamorous.

"What is there to see in Monte Carlo? What do you do there?"

"What *I* do, and what *you* will are probably different things," he teased.

"Please, Rand, I really want to know."

He relented when he saw the eagerness in her face. "There are nightclubs and museums and fancy shops. You'll get to see everything. One day I'll drive you along the Grande Corniche. We'll stop at the Matisse Chapel and the village of Eze, and wind up in Nice. Would you like that?"

"I thought you were going back to Singapore."

"Only for a few days, if at all." He smiled into her dazzled face. "I have a feeling you're going to be my first priority for the next few weeks."

That seemed to settle the question of his marital status, but Dani thought she'd better make sure. "Isn't there anyone with a prior claim on your time?" she asked delicately.

Rand was amused. "Are you referring to Cleve, or asking about my love life?"

Dani settled for the direct approach. "I was trying to find out if you were married. I'm allergic to other people's husbands."

"You can put away your antihistamine pills. I'm free as an eagle."

And just about as hard to tame, she thought cynically.

It wasn't until she got on the plane that Dani started to panic. The events of the past two days had driven the recent crash from her mind. The spacious first-class section was completely different from the cramped little rows of seats on the excursion flight she'd taken to Lake Placid to go skiing. But when the motors roared to life and the giant airplane taxied down the runway, all the horror came rushing back. She gripped the arms of her seat, reliving the terrible, screaming sounds of descent onto a snowcapped peak.

"We'll be serving drinks as soon as we're airborne," the pretty stewardess told Rand. "What can I get you?"

He turned to Dani. "Would you like—" Rand paused as her rigid pose registered. "We'll order later," he told the stewardess.

Dani scarcely felt Rand pry her fingers loose from the arm and warm them in his big hand. She was caught in the grip of unreasoning terror. It was useless to remind herself that thousands of planes flew millions of miles every day without mishap. She was trapped in her own personal hell.

"It's all right, honey," Rand said softly. "Nothing's going to happen."

"I know." She had to force the words past her numb lips.

"I'm sorry to have to put you through this, but it's better to get it over with right away."

Dani nodded, watching the ground disappear. Her slender body was taut, braced to take a shock. It came from an unexpected direction. Rand's hand cupped her chin and forced it gently toward him. His mouth covered hers, demanding full attention as his tongue slowly traced the closed line of her lips, coaxing them to part.

Dani's immediate impulse was to draw back, but his hand curled around her neck, immobilizing her while he gently massaged her tense muscles. His mouth continued its persuasion until her lips opened like an unfurling flower. When his tongue entered the moist opening, it gave sensual pleasure. Rand filled her entire consciousness. The sensations he was causing made her forget everything else. There was no fear, no tension, only tactile enjoyment. She made a small sound of protest when he relinquished her mouth.

He urged her head against his solid shoulder and kissed her temple. "That's what you have to think about, sweetheart, living instead of dying."

Reaction set in, and a shudder shook her slender body. "I came so close."

He pushed up the divider between them and took her in his arms. "Don't think about it, angel. From now on, I'm going to take care of you. Nothing bad will ever happen again."

Everything about him inspired confidence. Dani buried her face in Rand's neck and permitted herself the joy of letting someone else take over. She had fought her own battles for so long.

His caressing hand down her back was soothing, but eventually she returned to reality. He was a very new acquaintance, and they were in a public place.

Dani drew back self-consciously. "I'm all right now."

"There's no hurry about proving it," he teased gently as she moved back to her own seat.

"I didn't realize it would affect me like this."

"It's understandable," he said compassionately. "Just look at it this way—you've used up all your bad luck."

She sighed deeply. "I wish I could believe that."

"Aren't you on your way to one of the most glamorous spots on the Continent?"

"I didn't have much choice in the matter." She smiled wryly.

Rand was quietly reassuring. "We all want what's best for you."

Dani shook her head. "You want what's best for my grandfather."

"It's the same thing."

"And if it weren't, it wouldn't matter to you," she said wearily. "I'm just an assignment—another merger to put together."

"You don't have a very high opinion of me, do you?" he asked quietly.

Dani stared down at her intertwined fingers. "I think you're very good at what you do."

He tipped her chin up with a long forefinger. "But you don't like me much."

"I didn't say that." Her eyes darkened. "I'm just . . . wary of you."

"Which is another word for frightened." He stroked her cheek. "Don't be afraid of me, little one. I won't ever hurt you."

His feathery touch was purposely light, as though assuring her he'd be gentle. Dani wanted to believe him, but when she looked into his compelling topaz eyes, she had a feeling this man could hurt her very much.

It was four in the morning, European time, when they landed in Nice. Rand had explained that Monaco's airport couldn't accommodate the big jetliners. The easiest way to get to the small principality was to fly to Nice and then take a helicopter to Monte Carlo.

The short ride was fascinating. Dani stared out at the lights that marked small towns along the Grande Corniche. The famous highway ran along the water before turning to wind up into the mountains. To the right was the Mediterranean, black as a crushed-velvet cloak edged in swirling white ermine.

In spite of the fact that it was almost morning, a chauffeur-driven limousine was waiting when they landed. Dani was beginning to get some idea of how the very rich lived.

"We've taken everything but a bicycle to get here," she remarked as Rand helped her into the car.

"You don't get into paradise easily," he said with a smile. "You have to work for it."

"I'm not ready for paradise yet," she commented.

"You'd be surprised at how easily people get used to it." The expression on his face was sardonic.

"That sounds very cynical."

He shrugged. "I've seen the power of money."

"So have I," Dani answered grimly.

"Give him the benefit of a doubt, Dani," Rand coaxed.

"I never had any. You're just a great salesman."

"It appears I still have a selling job to do," he said lightly.

"I'm here, Rand. Please, just leave it at that."

"Okay, honey, if you say so."

Dani wasn't deceived by his ready agreement. She was beginning to know Rand well enough to realize that he played to win. All that charm and solicitude were merely expediency. He was a very dangerous adversary because he didn't care if his cause was just—only that he triumphed.

The limousine had left the beach road and was climbing a wooded hill. It was dark and quiet in the predawn. Dani caught only glimpses of shuttered houses behind flowering shrubbery that filled the air with perfume. They turned into a driveway and stopped in front of a long, low villa.

"We're home," Rand announced.

Dani wanted to protest the term "home" but she knew it would be useless, and she needed to conserve her energy. Lights shone from the house. Could her grandfather be waiting up at this hour?

As Rand led her to the front door, it opened, and a man stood in the entry. Dani hadn't known what to expect, but certainly nothing like this. She had unconsciously pictured Cleve Barringer as a stooped old curmudgeon. This man had wings of gray at his temples that made him look distinguished rather than old. He was tall and trim, with an erect carriage. There were lines in his deeply tanned face, but his dark eyes weren't the least bit faded.

Her grandfather's voice was filled with emotion as he said, "My dear child, thank you for coming."

"I . . . It was nice of you to invite me."

The polite reply was the result of good upbringing. But when Cleve advanced toward her with his arms outstretched, Dani backed away, bumping into Rand.

His arm went around her automatically. "Someday I'm going to figure out how to beat the time lag. We had our choice of leaving New York at the crack of dawn, or arriving here at this ungodly hour." Rand ushered her into the house, keeping up a steady flow of conversation to ease the tension.

Cleve silently indicated the way to a cozy sitting room furnished like an indoor garden. When Dani had recoiled from him, a look of pain crossed his face, but he didn't press the point.

The tiled entry hall they passed through had magnificent paintings on the walls and graceful statuary on marble pedestals. A hallway on the left led to the informal sitting room that was furnished in white wicker with green and white cushions. Large pots of geraniums gave splashes of color. The floodlit patio beyond sliding glass doors seemed like an extension of the room. Beyond it was an oval swimming pool that gleamed like an aquamarine set in green velvet.

There were trays of sandwiches and pastries on a round glass table that also held two electric silver urns.

"I thought you might be hungry after your long trip," Cleve said. "There's coffee and tea, too."

"Just a cup of tea will be fine," Dani answered.

Rand was inspecting the food appreciatively. "You should try some of Henri's pâté. He's the best chef in Monte Carlo."

"No, thank you," she declined. "I couldn't eat anything."

Dani's nerves were wound too tightly. It didn't seem possible that the distinguished older man acting the solicitous host was actually her grandfather—or that she was here in his house. He obviously expected her to forgive and forget, but she couldn't.

This luxurious mansion was a far cry from the modest apartment she grew up in. Just a fraction of the money he spent on limousines and first-class travel would have made all the difference in her mother's life. Dani didn't regret the advantages she might have had. What she bitterly resented was the drudgery and loneliness Cleve Barringer had inflicted on her mother.

"You're probably too tired," he was saying. "When you've finished your tea, I'll show you to your room."

Dani glanced around at the deep pile throw rugs and white silk draperies. "You have a beautiful home."

"I hope you'll enjoy it here," Cleve said with feeling.

"I'm sure it will be a memorable visit," she answered pointedly. He might as well know from the beginning that she had no intention of staying.

"I told Dani she was in for a treat," Rand interposed smoothly.

"You haven't been to Monte Carlo before?" Cleve asked.

"I've never been to Europe," she said.

He smiled. "What a pleasure it will be to show it to you."

Dani lifted her right foot slightly. "I don't get around very well yet."

"We must have a specialist look at that leg." He turned to Rand. "Did you get a transcript of her medical records?"

"That wasn't necessary," Dani protested as Rand nodded.

"I want you to have the finest care," Cleve said.

"I *have* had." She raised her chin and looked at the older man squarely.

Rand's frown came and went almost immediately. "I think it's time we all got some sleep. Tell me where you put Dani, and I'll show her to her room."

Cleve looked suddenly tired. "I had the rose room made up for her."

"Okay, I'll be right back." Rand's firm grip on her arm was the only outward indication that he was annoyed with her.

Dani's room was actually a suite, decorated completely in a delicate blush pink. The carpeting and walls, the puffy bedspread and matching draperies, even the bathroom fixtures and tiles were all the same pastel tint. Throw pillows on the king-size bed and on the love seat in the sitting area were a deeper shade that was repeated by large bowls of roses in vibrant colors of garnet and vermillion. A dressing room with built-in drawers and shelves could accommodate far more clothes than Dani possessed.

"It's gorgeous!" she gasped.

Rand's mouth formed a tight line. "I'm glad *something* meets with your approval."

"Have I complained about anything?" she demanded.

"Actions speak louder than words. If I'd known you only agreed to come here so you could get revenge, I would have left you in New York."

"This was *your* idea, not mine. I'll be happy to go home tomorrow."

"Listen to me carefully, Dani." Rand's voice was menacing in spite of its softness. "I won't let you break that old man's heart."

"He doesn't look exactly doddering to me," she scoffed, refusing to be intimidated.

"Would that have made you more compassionate? Appearances are deceiving. Cleve's been through a great deal. He just doesn't show it."

"Poor baby," Dani said witheringly. "Did his yacht spring a leak?"

Rand moved closer, glaring down at her. "I'd like to shake some sense into that stubborn little head of yours."

She stood her ground, tilting her chin to look up at him. "It might make you feel better, but it wouldn't prove a thing. So far, I haven't seen anything to make me change my mind."

Rand swore softly under his breath. "I'm damned well going to do something about that! Go to sleep, Dani."

He stalked back to the garden room where Cleve was looking out the window, his shoulders slumped.

"You have to tell her the truth about Danny," Rand said without preamble.

Cleve's momentary weakness vanished. He was his usual imperious self when he turned to face the younger man. "It's out of the question. I explained my reasons."

"They're not good enough! You saw how she acted—like you had horns and a tail."

"Then it's up to me to change her mind."

"How can you, if you don't set the record straight?"

"She's my granddaughter," Cleve answered softly. "There must be some bond between us."

Rand sighed. "It would be so much easier to tell her the truth."

"For me, not for her." Cleve's face was stern. "I won't hurt that child."

"Even if it means losing her?"

Cleve nodded. "No matter what it costs," he said bleakly. "Promise you'll respect my wishes."

"How can I agree to something I know is wrong for both of you? Dani has guts. She can stand to hear the truth."

"Promise," Cleve repeated adamantly.

"Oh, hell!" Rand stuck his fists in his pockets, tightening the fabric over his taut thighs. "All right, I promise."

Dani didn't awaken until after noon. The heavy draperies kept the room dark, but she could hear birds singing outside, and the sound of hedge clippers.

The scene that greeted her when she opened the drapes was straight off a picture postcard. Green hillsides were dotted with pastel villas, like exotic flowers tucked into the foliage. The pools scattered about reflected the cloudless blue sky overhead. Everything sparkled in the sunshine that was so bright that it illuminated each jewel-colored marking on the butterflies that fluttered through the clear air.

Dani couldn't wait to get out and go sight-seeing. Excitement filled her, in spite of the awkwardness of her situation.

Rand's tirade the night before had been totally unwarranted. Even if there had been no bitterness between her grandfather and her mother, she couldn't be expected to feel love for a total stranger. Courtesy was all she could manage. It was unfortunate if that wasn't enough for Rand. Dani didn't intend to let him ruin her vacation. She refused to admit to herself how much his criticism hurt.

Trying to put it out of her mind, she went to take a bath. A generous sprinkling of the scented powder in a crystal jar on the ledge produced a tubful of bubbles. She tied her long hair on top of her head with a ribbon, and slid down the sloping side of the sunken tub, feeling very pampered. The bath was so large and deep that it was almost like a small hot tub. Dani was relaxing in the sheer luxury of it when Rand's voice made her tense up.

"I heard the water running, so I knew you were up," he called through the closed door. "Do you need anything?"

"No, I'm fine," she called back, relieved at his friendly tone. She was learning that Rand had a quick temper that flared and then was forgotten. "I'll be out in a minute."

"No hurry. Come out to the terrace when you're ready. We'll have brunch there."

"Wait, Rand. I want to ask you what to—oh!" Her voice broke off with a sharp exclamation.

Dani had just discovered that the bubble bath had been a mistake. She couldn't get out of the tub. Supporting herself on the good leg was no problem, but then she couldn't put her weight on the bad leg after she stepped over the side. The only solution would be to hoist herself up on her arms and roll out onto the floor.

When she stopped so abruptly, Rand called urgently, "What happened? Are you all right?"

"I guess so." Dani was glad he wouldn't witness what was going to be a very ignominious exit.

He opened the door and came in with a worried expression on his face. "What do you mean, you—"

She ducked under the bubbles, but not before Rand had glimpsed her soapy little breasts with great interest.

"You have a lot of nerve barging in here!" she raged.

"I was afraid something happened to you," he said innocently.

Dani's cheeks were the color of the pink tile. "Well, now that you see nothing did, would you please leave?"

"Why did you cry out like that? Did you hurt yourself?"

She could see he wasn't going to leave until he got an explanation. "I was having trouble getting out of the tub. This dumb thing is so deep I ought to have steps and a railing," she muttered.

"Why didn't you take a shower instead?"

She gritted her teeth. "Because I like to live dangerously. Will you please go?"

"And leave you here to a wrinkled fate?" His eyes sparkled with amusement as he squatted and held out his arms. "Come on, I'll lift you out."

She backed out of his reach. "Not on your life! I'll get out by myself."

"How?"

"It won't be graceful, but I'll pull myself up and roll over the edge."

"Okay, if that's what you prefer." He pulled over a small stool and sat down on it, resting his forearms on his muscular thighs.

"What do you think you're doing?" she asked in outrage.

"Waiting to see that you get out safely," he answered calmly.

"A likely story! You know what you are? A peeping Tom!"

His teeth gleamed in a wide grin. "You aren't the first nude woman I've ever seen. And with luck, you won't be the last."

Dani knew *that* was true! His complete assurance in this intimate situation told her how familiar he was with them. Rand was probably used to frolicking in these oversize tubs. The thought of sharing this one with him brought out goose bumps on her bare skin. Dani instinctively ducked lower in the water—too low. Bubbles got in her nose and she started to sneeze.

"All right, that's enough." He reached out for her. "Modesty isn't worth that kind of discomfort."

Before she could stop him, he put his hands under her arms and lifted her out of the water as easily as if she were a child. Dani's cheeks burned as he set her on her feet and reached for a towel.

"You had no right!" she sputtered, grabbing it away from him and holding it in front of her.

He smiled at her perturbed face. "It seemed easier than arguing endlessly. You're a very stubborn young lady."

"Then I wish you wouldn't waste your time on me," she stormed. "I'm sure there are a great many women who would be delighted by your advances. I just don't happen to be one of them."

He took a shining strand of hair that had escaped from her topknot and wound it around his finger at the nape of her neck. "I haven't made any advances to you—yet. When and if I do, you'll know the difference."

His smoky voice made Dani's heart race. She was tinglingly aware of his powerful body so close to her own totally vulnerable one. His dark head was poised over hers as though he meant to kiss her. Dani knew from experience what emotions his firm mouth could provoke. She didn't want to chance another demonstration in her present state. The possibility made her take a step backward.

Rand snaked a long arm around her waist and pulled her against his solid bulk, away from the edge of the tub. "Are you determined to wind up in the hospital?" he demanded, half amused, half irritated.

Dani squirmed helplessly against him, trying to dislodge his hand from her bare waist. "It might be worth it," she said through clenched teeth. "At least I'd be safe from unwelcome passes!"

Rand's eyes narrowed dangerously. He jerked Dani's towel aside and crushed her slender body against his long length. When she started to rage at him, he stopped the furious words with his mouth. Her efforts were useless. Rand's hand wandered down her back, stroking the rounded curve of her bottom while his tongue plundered her mouth.

Little by little, Dani's struggles lessened as a creeping warmth invaded her body. His sensuous caresses were destroying her will to resist. The prickling sensation inside her was growing in intensity.

When she stopped fighting him, Rand buried his face in her tousled hair for a moment. "Beautiful Dani," he murmured huskily. He gripped her shoulders and put her firmly away, although his tawny eyes were regretful. "Now you have something to complain about. *That* was definitely a pass." He picked up the big bath towel and wrapped her in it like a cocoon, since she seemed unable to do it herself.

Reaction set in after he left. Dani sank down on the stool, clutching the towel around her heated body and trembling uncontrollably. Rand's disgraceful behavior was inexcusable, but she was even more appalled by her own response to him.

For one incomprehensible moment, she was ready to surrender completely. Did he know it? Of course he did! Rand knew everything there was to know about women. Then why hadn't he made love to her? Dani assured herself she was grateful for the reprieve, but that didn't excuse him. She would never forgive him as long as she lived!

Her anger simmered all the time she was dressing in white pants and a brief top edged with a band of lace at the hem and short sleeves. She brushed her long hair until it crackled like the banked fire it resembled. Her green eyes sparkled in their frame of sooty lashes, and the high color in her cheeks was natural.

Hunger finally drove Dani out of the bedroom—that and pride. Rand should be the one who was ashamed to face *her*!

In spite of her righteous indignation, Dani paused reluctantly at the door to the terrace. He and her grandfather were in deep conversation, arguing some point forcefully. They looked very formidable, as though each was used to getting his own way.

Dani felt a prickle of apprehension. Rand and Cleve were clearly a match for each other. Was she a match for their combined wills? Or were they going to change her life drastically, whether she liked it or not?

Cleve looked up and saw her. He smiled and both men stood up. "How nice you look, my dear. Did you sleep well?"

"Yes, thank you," she replied.

Dani limped toward the round umbrella table that was set for three. When Rand pulled out a chair for her, she slipped into it without looking at him. Her grandfather rang a small crystal bell to summon a servant.

"You must be hungry," he remarked. "Would you prefer breakfast or lunch?"

"I'll have whatever you're having," she said.

"I had a late breakfast, so I'm only having iced coffee, but the chef will make whatever you'd like. A lobster salad? Mushroom crepes? A club sandwich? How can I tempt you?"

"It's a good thing you didn't offer her an apple." Rand's deep voice was filled with amusement. "She has a violent reaction."

"Are you allergic to them?" Cleve asked.

"No, that's just his idea of a joke. He has a weird sense of humor," Dani said grimly. "I'll have some toast and coffee."

"That isn't enough," Cleve protested. "You must eat more than that. You're too thin already."

Dani couldn't help smiling. "You sound like my mother." She regretted the words as soon as they were out. They hung in the air, adding to the existing tension.

"I was sorry to hear that your mother had passed away," Cleve said quietly.

Dani looked down at her place mat. How could he be so hypocritical? Both these men were her enemies in different ways. She wished with all her heart that she'd never gone there.

A uniformed maid appeared on the patio, momentarily defusing the situation. Rand ordered a hearty breakfast of strawberries, waffles and bacon. When Dani declined his suggestion that she have the same, Cleve instructed the maid to bring several other choices. Except for the absence of menus, they might have been in a restaurant in an exclusive hotel.

"You don't have to eat anything you don't want," Cleve assured her. "But perhaps something will appeal to you."

"Henri is an artist," Rand commented. "His food looks as good as it tastes. Are you having dinner home tonight?" he asked Cleve.

"The choice is Dani's. Would you prefer to go out?" he asked her.

"Whatever's most convenient," she said. "You don't have to entertain me."

It didn't sound as though Rand intended to join them. She was relieved in one way, but that meant spending an evening alone with her grandfather.

"You're a cherished guest. I want to do whatever will make you happy." To cover his emotion, the older man turned to Rand. "Will you be dining with us this evening?"

Rand slanted an oblique look at Dani. "I really should check in at my place. I haven't unpacked from the Singapore trip yet."

"Don't you live here?" Dani asked in surprise. He had stayed there the night before.

Rand laughed. "Home is anywhere I happen to be at the moment."

"Rand has quarters here, but he also has his own apartment," Cleve explained. He exchanged a smile with the younger man. "There are times when he feels the need to get away from my company."

Dani could imagine when those times were. She glanced through her eyelashes at the very virile man lounging in his chair with one arm draped casually over the back. It tightened the silk shirt over his broad chest, outlining the lithe muscles that Dani was becoming well acquainted with.

The sun made his eyes appear golden in his tanned face. They wore an amused expression now, but she had seen how they could glow under different circumstances. He probably had a steady procession of women in and out of his apartment.

Dani's resentful speculations were interrupted by the arrival of the maid pushing a tea cart loaded with food that lived up to its description. Dani found it hard to choose. A beautiful salad was a medley of pink shrimp, green avocado and yellow-and-white deviled eggs on a bed of crisp lettuce. But the mushroom crepes in a sherry cream sauce looked delicious, too. There were also tiny finger sandwiches surrounding a compote of fresh fruit.

"How do you stay so trim?" she asked both men. "If I ate like this every day I'd be as round as a butterball."

"You could handle a few extra pounds," Rand observed.

She looked at him sharply, but his expression was innocent as he poured cream on his strawberries.

They were almost finished when there was an unexpected interruption. A beautiful blond girl joined them. She was several years younger than Dani, but she had the sophistication of a much older woman. Perhaps because she had a lot to be confident about. Her brief shorts and tiny halter revealed a magnificent, curved figure, and the smile she flashed the men showed perfect white teeth.

She put her arms around Cleve and kissed his cheek. *"Bonjour, Papa."*

Dani's face expressed her shock. Rand said Cleve had never remarried, that Dani's father had been his only child.

The girl went over to Rand and framed his face in her palms. *"Bonjour, polisson."* She kissed him on the lips. A spate of unintelligible French followed.

"I didn't get in until almost dawn," he protested, smiling up at her. "Did you want me to call you at five in the morning?"

"I'd like you to meet my granddaughter," Cleve interrupted.

"Ta petite-fille?" The blonde's face reflected the same surprise Dani had felt.

"Speak English, please," Cleve instructed. "Dani is American. This is Roxanne Duprès." He completed the introduction. "Her mother is a friend of mine."

"Who keeps hoping to change her name to Barringer." Rand grinned. "That's why Roxanne calls Cleve Papa. She hopes he'll get used to the idea."

"She knows I'm too old for her mother." Cleve had evidently voiced the sentiment before.

"It would be a perfect marriage," Roxanne protested. "She would keep you young, and you would make us rich."

Dani gasped, but Cleve merely smiled and shook his head. "After all these years, I'm a confirmed bachelor."

"You've corrupted Rand, too," Roxanne said with a pout. "He refuses to take me seriously."

Rand chuckled. "I'm not rich enough for you."

"One's first marriage should be for love." There was no sign that she was joking.

Rand glanced at Dani. "You're shocking Dani. She believes love should last."

"I'm an American. We're not as sophisticated as the French in these matters," Dani remarked lightly, although she was hurt by the cynicism in his voice and appalled by the morals of these people. If this was how the rich behaved, Dani didn't mind being poor.

Roxanne was looking at her curiously. "Where do you live? And where have you been all these years?" She wasn't troubled by the fact that it was a personal question.

"Dani and I are celebrating our reunion," Cleve answered for her, vaguely.

"Are you here to stay, or is this just a visit?" Roxanne persisted.

This time Rand took over. "Dani is recovering from an accident. She's never been to Europe before, and we're hoping to keep her amused."

"I'll be glad to help." Roxanne was sitting on the arm of Rand's chair with her arm around his shoulders. She smoothed a lock of dark hair off his forehead with caressing fingers. "We'll get someone utterly dashing for Dani, and the four of us will do the town."

There was no mistaking her meaning. Rand was her property. The amused look he was giving the curvy blonde did nothing to dispel the idea. Dani felt an unaccountable sense of loss. Then her soft mouth thinned disapprovingly. When she remembered how Rand had held *her* in his arms only an hour earlier, she wanted to tell Roxanne she was welcome to him!

Chapter Three

After lunch, Rand went back to his apartment, and Cleve took Dani sight-seeing in the chauffeur-driven limousine. Any awkwardness between them was soon dispelled by the enchanting scenery.

They drove down a winding ribbon of road to the lower slopes where tall luxury apartment buildings rose like pastel fingers pointing at the blue sky.

"The view must be heavenly. Does Rand live in one of those?" Dani asked casually.

Cleve gestured at a building with a six-sided apartment on top, completely ringed by a wide terrace. It had a three-hundred-and-sixty-degree view. "That's his penthouse."

Dani gasped. "If I lived in a place like that, I don't think I'd ever leave it."

"It's rather wasted on Rand, I'm afraid. He's rarely home. But I suppose everyone needs a place where he can get away alone."

"I don't imagine he's alone too often," Dani commented primly.

Cleve chuckled. "No, he's a handsome devil, isn't he?"

"I suppose some women might think so," she answered neutrally.

Cleve started to say something, then changed his mind. He gazed at her thoughtfully instead.

When they reached the beach, Dani forgot her annoyance. It was like something out of a movie. All the people were tanned and beautiful, the water was as smooth as blue silk, and there were two large white ships riding at anchor.

"Are those cruise ships?" she asked.

"No, private yachts."

"They're tremendous!" Dani exclaimed. "I wonder who they belong to."

"One is owned by a Greek shipping magnate. It's moored here a good part of the year. The other one is mine."

When Rand had mentioned her grandfather's yacht, Dani never imagined anything that huge. She stared at him speechlessly, trying to adjust to the magnitude of his wealth.

"I'd take you aboard, but getting in and out of the tender would be a little tricky in your present condition."

"I suppose so." Her green eyes darkened. "You don't know how much I hate being a cripple!"

"You aren't, my dear." His hand covered hers. "This is only temporary. The doctor says you're going to be fine."

"He might just be saying that so I don't get discouraged."

"There would be no reason for him to lie to *me*."

"You spoke to Dr. Campbell?" she asked uncertainly.

Cleve nodded. "I called to find out what the situation was. I wanted to make sure you would get the best care, in case lengthy treatments were indicated. That's when he told me all you needed was rest."

"You didn't really expect me to come here, did you?" she asked slowly.

"I could only hope. But it wouldn't have made any difference. You're my granddaughter. I want to take care of you."

That was precisely what Dani *didn't* want. She carefully removed her hand. "You don't owe me anything," she said coolly.

"We both know that isn't true," he answered quietly.

"No, your debt was to my mother, and you can never repay that." Dani tried to steel herself against the pain in the older man's face, but it was useless. No matter how much he deserved it, she felt rotten about hurting him. "Why did you do it?" The anguished words burst out of her. "Didn't you know how desperately they loved each other?"

Cleve's sigh came from the depths of his soul. "There was so much I didn't know then. I'm sure you won't believe this, but I had Elizabeth's welfare in mind as well as my son's. She was so young," he said sadly.

Dani refused to accept that. "My mother was earning her own living. That proved she was mature enough to get married."

"Unfortunately, my son wasn't."

Dani was too impassioned to see the disgust in her grandfather's eyes. "She wouldn't have let him drop out of school, if that's what you were worried about! Why don't you admit she wasn't good enough for you?"

"No, Dani." Cleve's voice was stern, the placating note gone. His eyes burned into hers, commanding her to believe him. "That's not true. Think whatever else you like about me, but not that."

The unmistakable ring of truth in his words shook Dani's confidence. "Then *why?* Give me a reason," she pleaded.

His face became shuttered. "It doesn't matter now. As you pointed out, I can never make it up to your mother."

It was a terrible punishment. Dani couldn't help feeling sorry for him. By trying to play God, he had wound up with nothing—except money. It wasn't surprising that he thought it could buy anything, since money was a powerful lure. Roxanne had been quite frank about wanting it. Probably everyone Cleve knew wanted something from him.

Everyone except Rand. His devotion to the older man seemed genuine. Or was it only an act? Rand was obviously paid very well. That penthouse alone must cost a fortune. But suppose he wanted more? What if he planned to take over the empire after her grandfather's death? Dani had seen Rand's single-minded determination. Was all that solicitude merely the mask of a patient tiger?

Dani felt as though she'd stepped into a web of intrigue. There was no one she could trust.

"Would you like to go home?" Cleve broke the silence that had fallen between them.

"If you don't mind. I'm a little tired."

"It's the time difference. It might be best if we dined at home this evening."

Dani dreaded having dinner alone with her grandfather. What would they talk about? "Do you think... Will Rand be joining us?"

"Do you want him to?"

"I don't want you to order a command performance," she said hesitantly.

Cleve's smile relieved the strain on his face. "You don't know Rand very well. No one orders him to do anything."

"Not even you?" she asked doubtfully.

"No, Rand and I discuss things—sometimes rather loudly." Cleve chuckled.

"You think a lot of him, don't you?"

"He's like a son to me." There was pride in the older man's voice.

"Was my father like Rand?" Dani asked curiously.

"No." Cleve glanced out of the window. "Here we are at home. I think you should take a little rest now."

Dani found that she did feel tired, although she'd slept late. It was probably mental fatigue more than physical. The confrontation with her grandfather had been upsetting but inevitable. They hadn't resolved anything, though.

Dani had the nagging feeling that he was keeping something from her. His reluctance to talk about her father was strange, too. Or was she just imagining that?

She turned back the quilted silk bedspread before lying down on the bed with a book. There was no point in puzzling over questions that no one would answer.

* * *

Cleve had recognized Rand's red Ferrari in the driveway. He found the younger man sitting behind the big desk in the den.

Rand looked up and smiled, continuing his phone conversation. "It sounds promising. Send me the figures by courier, and I'll get back to you."

He started to get up, but Cleve waved him back and took a seat on the couch facing the desk.

"That was Stevens," Rand said. "The Amsterdam deal sounds like a bonanza."

"That's good," Cleve answered absently.

Rand took a closer look at him. "Is something wrong, Chief?"

The older man's mouth twisted sardonically. "What could be wrong? We're going to make another million dollars, aren't we?"

Rand settled against the high back leather chair. "It's Dani, isn't it?" he asked quietly.

Cleve sighed heavily. "I've never been a quitter—you know that. When people told me something was impossible, I considered it a challenge. But that child defeats me. I don't think I'll ever win her over."

"You know the solution."

"And you know I'll never take it." Strong wills clashed as the two men locked eyes.

Rand was the one to back down. "What happened today?"

"She asked questions."

"You knew she would. How did you expect to field them?"

Cleve's mouth twisted in the semblance of a smile. "I guess I hoped she'd see how much she meant to me and decide I wasn't all bad."

"Poignant, but scarcely realistic," Rand observed dryly.

"You're right. She can't even stand to be alone with me. She asked if you'd have dinner with us."

Rand started to laugh. "She *must* be desperate!"

Cleve frowned. "Did you two argue? She acted rather strange when your name came up."

Rand looked amused. "I'm not surprised."

"You haven't been up to your old tricks with my granddaughter, have you?" Cleve asked ominously.

"That depends on what you mean," Rand answered lightly. "I've tried to be charming."

"Dani's no match for you, Rand. I wouldn't like to think you'd take advantage of her."

Rand's mockery vanished. "I thought you knew me better than that, Chief."

Cleve was satisfied by what he saw in the other man's face. "I shouldn't even have asked. It's just that she's so...defenseless, somehow, in spite of her defiant attitude. I want to protect her from the world, but she won't let me get close to her," he said sadly.

"Give her time. This is only her first day. You can't expect an instant miracle."

"I'd settle for a small wonder," Cleve muttered.

"She's excited about being here. I know that. If Dani started to enjoy herself, she'd relax."

"Possibly, but how do I accomplish that?"

"This is a glamorous town. Take her gambling at the casino, introduce her to celebrities, keep her too busy to ask questions."

Cleve stared speculatively at him. Rand had unbuttoned his silk shirt halfway down and rolled up his sleeves. His muscled forearms and the glimpse of dark curling hair on his broad chest made him look very virile.

"There might be another way," Cleve murmured almost inaudibly. "She doesn't enjoy my company. Why don't you entertain her for me?"

Rand's eyes narrowed dangerously. "I wasn't hired as a paid escort."

"That's a ridiculous thing to say! I'm only asking you to do me a favor."

"You indicated Dani was off limits."

"It was just a misunderstanding," Cleve said placatingly.

"She's a very beautiful girl, and I'm a normal male. Don't push your luck too far, Cleve."

"I trust you."

"What am I, the palace eunuch?" Rand demanded angrily. "Why would you throw us together after I've admitted I'm attracted to her?"

"A mild flirtation wouldn't be the end of the world," Cleve remarked innocently.

Rand shoved his chair back so violently that the casters screeched protestingly. His flattened palms on the desk supported his weight as he glared at the older man. "Dani was right about you. You *are* a devil! You want me to seduce that innocent girl just so she'll remain here. What the hell kind of man do you think I am, anyway?"

"A very fine one," Cleve answered quietly. "I wish you were my son."

Rand swore violently. "Dammit, Cleve, don't try to get around me! I know what a pirate you are."

"I'll admit I'm a tough competitor, but have you ever known me to do anything dishonorable?"

"Not until now," Rand growled.

"Especially not now. I'll grant you it would give me the greatest joy if you and Dani fell in love and got married, but I realize I have no control over that."

"Well, at least you expect me to marry her," Rand said with heavy humor.

"All I want you to do is help me through the biggest crisis of my life. If I can't establish some kind of rapport with Dani, I might lose her forever." The lines in Cleve's face deepened. "Do you realize her children will be my great-grandchildren? How could I stand to be cut off from them?"

Rand sighed deeply. "Okay, you win—as usual. I'll give her the grand tour. But no romance," he stated firmly.

"Whatever you say." Cleve was uncharacteristically meek.

"I suppose you want me to start tomorrow."

"I was hoping you'd have dinner with us tonight."

"I might as well," Rand said disgustedly. "Before you get yourself in any deeper and make my job impossible."

Cleve hid a smile. Rand couldn't be made to do anything he really didn't want to do. For the first time since Dani had arrived, Cleve allowed himself to hope.

"It would be a good idea to invite Lulu and Keith to dinner, also," Rand was saying.

Cleve's smile vanished. "Why on earth would I do a thing like that?"

"Lulu is Dani's great-aunt, and Keith is her second cousin."

"I was hoping to keep it a secret," Cleve remarked dryly.

"That's the point—you can't. Roxanne has spread the news of Dani's arrival all over town by now. If I know

Lulu, she's already in hysterics, and Keith is having an anxiety attack. All that nice money flying out the window,'' Rand said mockingly.

"You don't honestly think they're my beneficiaries?'' Cleve's mouth thinned with disgust. "Keith would bankrupt the corporation in a year, and my sister would spend her share buying more titled husbands. I think she needs a baron to complete her list.''

"They're still going to look Dani over carefully, so it might as well be here at home instead of someplace like a party.''

"I suppose you're right.'' Cleve's eyes glinted dangerously. "They'd better not try to give her a bad time, though.''

Rand laughed. "You could always cut off their allowances.''

"Don't think I wouldn't!''

The phone shrilled and Rand answered it. "Well, speak of the devil.'' He grinned broadly. "We were just talking about you, Lulu.''

Cleve waved negatively, mouthing instructions.

"He isn't available at the moment,'' Rand said smoothly. He shuffled some papers around the desk as he listened. "Yes, your messages are here, but Cleve was out this afternoon.'' After a pause he continued, "Yes, it's true. Cleve wants you to meet her. He told me to ask you and Keith for dinner tonight.''

"I take it they accepted,'' Cleve remarked acidly, after Rand hung up.

"The whole Sixth Army couldn't keep them away.'' Rand grinned.

Cleve massaged his taut neck muscles. "It promises to be an enchanting evening.''

"Interesting, anyway.''

"You must love a trip to the dentist," Cleve replied sarcastically. "I think I'll take a nap."

"Good idea. I have to go home for a bit, but I'll be back for cocktails at seven-thirty."

Rand made a few phone calls first, and then stuffed some papers in his briefcase. When he glanced out of the window as he was ready to leave, he saw Dani standing on the terrace. She looked so dejected that his heart twisted. Poor little kid. She wasn't having a very good time, but he'd take care of that.

Rand slid open the glass door and walked out to join Dani. "Cleve tells me you went sight-seeing today. What do you think of Monte Carlo?"

"It's beautiful," she answered politely.

"Did you see the palace and the casino? Those are the most famous landmarks."

"No, we...we weren't out very long."

"Your grandfather didn't want to tire you."

"That was probably it." Dani looked away. Rand obviously didn't know they'd argued.

"Tomorrow I'll take you to see the changing of the guard, and then we'll have lunch and take a flutter at the casino. Would you like that?"

"Very much!" The droop was gone from the corners of her mouth. "But don't you have to work?"

"Things are slow right now," he lied. "I need some time off, anyway. My suitcases still aren't unpacked."

"I thought you went home this afternoon to do that."

"I did, but I got sidetracked."

"I see," she remarked distantly. Dani had a sudden, unwelcome picture of Rand and Roxanne, their superb bodies intertwined.

He laughed. "You have a very sexy imagination. As a matter of fact, I stopped at the office and never made it home."

"You don't have to explain to me," she mumbled, feeling obscurely better.

"No, I don't, but I couldn't bear the thought of your wasting all that imagination on an empty apartment."

Dani couldn't look at him. "Grandfather pointed out your apartment. It's beautiful. You must have a magnificent view."

"It was one of the things that sold me on the place—that and the bathtub," he teased. "Would you like to see it? The apartment, I mean. I'm on my way home."

"I'd like to, but then you'd have to bring me all the way back."

"I'm coming here for dinner tonight. Your great-aunt and her son will be here, too."

"What are they like?" Dani asked as Rand led her out to the car.

"You'll see for yourself," he answered noncommittally.

"It's so strange to have a great-aunt whose name I don't even know."

Rand started the car and drove out of the driveway. "Let's see if I can remember them all. I'm not sure of the order, but it's something like Lulu Von Neustein La Fromard Fontinelli. Everyone thought she married two with the same last initial so she wouldn't have to change the monogram on the towels."

"I don't mean to be disrespectful, but it sounds like a list of imported cheeses."

"Very perceptive. The gentlemen were definitely imported—also cheesy—and Lulu's always been considered crackers."

"Which one is she married to now?"

"None of the above."

"Well, which one is the father of her son?"

"Also none of the aforementioned, although Keith goes by the name of Von Neustein. He was adopted when Lulu felt a brief flutter of maternal instinct. She wasn't sufficiently carried away to go through all the inconvenience herself, however."

"You don't care much for them, do you?" Dani asked slowly.

"I shouldn't try to influence you." Rand was belatedly remorseful.

"Why don't you like them?" Dani persisted.

"It isn't important. I'll let you form your own opinions."

She was slightly uneasy. Wasn't anyone normal in this crazy world she'd stumbled into?

Dani forgot her anxieties when Rand opened the door of his penthouse. The huge living room had a circular arrangement of couches around a square glass-topped table that held fascinating ornaments. Scattered around the room were other artifacts gathered during his world travels.

Dani didn't know where to look first. The interior was as stunning as the exterior, which was dazzling. Thick white carpeting muffled her footsteps as she walked to the windows where a view of the city spread out beyond the broad terrace.

"I don't know what to say. It's just magnificent," she said simply.

He grinned mischievously. "You haven't seen the bathtub yet."

Rand's frequent references to Dani's mishap in the tub had blunted the trauma. While she couldn't be quite as amused by it as he, it no longer caused acute embarrassment. Was that why he did it, she wondered suddenly. She'd thought it was out of deviltry, but it might be an act of kindness. He was a very complex man.

"I don't know what this fixation is you people have with bathtubs," she said lightly.

"You'll have to admit they give a great deal of enjoyment."

"Your activities must be different than mine."

"I give lessons," he offered cheerfully.

It struck a nerve. "That's what I used to do," Dani said soberly.

"Hey, you're not going to get serious on me, are you?" Rand put a comforting arm around her shoulders.

"No." She gave him a rueful smile. "It was just my way of reminding you that I can't defend myself if you got me up here for ulterior purposes."

He turned her to face him. Linking his arms loosely around her neck, he looked down at her. "You don't ever have to worry about that. I'll always be completely aboveboard with you."

"If you say so." Dani wasn't foolish enough to believe him.

"I'll prove it. Right now I'd like very much to kiss you."

His long fingers trailed down her cheek to trace the shape of her mouth. It was a very sensuous feeling. By the essentially innocent gesture, Rand had made her remember the touch of his firm lips, the leaping excitement of his tongue. She shivered slightly.

"Do you want me to kiss you, Dani?" His husky voice fueled the slow fire that was beginning to smolder.

"No!" She clung tightly to her self-control.

"You're not being as honest with me as I am with you," he chided gently. His golden eyes gazed deeply into hers. "Tell me the truth. Do you want me to kiss you?"

She couldn't look at him and deny it. "Yes," she whispered, lifting her face.

"You see how easy it is to be honest?" He kissed her lowered eyelids. "From now on we know we can trust each other."

Dani had put her hands against his chest defensively. Her rigid arms relaxed now as she was drugged by the sound of his voice, the tangy male scent of his skin. Her palms started to move unconsciously over his shirtfront, enjoying the warm, firm feeling of his lean torso.

A startled look replaced Rand's indulgent expression, and his hands gripped her waist, pressing into the bare skin exposed by her hiked-up overblouse.

As she swayed toward him, Rand's arms went around her automatically, drawing her tightly against his hard frame. His mouth covered hers, moving sensually, savoringly. When Dani ran her fingers through his hair, uttering a tiny sound, Rand's kiss became more urgent.

His hands caressed her back, then moved lower to guide her body to the juncture of his taut thighs. She clasped her arms around his neck and clung to him as desire raced through her like wildfire.

"My sweet, passionate Dani," he murmured, raining kisses over her rapt face. "You're so perfect, every exquisite inch of you."

His hand cupped her breast, creating ripples of pleasure. Dani dimly realized that she should stop him, but when his fingertips gently circled her sensitive nipple, she could only murmur his name over and over.

"Do you like that, darling?" His husky voice was low and vibrant. "Tell me how to please you. I want to bring you more pleasure than you've ever had before."

He kissed the hollow in her throat while he lifted the hem of her brief top. Lowering his head, he touched the tip of his tongue to the coral peak that strained against her thin lace bra. The molten sensation made her move restlessly. Without thinking, Dani shifted her weight to her right side. She cried out in pain as her leg gave way under her.

"Darling, what is it? Did I hurt you?" Rand caught her as she sagged.

"It's my leg," she whispered.

He stared at her as the passion receded from his face. "Oh, God, what did I almost do?" He lifted her in his arms and held her tightly.

As sanity returned, Dani felt waves of shame wash over her. She buried her face in Rand's shoulder. When he put her tenderly down on the couch and sat beside her, she turned her head away and hid her face in the cushions.

Rand gently forced her chin around. "I won't let you make too much of this."

Dani's eyelashes were feathery fans on her flushed cheeks. "Just take me home." The agonized words were scarcely audible.

"Not until we talk about it first," he said firmly. "What just happened was perfectly normal."

Her lashes flew open. "How can you say that? We almost—"

"Made love," he finished for her when she stopped. "Because we're very attracted to each other. I'm glad we didn't, since you'd have regretted it."

"It would have been a mistake," she said in a small voice.

"As long as you think so." He stroked her cheek caressingly. "You're very lovely and I want you very much, but not if you're going to be sorry afterward."

"How could I help but be? We hardly know each other," she murmured.

Rand laughed. "It would have been a great way to get acquainted." His laughter faded as he looked deeply into her eyes. "I don't know if we'll ever be lovers, Dani, but I want you to consider me your friend. What I said about honesty between us still goes." He got to his feet, smiling. "But that's how this whole thing got started. I think we'd better save any further discussions like this for public places. Come on, I'll take you home."

Rand's insistence on bringing everything out in the open had cleared the air. Dani no longer suffered from crushing humiliation. He had such a healthy attitude toward sex. It existed, so why try to pretend it didn't?

As she looked at his strong profile in the car going back to the villa, Dani wondered wistfully what it would have been like. There was no doubt that Rand would be a marvelous lover. She sighed unconsciously.

Dani changed to a simple pink silk dress with a square neckline. The pale color made her auburn hair seem to glow like wine, and the strand of imitation pearls that circled the base of her throat accentuated the creaminess of her skin. A pair of high-heeled pink sandals completed the outfit. Dani teetered on them gingerly because her leg was still sending out twinges.

When she reached the living room where Rand had told her they'd meet for cocktails, Dani discovered the men had on dinner jackets. They both looked very handsome. Rand's white coat accentuated his deep tan, and her grandfather was distinguished enough to have been an ambassador.

"I didn't realize it was a formal party," she said, faltering.

"You look perfectly charming, my dear," Cleve assured her.

"I'll drink to that." Rand held up his highball glass while his tawny eyes went over her slender figure admiringly. "But I know how women are. If it's going to make you uncomfortable, why don't you go in and change?"

"I don't have anything dressier," she said simply.

"No problem," Rand said. "We'll include a shopping spree in our excursion tomorrow."

"I doubt if I could afford the prices here," she remarked.

"It would give me great pleasure to buy you a new wardrobe," Cleve offered.

"No, thank you," Dani declined firmly.

"Better take him up on it," Rand advised. "You're right about the prices in Monte Carlo."

She shook her head. "I'll just have to struggle by on what I brought with me."

A look of irritation crossed Rand's face. "You're being ridiculous!"

"I don't happen to think so," she answered coldly.

"There's a difference between independence and stubbornness." They glared at each other, neither giving an inch.

"I understand how Dani feels," Cleve said gently.

"It would be nice if she accorded you the same courtesy," Rand muttered.

"That's enough!" Cleve said sharply.

A muscle jerked at the side of Rand's square jaw. Although he lapsed into silence, the brooding look he turned on Dani was definitely annoyed.

Was this the man who was so tenderly understanding just a few hours ago? The one who promised to be her friend? All he really felt for her was sexual attraction, Dani thought bitterly. In any conflict, Rand would be on her grandfather's side. It was something to remember.

Fortunately the doorbell rang and a servant ushered in Cleve's sister and nephew, providing a diversion.

Dani had no idea what to expect. She looked at the newcomers curiously. They were a glittering pair. Lulu was a woman of indeterminate age. Perfectly arranged blond hair framed a smooth, vapidly pretty face, but her neck added years to Dani's first estimate. She had to be middle-aged, yet her figure didn't show it. She was an impressive example of what skillful plastic surgeons, masseuses and couturiers could accomplish—also money. The beaded dress she wore cost thousands.

"I'd like you to meet your great-aunt," Cleve said, making the introductions.

"So you're Cleve's grandchild. It doesn't seem possible." Lulu's hard eyes inspected her thoroughly, pausing speculatively at the strand of pearls around Dani's neck. She dismissed them immediately as being imitation.

"And this is Keith," Cleve was continuing.

Lulu's son was not only a very attractive man, but he was also a lot friendlier than his mother. His inspection was as thorough, but the conclusions were more favorable. His blue eyes reflected frank admiration. Dani couldn't help returning the compliment. The combination of sun-bleached blond hair and light eyes in a tanned face was outstanding. Like his mother's, Keith's age was hard to pinpoint, but he was somewhere in his thirties.

He took Dani's hand in both of his, squeezing it slightly as he looked down at her with a smile. "We aren't really blood relatives, you know."

"I wondered how long it would take you to mention it," Rand said sardonically.

The look that passed between the two men was hostile. Dani realized there was no love lost on Keith's part, either.

"Which one of Daniel's wives was your mother?" Lulu asked, accepting a glass of champagne.

"His first one," Dani answered evenly.

Lulu frowned. "I don't remember Margo having any children."

"Dani's mother was named Elizabeth," Cleve said. "She and Danny were married while he was in college."

Lulu's eyes narrowed suspiciously. "According to this girl?"

"This girl happens to be my grandchild." Cleve's soft voice didn't conceal the steel underneath. "You will treat her as such."

Lulu did a nervous turnaround. "Well, of course! No offense intended, brother dear. It's just such a surprise! I mean, we had no idea."

"You're babbling, Mother." Keith's voice carried a note of warning. He turned to Dani with a smile. "We couldn't be more delighted to welcome you into our little family. I hope you'll consider me your kissing cousin."

Dani smiled back. "I'm having a little trouble adjusting to the idea that I have *any* cousins."

"I'm sure the surprise was universal." The remark was a conventional one, but there was a mischievous gleam in Rand's eyes.

"How could you keep this adorable girl a secret all these years?" Lulu asked Cleve, trying to make amends. Her arch tone was meant to imply that she accepted Dani's claim unhesitatingly.

"Unfortunately, we never got to know each other. Her mother moved away when Dani was only a baby," Cleve answered vaguely. "It was just a stroke of luck that I happened to see her name in the paper."

Lulu slanted a narrowed glance at Dani. "I suppose your mother must have remarried and you took your stepfather's last name. So clever of you to have known she was Danny's child, Cleve." Lulu knew she was on thin ice, but there was too much at stake not to risk raising the question.

"Can you look at her and doubt it?" he asked.

Dani flushed as they all stared at her. "Mother always said that, but I've never even seen a picture of him."

Lulu's raised eyebrows expressed astonishment. "You never met your father?"

"No. Their marriage was... They weren't married very long," Dani concluded awkwardly. Lulu obviously didn't know the wretched story, and Dani preferred to keep it that way.

Rand came to her rescue. "Is everyone ready for dinner? I can't wait to see what Henri cooked up for us tonight." He stood up and held out his hand to Dani.

The dining room table looked like a picture in an expensive magazine. It was beautifully set with magnificent crimson-and-gold service plates flanked by gold flatware. The same color scheme was echoed by the centerpiece of fringed red tulips with yellow centers.

At first Dani was too tense to fully appreciate the elegant surroundings. She kept anticipating more awkward questions. But Rand adroitly steered the conversation away from her. After a while she was able to relax and enjoy the excellent food.

They were having coffee when the maid came in to say there was a long-distance call for Cleve.

He instructed her to take a message, but Rand said, "That might be Stevens. I told him to phone if there were any new developments on the Amsterdam deal, no matter what time it was."

"You'd better come with me, then. I must apologize, ladies," Cleve said. "We'll make this as brief as possible."

"We understand," Lulu assured him. "Business before pleasure." She waited until they left the room before turning to Dani with hard purpose masked behind an innocent manner. "They're both such high-powered men, aren't they?"

"Yes, they are." Dani could certainly agree with that statement.

"It must have been a surprise to discover your grandfather is one of the wealthiest men in the world," Keith observed.

"I always knew that," Dani said quietly.

"And you never tried to get in touch with him?" Keith asked incredulously.

"No."

"What changed your mind?" Lulu demanded.

"I didn't. Grandfather contacted me. He asked me to come for a visit."

"A visit?" Keith asked. "You don't intend to live here?"

"No, I'm just staying for a few weeks," Dani said reluctantly.

There was something unpleasant about the avid way they were cross-examining her. It was hurried, as though they wanted to find out all they could while they had her alone.

"That isn't much time," Keith said, exchanging a glance with his mother.

When the two men returned, Rand said to Dani, "I'm afraid our sight-seeing trip is off for tomorrow, honey. I have to fly to Amsterdam. But I'll make it up to you."

"No problem," Keith said smoothly. "I'll be glad to pinch-hit. Will you accept me as an eager substitute, cousin?"

There was nothing else she could do, although Dani was terribly disappointed. She hadn't realized until then how much she'd been looking forward to being alone with Rand for a whole day. He bullied her and argued with her. They didn't agree on a single thing, but he made life exciting.

"It's very kind of you to offer," she told Keith politely.

"I welcome the opportunity," he answered with satisfaction. "It will give us a chance to get acquainted. I have a feeling this is going to be the start of a beautiful relationship."

The expressions of the other two men were enigmatic.

Chapter Four

Keith called for Dani the next day at one o'clock. After she'd resigned herself to the change of escorts, Dani looked forward to the day with anticipation. There was so much she wanted to see.

Keith was very handsome in white slacks and a light-weight navy sport jacket. Instead of a tie, he wore a navy-and-white polka-dot ascot knotted in the open neck of his white silk shirt. His outfit was so dauntingly elegant that Dani had second thoughts about the simple khaki shirt dress and low-heeled sandals she'd thought would be appropriate for sight-seeing.

"Maybe I should change," she said hesitantly.

"Not at all. You look charming," he assured her.

Dani sighed. "I never seem to wear the right thing."

"A girl as beautiful as you doesn't have to worry." His eyes glittered. "You could wear anything and get away with it."

It was rather a left-handed compliment, but Dani knew he meant well. She decided not to let unimportant things spoil the day.

"Are we going to see the changing of the guard?" she asked eagerly as Keith led her outside. A two-tone, black-and-gold Cadillac convertible was parked in the circular drive.

"That sort of thing is for tourists," he said disparagingly as he helped her into the car.

"That's what I am," she pointed out.

"Not if you stick with me." He patted her hand. "I'm going to show you the *real* Monte Carlo."

"I really do want to see the changing of the guard," she said tentatively.

"It's too late today, anyway." Keith looked at his watch, taking his eyes off the curving mountain road they were traveling down. "The show goes on before noon, I think. Believe me, you wouldn't like it. The whole square is a clutter of tacky people with cameras draped around their necks."

"It sounds as though you don't care much for tourists. Aren't they Monaco's leading industry?"

He shrugged. "I suppose they're a necessary evil, especially for the tradespeople. To the rest of us, they're just a bloody nuisance."

Dani frowned. "That doesn't sound very friendly."

He glanced sideways at her disapproving face. "I was just joking. I have the reputation of being a very friendly fellow." He smiled fondly at her, covering her hand where it rested on the seat next to him.

Keith was taking the curves at a rather alarming speed. "This road is very twisty," Dani remarked. "Don't you think you should use both hands?"

"Whatever you say, little cousin." He did as she suggested.

"Where are we going?"

"I thought we'd have lunch first at a place called Chez d'Or. It hasn't been open long enough to get written up in the guidebooks, so it isn't overrun by the camera crowd. I think you'll like it."

"If the food is anything like Henri's, I'll love it! Isn't he marvelous?"

"He should be. Uncle Cleve pays him a fortune. But that's what money's for, isn't it? To spend."

"I wouldn't know." Dani laughed. "I've never had any."

"That's all changed now. You're an heiress."

Her first impulse was to deny it. She would never take a penny of Barringer money. Yet if she told Keith that, he'd want to know why.

"You certainly picked the right family to be born into," he was continuing lightly. "Have you thought about what you're going to do with all those millions?"

"That's called counting your chickens before they're hatched." Dani tried to match his light tone, although the subject was distasteful.

"I wish *I* could be as sure of everything in life." There was a sudden bitter note in Keith's voice. "Uncle Cleve idolizes you."

"He barely knows me," she protested. "It's just that I remind him of his son."

"Is that what you think?" Keith slanted her an amused glance.

"Everyone says I look like my father," Dani said uncertainly.

"You do. Even Mother had to admit that." His expression was sardonic.

"You knew him. What was he like?"

"Danny? He was a great guy."

It was the first time anyone had ever answered her question. "Tell me about him," Dani said eagerly.

"What would you like to know?" Before she could reply, Keith pulled up in front of a restaurant. "Here we are, safe and sound."

There was no time to continue the conversation. A parking attendant opened the door for Dani and helped her out of the car. Then Keith led her inside where they were met by an obsequious maître d'.

"*Bonjour, Monsieur Von Neustein.* Your table is ready and I have your favorite wine chilling."

"Excellent, Armand," Keith replied.

Instead of showing them to their table, the man glanced uneasily at Dani. Lowering his voice he said, "I think you should know that Mrs. Stanhope made a reservation for two o'clock."

Keith's smile was replaced by a frown as he, too, glanced at Dani. Then his expression cleared. "No problem, Armand. We'll sit down now."

The room was so dark that Dani's eyes were having trouble adjusting to the gloom. The white tablecloths were ghostly blurs faintly illuminated by small rose-shaded lamps. There were tall windows along one wall, but velvet draperies covered them almost completely, letting in just a glimmer of light. This was clearly not one of the restaurants that took advantage of Monte Carlo's fantastic views. Keith was safe, she thought with amusement. Chez d'Or wasn't one of the spots that would catch on with the tourists.

"This looks like a place where men bring women they don't want to be seen with," Dani commented as she proceeded cautiously toward their table.

"Why would you say a thing like that?" Keith asked sharply.

She laughed. "It's so dark no one could recognize you."

"We can go somewhere else if you'd rather." He took her arm and started to lead her back to the entry.

Dani realized belatedly that she hadn't been very polite. Keith had been so proud of his "in" place. "I was just joking." When he still hesitated, she said firmly, "I wouldn't think of leaving."

"May I bring you a cocktail?" a waiter asked soon after they sat down.

"Not for me, thanks," Dani declined. "It makes me sleepy to drink in the afternoon."

"Then I'll just have to think of some stimulating way to keep you awake," Keith murmured.

Was she imagining the suggestive note in his voice? Dani decided to ignore it. "What are we going to do after lunch?"

"It depends on what time it is. French food has to be savored slowly to appreciate the delicate nuances of the sauces."

A feeling of frustration began to build in her. Spending the day in a dark restaurant was a total waste of time. Wasn't she *ever* going to see Monte Carlo?

"I've heard a lot about the Oceanographic Museum," Dani persisted. "Could we go there?"

"I have something much more intriguing in mind," he answered with a slow smile.

"Like what?" she asked warily.

"It's a surprise, but I guarantee to keep you amused." He reached over and took her hand.

Dani pulled it away. "I think you'd better tell me. We seem to be on different wavelengths," she said evenly.

Keith was instantly attuned to her change of mood. "I didn't realize you had your heart set on the museum. Of course we can go if that's what you want."

"It isn't that, Keith." She gave him a troubled look. "It's the little things you say. Maybe you thought I expected a romantic afternoon. Casual sex seems to be a way of life around here, but not for me. I'd just like to set the record straight before things get unpleasant."

He looked shocked. "Dani, my sweet! You don't honestly think I was leading up to anything? We're family!"

"Not really. You were the one who pointed it out."

"I only meant we don't share the same blood. And when I saw you I couldn't help being glad there are no obstacles between us." His voice dropped a note. "You're divinely beautiful. But how could you think I'd even consider having an affair with you? It would be like violating my own sister!"

Dani couldn't help laughing. "You're contradicting yourself. First you say we're not relatives, and then you say we are."

"I hope we're going to be related in a different way," he murmured significantly.

"You must be joking!" She looked at him incredulously. "We only met last night."

"I always thought love at first sight was just an expression, but now I know it can happen."

"Keith, this is ridiculous," she said helplessly.

"I knew it would sound that way. That's why I wasn't going to tell you yet. But I'm glad it's out in the open. Tell me there's a chance for me, darling."

"How can I tell you that when I barely know you?"

"Is there someone else?" he asked urgently.

Rand's darkly handsome face appeared before her, but Dani tried to banish the vision. He was the stuff dreams were made of. Rand would bring ecstasy—and then heartbreak.

"No, there's no one else," she said firmly.

Keith looked visibly relieved. "Then there's hope for me. I won't rush you, kitten. Just let me try to make you love me."

She smiled ruefully. "You'll have to work fast. I'll only be here a few weeks."

His eyes held a determined glint. "You'd be surprised at how fast I can work when there's something this important at stake."

Dani seized the opportunity to change the subject. "What kind of work do you do, Keith? I don't believe it was mentioned last night."

He laughed. "As little as possible."

"You and Rand are at opposite ends of the spectrum, then," she commented lightly. "He's a workaholic."

"Or so he'd like everyone to believe." Keith's face hardened.

"What else would you call it? He's in Amsterdam right now. Last week he was in Singapore and New York. He travels all over the world on business."

"Monkey business! It wouldn't surprise me if he took Roxanne Duprès with him on this trip. She's a sexy little number he's been romancing."

"So I gathered," Dani said distantly.

"It's remarkable how often Roxanne leaves town when Rand does—coincidentally, of course." Keith's mouth twisted sarcastically. "And poor old Uncle Cleve thinks he's working."

Dani knew that criticism at least was undeserved. Rand would attend to business before pleasure. It didn't loosen her clenched jaw. There were all the long nights in hotel rooms with Roxanne curled up in his arms. Dani didn't want to think about the molten excitement his hands and mouth could generate, or the ultimate moment when his hard body took possession.

"Your concern is admirable, but misplaced," she said grimly. "I don't think anyone can pull the wool over Grandfather's eyes."

"Nobody except Rand. He's turned Uncle Cleve against his own family." There was bitterness in Keith's voice.

"I didn't know he had any, other than you and your mother."

"He hasn't—that's what I'm saying. I should be the one he depends on, but Rand has his ear. He's filled the old boy so full of lies about me that I've been squeezed out of the business."

"Did you ever work for the corporation?"

Keith's eyes slid away from hers. "They offered me menial jobs, knowing I'd turn them down."

"What do you do instead?"

"Stocks and bonds...things like that," he answered so vaguely that Dani didn't know if he sold them or clipped coupons.

A woman came up to their table. In the muted light her face was unlined, but like Lulu, she showed signs of age that couldn't be eradicated. The heavily jeweled hand she put on Keith's shoulder had prominent veins, and her voice was no longer youthful.

"What a surprise seeing you here today, Keith." Her tone didn't indicate it was a pleasant one. "I thought you were all tied up with family." The look she gave Dani didn't miss a detail.

He stood up with a pleased smile. "How nice to see you, Blanche. I'd like you to meet my cousin Dani."

"Really, Keith! I expected better than that from you."
The woman's lip curled contemptuously.

"Dani is Uncle Cleve's granddaughter," he continued
smoothly, ignoring her sarcasm. "She's staying with him
at the villa. I'm surprised Mother didn't mention it."

Blanche's hard expression changed to uncertainty.
"Well, I...I haven't spoken to Lulu in a couple of days."

"That would explain it," Keith said. "Dani just arrived yesterday. She's never been to the Continent before, so I'm showing her around."

"How nice." There was no sarcasm this time. The
older woman turned to Dani with the first show of
friendliness. "Don't you just adore Monte Carlo?"

"I haven't seen very much of it yet," Dani answered.

"I'm sure Mother is planning a luncheon for you,"
Keith said. "After you're introduced to everyone, you
won't have a minute's free time."

Keith's idea of seeing Monte Carlo was evidently the
inside of restaurants, nightclubs and people's villas. It
didn't sound very appealing to Dani.

"You came at a wonderful time of year," Blanche informed her. "The parties are in full swing." She turned
back to Keith. "I'm expecting you tomorrow night."
There was a note of steel in her voice.

"I'm looking forward to it," he replied pleasantly.

After she'd left, Keith gave Dani a rueful smile.
"Blanche is a friend of my mother's, as you must have
gathered."

Dani had noted that, but she couldn't figure out the
woman's possessive attitude toward him. Surely Keith
wasn't romantically involved with her. She had to be
around Lulu's age.

"Do you see much of her?" Dani asked tentatively.

"More than I like! Mother feels sorry for her, so she keeps roping me in to make a fourth at bridge, or take Blanche to a party when she doesn't have an escort."

"Is she here alone? You introduced her as Mrs. Stanhope."

"She's a widow." Keith sighed. "I suppose it's a lonely life. I shouldn't be so impatient."

"Why don't you try to fix her up with someone her own age?"

"It's an idea," he said lightly.

Keith seemed to want to drop the subject after that, and Dani could understand why. A man with any backbone didn't let himself be pushed repeatedly into doing something distasteful. It surprised her somewhat. Keith had struck Dani as being rather self-centered, but evidently he had a compassionate side to his nature.

Although the food was delicious, lunch seemed to drag on interminably. It was almost four o'clock when they finally left the restaurant. Dani blinked in the bright sunshine, rather startled to find it was still daytime.

She was about to mention the museum again when Keith announced, "Now for the diversion I promised you."

"Anything, as long as it's outside. I need some fresh air—to help me digest all that wonderful food," she added hurriedly.

"You'll get it," he promised.

They drove to the marina where Keith led her to a small yacht moored to the dock. It was only a fraction of the size of her grandfather's yacht, but it was a sleek little craft. Loud music was blaring forth, and the decks were crowded with people carrying cocktail glasses.

Dani looked at Keith in bewilderment. "Where are we?"

"You're about to meet the fun crowd of Monte Carlo," he said with satisfaction.

Dani wanted to protest that she wasn't dressed for a party—not to mention the fact that it was the last place she wanted to go. But Keith didn't give her a chance. He hurried her up the plank gangway, and she was too busy trying to keep her footing to voice any objections.

Keith was greeted with loud shouts of welcome. As he responded to them, Dani had a chance to inspect his friends. They all looked like people in a movie magazine. The men were handsome and well built, and the women were beautiful and glamorous. Both sexes wore a great deal of jewelry with clothes that were in such high style that they were slightly bizarre in some cases.

Dani was uncomfortably aware of her simple cotton dress. She was gazing longingly at the dock when Keith pulled her into a group.

"I want you all to meet my beautiful cousin Dani." After his announcement was met by jeers of laughter and derogatory comments, Keith said, "A little more respect please. Dani just happens to be my Uncle Cleve's granddaughter."

Dani was getting a little weary of all the skepticism that greeted her. Didn't anyone here ever say a simple hello? She had to admit, however, that her grandfather's name was magic. Avid interest replaced the snickers.

"Cleve Barringer is quite a celebrity around here," one of the men told Dani. "His yacht makes my little cruiser look like a rowboat."

Dani gathered this was the host of the party. He was a good-looking man about Keith's age. A heavy gold chain around his neck was nestled in the dark chest hair exposed by his deeply unbuttoned silk shirt. He looked very fit, but the bright sunlight showed tiny lines around his eyes and mouth. Keith had the same lines, Dani noticed for the first time.

"I'd sure like to go out on the *Sea Siren* sometime," the man remarked casually. That was the name of Cleve's yacht.

"Wouldn't we all!" a woman exclaimed. She was a gorgeous brunette in an off-the-shoulder blouse, skin-tight pants and stilt-heeled shoes. "What a great place for a party! We could cruise to Cannes for the film festival."

"The festival isn't for another month," someone remarked.

"Can you think of a better place to wait?" the brunette asked.

Amid general laughter and agreement, their host said to Dani, "I think Elyse is on to something. How about having dinner with me tonight so we can discuss it?"

"Back off, Harrison." Keith draped his arm around Dani's shoulders. "In case you've forgotten, Dani is with me."

The other man's smile was unpleasant. "I didn't know Blanche had given you the night off."

"That was uncalled for!" Keith replied sharply.

A distraction was created by Roxanne's arrival. The short, sarong-type dress she was wearing had huge flowers on a fuchsia background that was echoed by ankle-strap sandals with spike heels. It would have been a garish outfit on anyone with a less superb figure, but she managed to look exotic and sexy.

Dani's heart rose when she saw her. Keith had been wrong. Rand hadn't taken Roxanne with him! There were any amount of reasons to explain the fact, but it still made Dani feel better.

After she'd made the rounds of the men, Roxanne came over to Dani. "What a surprise to see you here. Who brought you?"

"I'm the lucky fellow. Dani and I spent the day together." Keith gave Dani a melting smile. "We have a lot of ground to cover in a short time."

"Fantastique!" Roxanne's white teeth flashed. "Now we have our foursome."

"Who's the other member of this chummy little group you're planning?" Keith drawled.

"Rand, naturally." She smoothed her long blond hair. "Everyone knows we're inseparable."

"There's no accounting for tastes," Keith said derisively.

Roxanne's blue eyes narrowed. "That's true. People have been saying the same thing about *your* choices for years."

Keith's mocking smile faded. "Meaning your macho boyfriend? I can guess what kind of things he whispers in your ear."

Roxanne smirked. "I don't think you're that imaginative, darling."

"Your glass is still full, Dani." Harrison was standing over her with a bottle of champagne. "Drink up so I can give you a dividend."

Someone had put a glass in her hand as soon as she arrived. "No, thanks. I have plenty," Dani said.

"The sun's over the yardarm," Keith told her. "It isn't afternoon anymore."

It seemed easier to drink the now-tepid champagne than argue about it. Dani drained half her glass and watched in resignation as Harrison refilled it. She only hoped it would get her through this ordeal. Nothing in

Dani's experience had prepared her for the nasty innuendos that passed for conversation in this crowd.

Things got better after Roxanne drifted away, but Dani wasn't enjoying herself. She didn't know any of the people they gossiped about, and hadn't been to the parties they discussed. Her leg was starting to ache from standing too long, and a combination of champagne and hot sun had given her a headache. If this was la dolce vita, she wasn't cut out for it, Dani decided.

She touched Keith's sleeve finally. "Could we leave now?"

"The party's just getting started," he protested.

"Not for me," she answered grimly. "I'll get a taxi."

"What's all this about leaving?" Harrison appeared at her side. "You can't go yet. We haven't had a chance to get acquainted."

"Perhaps some other time," Dani murmured.

"What's the matter, Keith? Can't you stand the competition?" Harrison asked.

"It was Dani who wanted to leave, and I'm beginning to think it's a good idea to get her away from you vultures," Keith said coolly.

"It takes one to know one." Harrison smiled sardonically. "Come on, Dani, we're all going on to Jimmy'z later."

"Grandfather is expecting me back," she said desperately. It proved to be an inspiration. None of them was willing to argue about that. "You don't have to come with me, Keith. Just put me in a cab."

"I wouldn't think of it. I only suggested staying because I thought you wanted to."

Dani knew that wasn't so, but she didn't care to argue the point. On the way home she closed her eyes to ease her throbbing headache.

Keith glanced sideways at her, frowning. "You didn't like that crowd much, did you?"

"They were very friendly," she said defensively. "It's just that we come from different worlds."

"A lot of them were Americans."

"That's not what I meant. Their whole life-style is different."

"In what way?" he persisted.

"They don't seem to be interested in anything except parties. Is that all people in Monte Carlo do?"

Keith shrugged. "What's wrong with enjoying yourself?"

"I guess I'm used to pleasure being a reward, not a way of life," she explained haltingly. "I've always had to work."

"But that's all changed now." His hand gripped her fingers firmly. "I can introduce you to pleasures you've never dreamed of!"

She shook her head. "I'm a lost cause. I grew up on the work ethic."

"But you don't have to work anymore. Uncle Cleve will give you anything you want."

"I'm sure he would," she answered evenly. "But I don't want anything."

"Dani, my sweet, you're adorably unworldly."

"I suppose you're right," she agreed, hoping he'd drop the subject.

"I'll have to stay very close so no one takes advantage of you."

Dani could have told him she'd been taking care of herself most of her life, but she merely said, "You'll have to follow me to New York, then."

"You're not really going back, are you?"

"In a month," she said firmly.

"Does Uncle Cleve know?"

She nodded. "I told Rand before we left New York."

As usual, mention of Rand was like a red flag to a bull. Keith's face turned ugly. "I might have known he was behind this. Don't you see what he's doing? Rand wants to get rid of you. If you go home, you'll be playing right into his hands."

"Why would it matter to him one way or the other?"

"Can't you guess? He doesn't want anyone to come between him and Uncle Cleve. Until you showed up, Rand was the heir apparent. He has the old man so buffaloed that he's a cinch to take over the corporation when Uncle Cleve dies. Rand has already undermined Mother and me. Now he's after your scalp."

"That's ridiculous! Grandfather wouldn't leave the corporation to me."

"He would if you played your cards right. That's what Rand is out to prevent—and he'll use any means. He's a ruthless devil. If he can't get rid of you, I wouldn't put it past him to try seduction to get you on his side."

Dani bit her lip as she remembered how he already had. Could Keith possibly be right? Everything inside her rebelled at the thought, but there was no denying she could be a pawn in a very high-stakes game—and Rand wasn't overly scrupulous when it came to getting his own way.

Then she remembered how annoyed he'd been at her coolness to her grandfather. That didn't jibe with Keith's theory. On the other hand, there was Roxanne. If Rand was as involved with her as the girl claimed, he couldn't make love to someone else unless he was completely unprincipled.

Keith glanced at Dani's troubled face with barely concealed satisfaction as he drove up to the villa. "What time shall I pick you up tonight?" he asked.

"I'm sure you have other plans," she said. Keith's company was beginning to pall. Besides, she needed time to sort things out in her mind. "Don't worry about me. You've done enough already."

"This is only the beginning," he murmured meaningfully.

"I really have to go in now, Keith."

"First say you'll have dinner with me tonight," he coaxed.

"No, Grandfather's expecting me to spend the evening with him. I'm sure you understand."

The excuse had worked before, and it worked again. Keith stopped urging her. He did try to make another date, but Dani managed to put him off.

Cleve came out of the den when he heard her coming in. He was smiling, but something about her face sobered him. "Did you have a good time?" he asked tentatively.

"Yes, it was very nice," she answered politely.

Cleve hesitated. "You look tired."

"Maybe a little," she admitted.

"Is your leg bothering you?"

"Just slightly." Actually it was paining her a lot.

He looked concerned. "I should have warned Keith not to let you overdo it. Where did he take you?"

"To lunch, and then to a cocktail party. I guess I stood up too long."

Cleve frowned. "I thought you were going sightseeing."

"I did, too," she said with a sigh.

He made a sound of annoyance. "You'd better get right to bed. I'll have Marie bring your dinner there."

He was so solicitous that Dani felt guilty about her own reserve. It was difficult for them to converse normally, but her grandfather was trying and she wasn't. He had looked so eager when he came out to greet her. Dani suddenly realized that Cleve had probably been waiting for her all day.

"I'll be fine after I take a shower," she assured him. "And I hate eating in bed. I'd like to have dinner with you unless you have other plans."

He looked almost pathetically pleased. "Only to take you wherever you want to go."

"Could we have dinner here? I'll bet this is the best food in town."

He chuckled. "So Henri tells me every time he asks for a raise. What would you like him to make?"

"Surprise me."

As she went to take a shower, Dani reflected that it was the first relaxed exchange they'd had. Maybe the next few weeks wouldn't be as bad as she'd feared.

After showering and changing to a comfortable caftan, Dani joined Cleve on the terrace. The table had been set there, as beautifully as though they were eating in the dining room.

"I thought this would be cozier," he explained.

"It's lovely!" Dani exclaimed. "What a heavenly view."

The city was a spilled jewel chest of diamond, emerald and ruby lights that winked in the velvet darkness. Overhead was a canopy of more diamonds, and the floodlit swimming pool was an oval aquamarine.

"I'm glad you like it," Cleve said quietly.

"How could I help it?"

"I thought something was troubling you when you came in this afternoon."

Dani looked down at the artful centerpiece of daffodils and lilacs. The china was again coordinated. Delicate white plates were sprinkled with violets and banded in gold.

"Did Keith do something to upset you, Dani?" Cleve's face was stern.

She caught a glimpse of the implacability her grandfather could display. "No, he was charming," she said hastily. She knew Keith had tried to be, anyway.

"Then what is it?" Cleve asked searchingly. "If anything's wrong, I want to know about it."

Dani sighed. "It's just me. I don't belong here."

"Why would you say a thing like that?"

"At the cocktail party today...those people were so...so..."

"Useless?" he asked contemptuously.

She looked startled at his perception. "You don't know who was there."

"I could make an educated guess. I know who Keith's friends are. There are people like them all over the world, Dani—pleasure seekers with no scruples or sense of responsibility. Thank God they aren't in the majority."

Dani hadn't meant to get Keith in trouble. "They were really quite nice to me," she said hurriedly.

"I don't doubt it." There was irony in his voice.

"I guess it was just that I don't dress like them or speak a foreign language. I haven't been any of the places they have. That's what I meant about not belonging."

Cleve frowned. "This never would have happened if Rand hadn't gone to Amsterdam. I shouldn't have permitted it."

"You don't have to disrupt your life for me. Besides, these were his friends, too."

"I can assure you they aren't," Cleve replied crisply.

"Roxanne was there," she murmured, concentrating on lining up her silver precisely.

He laughed unexpectedly. "Roxanne is in a category all her own." Since Cleve sensed that wasn't calculated to gladden Dani's heart, he contained his amusement. "I suppose she gave you the impression that Rand's devotion is something like Anthony's was for Cleopatra, but it's wishful thinking on her part."

"They seemed quite...friendly...yesterday. Not that it's any of my business," Dani added carelessly.

"Or mine," Cleve agreed, just as casually. "But Rand's a fascinating subject. There are so many facets to him."

"He's very ambitious, isn't he?" Dani asked slowly.

"I don't know that I'd describe him that way. He's accomplished everything he set out to do. Rand knows the business as well as I do."

"So he could logically expect to head the corporation when you—" She broke off abruptly.

Cleve smiled. "It's all right, my dear. Contrary to public opinion, I don't consider myself immortal. The answer to your question is yes, Rand expects to succeed me."

"Isn't it unusual that Keith's not involved in any way? After all, he's your nephew."

Cleve's eyes turned cold. "We're operating successfully without him."

Although his manner didn't invite further questioning, Dani had to settle some of the doubts Keith had raised. "I couldn't help noticing that Rand and Keith don't care for each other." When her grandfather didn't respond, Dani persisted. "Would things be different if they got along?"

"You think Rand turned me against my own family?"

That was what Dani wanted to find out. But if Cleve had been brainwashed, he'd scarcely know it. "I'm mixing into something that doesn't concern me," she said apologetically.

"You're wrong, Dani. As my principal heir, this concerns you vitally." When she tried to interrupt, he overrode her protests. "I intend to see that you have all the material things you've been denied. I know they won't guarantee happiness, but at least they'll bring comfort. I trust Rand to guard your fortune and carry out my wishes." He smiled sadly. "Maybe after my death you won't mind accepting the benefits you couldn't take while I was alive."

Dani felt tears threaten. "I wish things could have been different."

"No more than I do, child." There was no mistaking the deep sorrow on his face.

Dani was drawn to her grandfather for the first time. But their detente was so new that they were both wary of showing too much emotion. By common consent they changed the subject and avoided any topics that might turn personal.

As the excellent meal progressed, Cleve exerted himself to be entertaining, and Dani discovered just how charming he could be. She found herself laughing and talking quite naturally.

It was only when she was alone, away from the influence of his magnetic personality, that Dani's doubts returned. Her grandfather had never really answered any of her questions.

She was getting into bed when the phone rang. Rand's low, slightly husky voice made her heart beat faster.

"I thought you were in Amsterdam," she said breathlessly.

"I am."

"Oh." Disappointment made her voice flat. "I guess you want to talk to Grandfather."

"No, I called to talk to you. How was your day?"

"It was all right."

"Just all right? Did you miss me?" he teased.

Dani suddenly realized how much, but she didn't want to admit it to him. "I didn't have a chance. Keith was very attentive."

"I'll bet! Where did he take you?"

"To a cocktail party on someone's yacht."

"With those trashy friends of his?" Rand swore pungently. "Keith's poor judgment is exceeded only by his stupidity—which is monumental!"

"I don't know what you mean," Dani replied coolly. "Your little friend Roxanne was there."

"I'm not surprised. She spends her life going to parties," he said impatiently.

"Then you must, too." Dani tried to keep her voice light. "She said you were inseparable."

"Roxanne never lets the truth interfere with her fantasies."

Maybe Rand and Roxanne weren't as close as she'd indicated, but no man ever turned down a body like hers. Dani felt anger sweep over her. "You don't have to deny it to me. I couldn't care less!"

Rand sighed. "I didn't call up to argue with you, Dani. I just wanted to know if you were getting along all right. Is your leg okay?"

His thoughtfulness made Dani ashamed of herself. "Yes, it's fine," she murmured.

"That's good. Well, take care of yourself."

"Rand, wait!"

"Yes?"

She couldn't let the conversation end this way. "Are you . . . I mean, when are you coming home?"

"Probably in a couple of days. Why?"

"No special reason. I just wondered."

"Well, now you know. Enjoy your vacation."

"But I'm not! Keith wouldn't take me to see the changing of the guard and my leg doesn't feel fine, it feels rotten. And I miss you!" The words came out in a rush.

"Why didn't you say that in the first place?" The gently teasing note was back in his voice.

"Would it have made any difference?" she asked forlornly.

"I'll be back in the morning. What shall I bring you?"

Dani's heart took a giant leap. Just yourself, she wanted to say. It didn't matter if Rand was a latter-day Machiavelli, or that maybe he wasn't being fair to Keith. She wasn't interested in the money or the corporation. All she wanted was to be with him, to see those topaz eyes glow just for her, to have him bring color into her life. Dani was startled by the intensity of her longing. Was she falling in love with Rand? It was all right to appreciate him as a superb male, but anything else would be sheer insanity!

"You must have a lengthy shopping list," he commented.

"What?" She was startled out of her introspection.

"I asked what you wanted me to bring you from Holland."

"How about a tulip?"

He chuckled richly. "You're a very inexpensive lady. Remind me to marry you some day."

After he hung up, Dani held on to the receiver for a long moment, as though to prolong the contact. There was a dreamy look in her eyes when she finally relinquished it and slid under the covers.

Chapter Five

Cleve insisted that Dani have breakfast in bed every morning. It felt sinfully rich, like the pale silk sheets that were changed every day. As her grandfather said, money couldn't buy happiness but it sure provided a lot of creature comforts. It was going to be difficult to get used to her tiny apartment again. Dani pushed the thought out of her mind as she rang the bell beside her bed.

Marie appeared promptly, but instead of a breakfast tray she brought a huge basket of pink tulips. It was so large that the little French maid was almost completely hidden behind it.

"Where did that come from?" Dani gasped.

"Mr. Stryker brought it."

"He's here?" Dani jumped out of bed. "Never mind breakfast this morning, Marie. I'll have it out on the terrace."

She showered and dressed in record time, choosing a yellow cotton dress with white sandals that matched the braided white belt. The simple outfit couldn't compare to Roxanne's high style, but nothing could bother Dani that morning.

Her eyes sparkled like flawless emeralds as she hurried down the hall as fast as her leg would allow.

Rand was alone on the terrace, going through some papers with a look of total concentration. Another place at the table indicated her grandfather had been there, but he must have gone into the house for something.

Dani stood in the doorway staring at Rand. There was a controlled energy about him that she had never encountered in another person. She drank in the clean line of his jaw and admired the wide set of his powerful shoulders under the black pullover that hugged his lean chest. With it he wore jeans.

Dani had never seen Rand dressed this casually before. His perfectly tailored outfits had always made him seem the epitome of urban sophistication. She could see him now at the prow of a pirate ship, dark hair ruffled by the wind, ready for any challenge.

When he looked up and saw her, his white teeth flashed in a welcoming smile. "I didn't think you were up yet."

"I would have gotten up earlier, but I didn't expect you back so soon. Thanks for the tulips. They're incredible! How did you ever get them here?"

"I bought another seat."

"You didn't!"

Rand laughed. "No, actually I romanced the stewardess into putting them in the galley."

"I'd rather you'd bought another seat."

"Would you really, Dani?" He cupped her chin in his palm, looking down at her with pinpoints of light in his tawny eyes.

She was afraid she'd revealed too much. "I don't want you to get sidetracked. No one else will take me sightseeing. You're my last hope."

Rand reverted to his joking manner. "I knew it was too good to be true. You don't want my body, you just want wheels."

"I'm in no condition to climb up to the palace," she commented lightly. "It's at the top of the hill."

"Okay. Since you're a needy case, I'll let myself be used." He held out a chair for her. "Have you had breakfast? Henri's eggs Benedict are fantastic."

"That takes too long. I don't want to miss the changing of the guard. Keith says they do it before noon."

"For once he's right. Even a blind pig finds an acorn once in a while," Rand commented mockingly.

"Don't you think you're being a little hard on him?"

Rand raised one peaked eyebrow. "I see he didn't waste any time."

"What do you have against Keith?" Dani asked curiously.

A curtain descended behind his topaz eyes. "We don't really see very much of each other."

As usual, Rand hadn't answered her question, but Dani was too happy to have him back to pursue the subject.

Cleve came out of the house carrying a thick manila folder. "What a nice surprise. Are you having breakfast with us, my dear?"

Dani looked dubiously at the paperwork on the table. "If I'm not interrupting anything."

"Not at all. Rand was just giving me a report on his trip. But don't worry, I won't keep him long. I know you two have an outing planned."

"Have something to eat while I brief Cleve on a couple of things," Rand told Dani. "It'll only take a few minutes, and then we'll be on our way."

Dani was too impatient to eat more than toast and coffee. And for once, her grandfather was too preoccupied to ply her with food. Dani watched the absorbed faces of the two men as they dealt with millions of dollars. There was no exultation over another fortune to be made, no tension that it might be lost, only supreme confidence in themselves. It was an impressive sight.

They kept their promise to be brief. Rand was ready in just a short time.

As they were leaving, he said to Cleve, "How about the Vistaero for dinner tonight? I think Dani would enjoy it."

Cleve nodded. "I'll make a reservation for you."

"You'll come with us, won't you?" Dani asked impulsively.

His pleasure was evident. "I'd like that very much."

"That was very nice of you," Rand said gently as he helped her into the Ferrari.

"Well, after all, he is my host," she answered carelessly. "It was the polite thing to do."

Dani wasn't ready to admit she was softening toward her grandfather, or that she'd enjoyed his company the night before. She still didn't trust either man.

Rand frowned. "Was that the only reason?"

"Let's not argue," she pleaded.

His face cleared. "Okay, honey, this is your day. You deserve it."

The massive stone palace had grace and dignity. It dominated the crest of the hill, looking out over its domain. Two soldiers, dressed all in white except for the red plumes on their hard helmets, guarded either side of the impressive front door. They faced a broad courtyard that was filled with people aiming cameras.

"You must hate looking like a tourist," Dani remarked apologetically.

"What's wrong with being a tourist?" Rand asked. "How else are you going to see anything?"

"It isn't very sophisticated."

"Who would worry about a thing like that? Let's get up close so you can see."

As Rand maneuvered her to a choice position, Dani compared his attitude to Keith's. Rand obviously had no insecurities, while Keith was riddled with them. She put it out of her mind as the ritual of the changing of the guard began.

It was so charmingly old-world that Dani was captivated. A small troop of soldiers marched out of an archway as music played over a loudspeaker. They advanced with precision down the courtyard and back, eyes straight ahead, oblivious to the frantically clicking cameras. After going through the stylized routine of presenting arms, the watch was changed and two new soldiers were left to guard the portals while the rest marched back into the armory.

"Not quite as much pomp as Buckingham Palace, but Monaco is a small country," Rand commented.

"I loved it!" Dani exclaimed. "I just wish I'd brought a camera."

"We'll get some picture postcards in the gift shop. It's better photography than you can do yourself."

Dani picked out a dozen different views. "I'm going to start a scrapbook when I get home. Although there isn't any chance I'd forget this trip!"

"You haven't changed your mind about staying?"

Her animation faded. "It wouldn't work, Rand."

"You've only been here a few days. Who knows? You might have a change of heart." Before she could deny it he said, "Are you ready for lunch? You didn't have much breakfast."

"I'm a little hungry," she admitted. "But I hate to waste time in a restaurant."

"How about a picnic in the park?"

"That would be super!" she agreed eagerly.

Rand telephoned ahead to a place that prepared picnic lunches. By the time they got there, a wicker hamper was waiting for them. After that, he drove to a lovely park with tall shade trees.

When he took a blanket out of the trunk of the car, Dani commented dryly, "You're prepared for anything, aren't you?"

He grinned. "I was a Boy Scout."

"I'll bet you didn't get the good conduct award."

"Maybe not officially." He chuckled reminiscently.

"Stop bragging," Dani told him as she helped spread out the blanket.

His eyes gleamed wickedly. "Just guaranteeing satisfaction, ma'am."

Dani knew from the sample she'd received that Rand could deliver what he promised. It made little chills run up her spine to think what it would be like.

"Can you also guarantee lunch?" she asked lightly. "I'm starving."

It was a very elegant picnic. There was pâté with French bread and the little pickles called *cornichons*. Also roast squab, a bottle of chilled wine and fruit and cheese for dessert.

After they'd eaten and packed away the debris, Rand stretched out on the blanket, propping his head on his crossed arms. "This was an inspired idea, if I do say so myself." His drowsy lion's eyes smiled at her.

"You look sleepy," Dani noted.

"Maybe a trifle. I was up at five this morning." His thick lashes drooped a little lower.

"Why so early?"

"I had a date with a lovely lady." He reached out and took her hand.

"You could have taken a later plane," she protested.

"Not and gotten here in time for this."

"We could have postponed it," Dani said weakly. Rand's thumb was moving lazily over her wrist, making her pulse beat so rapidly that she was afraid he could feel it.

"You're worth missing a little sleep for any day." His husky voice curled around her like a caress.

"Why don't you take a nap?"

"Only if you take one with me." He tugged on her wrist, pulling her down beside him.

"I'm not tired," she said breathlessly.

Rand had pillowed her head on his shoulder and drawn her body close to his. She was joined to him along her entire right side, her soft curves molding to his hard angles.

"You're just afraid I'll say we slept together," he teased.

She shifted her head to look up at his strong profile. "I don't think you'd kiss and tell."

"You can count on that, honey." Laughter rumbled in his deep chest.

Dani envied Rand his ability to be so relaxed when she was tied up in knots. It would seem to indicate that she didn't turn him on. Yet there had been memorable moments when she had. Rand was a very virile man who would take whatever came his way, but was she merely an assignment, as she'd first suspected? The idea brought a deep sigh.

He opened his eyes immediately. "This isn't any fun for you. Come on, we'll go to the Oceanographic Museum." He turned on his side, preparing to get up.

"There's lots of time."

She turned toward him and put her hand on his shoulder to push him back onto the blanket. Their bodies were only inches apart. Then they were touching as Rand's arms closed around her. He buried his face in her hair and held her so tightly that she could feel the accelerated beat of his heart.

"Do you know how beautiful you are? I want to make love to you," he groaned.

"We're in the park."

It was only a faint objection. His hard body had set up a clamor inside her the minute Rand had pulled her down next to him. Now that they were joined at every point, the urgency grew in volume. The contact with his rigid loins and taut stomach lit a spreading fire.

Rand kissed her slowly, drawing out the pleasure. "It's the only safe place for us," he muttered.

His breath entered her parted lips. It was a seductive feeling, a suggestive invasion that tantalized. Dani moved against him unconsciously.

He lifted his head slightly to look down at her. "We could go to my place. Would you like that, sweetheart?"

If they'd been at Rand's apartment, there was no doubt in Dani's mind that they would have made love. But she'd been given a respite. Rand was already a fever in her blood. If she made the ultimate surrender he might own her completely—and she still didn't trust his motives.

The blaze went out of his eyes as she hesitated. "I guess that answers my question."

Dani's lashes fluttered down self-consciously. She sat up. "I thought we decided it wasn't a good idea."

"I think it would be a fantastic idea," he said huskily. "But not if you don't agree." He got to his feet and reached for her hands to pull her up.

Dani felt awkward with him at first, but Rand was completely natural. She was grateful, yet perversely, his unconcern angered her. How could he turn passion on and off—unless it was calculated? She decided to make a stab at finding out.

"It was very nice of you to take the whole day off to show me around," she began innocently. "It looked as though you and Grandfather had a lot of work to go over."

Rand chuckled. "He'd have me gift wrapped and hand delivered if he thought it would make you happy."

"Grandfather's lucky to have someone so devoted," she commented lightly.

"I didn't say I'd go along with it."

"You're here," Dani pointed out.

He frowned. "I get the feeling you're trying to say something. What is it, Dani?"

She didn't want an open confrontation. "I was just surprised that either of you would let anything interfere with business," she said hastily. "You're both so single-minded about it."

"Is that what you think—that all we care about is making money?"

"Well...I guess when you deal in millions you have to give it your full attention."

"I'm not going to apologize for being rich, Dani—it's better than being poor. I was an orphan, so I know what poverty is all about. But money for its own sake doesn't impress either your grandfather or myself. Have you ever thought about the jobs we create for literally thousands of people? The corporation also has a charitable foundation that helps thousands more."

"I didn't know that," she said slowly.

"You don't know about Cleve's private charities, either. Very few people do. He goes to great lengths to remain anonymous."

"I wasn't criticizing," she said defensively. "It just seems..."

"What?" Rand asked when her voice trailed off.

"It isn't important," she murmured.

"Tell me," he insisted.

"All right. I was wondering why Grandfather can't find a place for Keith in his huge organization. It seems odd to be concerned about strangers and not your own family."

The familiar mask descended over Rand's face. "Keith's talents don't run toward industry."

"There must be *some* position he could fill."

"Nothing he'd accept, I'm afraid."

"You can't blame him for not wanting to take a menial job."

"What's wrong with working your way up? I did. It's the only way to learn."

Rand was watching the twisting road they were navigating. Dani gazed at his firm mouth and squarely set jaw. He looked equal to any challenge. Rand might have started at the bottom, but he was at the top of the heap now. How far would he go to stay there? One thing was certain, poor Keith was no match for him.

"How long have you worked for Grandfather?" she asked.

"I joined the organization right out of college." He stopped to figure. "It will be thirteen years in June."

"And now you're the heir apparent." Dani unconsciously echoed Keith's words.

Rand shrugged. "You never know. The world is full of surprises."

"I suppose I was one of them."

He turned his head to smile warmly at her. "One of the good kind. You've given Cleve's life new meaning."

"He has a lot going for him without me," she observed.

"Only material things. You can give him love."

"You mean because he's rich I should let bygones be bygones?" she asked sharply.

"No, because he's your grandfather and he loves you. He has so much love stored up. Let him lavish it on you, Dani."

"Too bad he didn't give some of it to my mother."

"He regrets the lost opportunity as much as you do. Cleve told me about your evening together last night. He was so thrilled that you opened up to him a little. Surely you discovered he isn't a complete monster. Don't close your heart to him, honey," Rand said urgently.

She turned her head away. "Don't rush me, Rand. I'll admit he's a very charismatic man, but it isn't easy to forgive what he did."

Rand smothered an oath. "Just keep an open mind. Maybe someday you'll understand."

Dani didn't share his belief, but she'd settled her doubts about one thing. Keith was off base. Rand's devotion to her grandfather was total. It didn't preclude fulfilling his own ambition after Cleve was gone. But for now at least, he wanted her to stay and keep the older man happy.

They both realized there was nothing further to say on the subject. Anything more might lead to an argument, which wouldn't change either's opinion.

"After the museum, how would you like to see the exotic gardens?" Rand asked.

"I'd love it, but you must be dead tired. Are you sure you can stay on your feet?"

His mouth curved in a rueful smile. "That seems the safest position when I'm with you." As her color rose he said, "How about you? Is your leg up to it?"

"It isn't bothering me at all today," she assured him.

The day was a continuing delight. They visited all the tourist spots and bought little souvenirs at each one. Keith would have turned pale with mortification. They were interchangeable with all the other sightseers. Rand even took a picture of an Italian family for them, and then advised them of inexpensive places to eat.

"You're a very helpful fellow," Dani observed. They were walking hand in hand through the gardens.

"Maybe someday you'll avail yourself of my services."

"I don't want my picture taken."

He grinned mischievously. "I perform other services."

"Very well, I'm sure. But no, thank you."

"Are you afraid I might become habit-forming?" he teased.

Dani was convinced of that! "It would be inconvenient with an ocean between us," she remarked lightly.

There was an enigmatic look in his eyes as they wandered over her delicate features. "If it got to that point, I don't think I'd let you go," he said slowly.

Dani's breath caught in her throat at the thought of endless joyous days and ecstatic nights, although she knew it was unrealistic. Some of those nights would be claimed by Roxanne.

"With a little work that could be a song title," she said, forcing a laugh.

"You may have something there. I'll do the words and you do the music." Rand's moment of seriousness was gone.

It was late afternoon when he brought her home. Dani turned a shining face to him in the car. "Thank you for a wonderful day. You'd make a perfect tour guide."

Rand chuckled. "Not if all my passengers were like you. Our tour almost ended with lunch."

"I won't let you spoil things by making me feel embarrassed," she said firmly.

"I don't ever want you to be embarrassed with me, honey." His long fingers stroked her cheek. "We're friends, remember?"

She smiled wryly. "I guess we must be. I'd hate to think I got that intimate with a stranger."

"I do believe your inhibitions are breaking down," he said approvingly. "Pretty soon you'll even admit that sex is a normal part of life."

Dani's gaze faltered. "Not casual sex. At least not for me."

"Or me." His hand cupped around the back of her neck, moving in slow circles. "If we ever make love there won't be anything casual about it, little angel."

"I'd better go in," she murmured.

"You're right." He sighed. "I'm acting like a high school boy trying to make out in a car. I'd forgotten how frustrating it is."

"You started it," she protested.

"True." He kissed the tip of her nose. "I'll be back at seven-thirty."

Dani was glad Cleve was out. He was very perceptive, and she was afraid her face might reveal her feelings. She went to her room, trying to shake off Rand's spell. When she was with him, there was a constant ache to be in his arms. But when she was away from him, common sense told her it would be a disaster. Why was the one man she could fall in love with so complex?

Dani inspected her limited wardrobe discontentedly. It was a disaster compared to the way high society dressed in Mônte Carlo. Her inexpensive things looked like the outfits of the tourists Keith despised. She knew it wouldn't bother Rand or her grandfather, but she hated to look like a poor relation.

Since it couldn't be helped, she chose the best of the lot, a white silk sheath with simple lines that made it look more expensive than it was. It wouldn't fool Lulu or Roxanne, though. That silly outfit Roxanne had worn to the cocktail party cost more than everything Dani'd brought with her. How could Roxanne afford it? She couldn't be rich if her mother was trying to marry for money. Did Rand buy her little goodies? Dani refused to pursue that line of thinking.

To distract from her simple outfit, Dani created an elaborate hairdo. She pinned her long hair into a cascade of curls that spilled from her crown, then tucked two perfect white camellias above her left ear. The garden outside her window was as good as a florist's.

She applied more makeup than usual, too, brushing her long lashes with mascara and using green eye shadow to deepen the color of her eyes. When she was finished,

Dani was satisfied with the result. She hoped Rand would be.

The men were waiting for her in the living room, and their reactions were flattering.

"Is this the tourist I took sight-seeing today?" Rand's admiring eyes roved over her from head to toe. "You should have been inside the palace, not outside."

"You look lovely, my dear," Cleve said. "There's only one thing I could think to add. Will you excuse me for a moment?"

"Did you take a nap?" Dani asked as the older man left the room.

Rand smiled. "Yes. It was easy once there were no distractions."

"It's a good thing your little friend didn't know you were back."

"Meaning Roxanne?"

"She seems to keep track of your movements." Dani tried to sound unconcerned.

"If you say so."

Dani wanted *him* to say it *wasn't* so. "I wonder where Grandfather went," she remarked, wishing she'd never brought up the subject.

He returned at that moment, carrying a square velvet box. He opened it to disclose a magnificent diamond-and-emerald necklace. The thumbnail-size green stones were surrounded by diamonds that winked like cold fire.

Cleve lifted the circlet from its bed of white satin. "I gave this to my wife when your father was born. I'd like you to have it."

Dani gasped. "It's gorgeous, but I couldn't possibly accept something that valuable. It must be worth a fortune."

"The value for me is sentimental." He walked toward her. "It would give me great pleasure to see it on you."

As she backed away, Rand remarked, "Cleve's right. It would look terrific on that dress, and the color matches your eyes. At least wear it this evening."

"I'd be worried all night! What if I lost it?"

"It's insured," Rand said. "Wear it for your grandfather."

As his persuasive voice coaxed her, Cleve fastened the necklace around her neck.

His eyes were misty as he looked at her. "I wish Irene could see you."

"Was that your wife's name?" Dani asked in a muted voice.

He nodded. "Your grandmother."

Dani touched the glittering stones, feeling a sense of continuity. Her grandmother had worn this necklace. It was a tangible link to the past. She was part of her father's family whether she denied it or not.

Rand defused the emotion-charged atmosphere. "We'd better get going or we'll be late for our reservation."

The Vistaero was an elegant hotel on top of a hill. It had a first-class restaurant on the first floor. The bar on a balcony above was reached by a wide curving staircase. Since it was difficult for Dani to climb stairs, they decided to have drinks at the table.

They were shown to a choice table beside a large square pool. When she noticed ripples in the water, Dani glanced over, expecting to see goldfish. Instead, she found the pool was filled with lobsters.

"You select the one you want and they cook it for you," Rand explained.

"That's horrible!" Dani exclaimed. "I'd feel like a murderer."

"Haven't you ever eaten a lobster?" he asked.

"Not one that was practically sitting at the table with me!"

Rand was having trouble containing his amusement. "You haven't been formally introduced. It isn't like losing a friend."

"Will you stop teasing her?" Cleve patted her hand. "The breast of duck is very nice here."

"Yes, the chef waits until it dies of old age," Rand said.

"Are you trying to turn Dani into a vegetarian?" Cleve demanded. "Henri will give notice."

In deference to her sensibilities, neither man ordered lobster, but there was a wealth of other choices. The food was delicious and beautifully served. But most of all, Dani enjoyed the company of her two distinguished escorts. They were interesting, witty and very well informed on a variety of subjects, not just the world of finance.

As they were finishing their coffee, Rand asked Dani if she'd like to go to the casino.

"I was hoping we could," she said eagerly. "I've seen it in old movies on television. At least it was supposed to be the casino at Monte Carlo. The men were in white tie and tails, and the women wore evening gowns. Someone always lost his entire fortune and then simply shrugged and said, *'C'est la vie.'* It was terribly sophisticated."

"What did they say when they won?" Rand asked.

"I don't think they ever did."

Cleve chuckled. "That's called cinema verité."

At first Dani was disappointed in the royal casino. It was a large, imposing building set in beautiful grounds, but it was swarming with tourists in jeans and T-shirts playing slot machines. Where were all the glamorous people?

She found out when Rand and Cleve led her to an inner room where an entrance fee was required. It was quiet inside, and the people were elegant and well mannered. There was a country club ambience to the large room with its tall draped windows and comfortable couches placed along the walls.

The gaming tables were widely separated from each other so no one would be disturbed, although the players were sedate. There was none of the carnival atmosphere characteristic of American gambling casinos. This might have been a large private party of genteel guests.

"What would you like to play, my dear?" Cleve asked Dani.

"I'll just watch."

"That's no fun," Rand objected.

"I don't even know what some of these games are," she explained.

"You know how to play roulette," Rand said. "All you do is put your chips on a lot of numbers and then watch the little ball land on the one you're not on."

"Stop discouraging the child," Cleve admonished. "Perhaps she'll break the bank."

"How much do the chips cost?" Dani asked cautiously.

"Don't worry, I'll back you." Rand grinned at Cleve. "If you lose, I'll just put it on the expense account."

"At least I'll know where my money's going this time," the older man replied dryly, but there was a twinkle in his eyes.

Their discussion was interrupted by friends coming up to greet the two men. They all politely acknowledged the introduction to Dani, which was a welcome novelty. She had gotten exceedingly tired of the derisive comments Keith's friends had directed at her.

Dani found a woman named Charlotte Langlois especially interesting. Her dark hair was drawn back from a face with exquisite bone structure, and her eyes sparkled with intelligence. The dress she wore was obviously expensive but understated and elegant.

After they'd chatted for a few moments, Charlotte said to Dani, "I can't imagine ever tiring of two such gallant men, but if you ever feel the urge for some female companionship, do come and have lunch with me."

"I'd like that very much," Dani said.

"I suppose it would defeat the purpose, but I'd like to come, too. I want to see your latest work. Charlotte is a very talented artist," Rand explained to Dani.

Charlotte smiled at him. "Rand always says the right thing. It's one of the reasons he's in such great demand."

"What a fascinating woman!" Dani exclaimed after she'd left.

"Yes, and I wasn't just being polite about her talent. Charlotte isn't a dilettante. She really works at her craft."

"I didn't know anyone in Monte Carlo worked except you and Grandfather."

"You haven't met the right people." He put his arm around her shoulders. "Let's try our luck."

All the people at the roulette table had different color chips so they could keep track of their bets. Dani's were white and Rand's were red. He played seven or eight chips on each spin of the wheel, placing them all over the board, while she doled out one chip at a time.

"That's no way to play," he admonished. "You have to go for it, be bold."

"You're almost out of chips," she pointed out.

"It's still the right way to play," he said calmly. "You have to take risks in life to win."

Rand casually distributed the last of his chips. His rugged face was completely relaxed as he watched the little bouncing ball. Of course he could afford to lose, Dani reminded herself, but somehow she knew that had nothing to do with it. Rand was stimulated by the element of risk, confident of his ability to beat the odds.

She wasn't surprised when the ball landed on one of his numbers. The croupier slid over two large red stacks, putting Rand back in business.

To Dani's delight, she also had a winner. Beginner's luck smiled on her, and she soon had several more. By the time Cleve came to join them, both she and Rand had piles of chips in front of them.

"I think I should have been playing roulette instead of chemin de fer," Cleve said with a smile. "I don't suppose you two want to leave since you're on a winning streak."

"I'm ready," Dani said promptly.

"You're on a roll," Rand protested.

"I know, but my luck could change. I might lose everything."

"Or you could win. You have to learn to take chances, Dani," Rand said softly.

As their eyes held, she had a feeling he was talking about something else.

"Leave her alone," Cleve said, dispelling the moment. "She's displaying good sense."

After he cashed them both in, Rand handed Dani a thick sheaf of bills with large numbers in the corners. It looked like a fortune.

"This is yours," she objected. "You bought the chips."

"I was only your banker."

"Take the money," Cleve advised. "If he gets any richer he might set up in business for himself, and I can't afford to lose him."

"What are you going to do with your windfall?" Rand asked in the limousine going home.

"I don't know. I've never had this much money before," she said happily.

Dani didn't see the shadow that crossed Cleve's face, or the look of commiseration Rand gave him.

"Do you know how much you have?" Rand asked.

"No, but it looks like a lot. Do you think I could buy a dress like Charlotte wore? Not exactly like it of course, but something elegant?"

"A whole bunch of them," Rand assured her. "Why don't I take you on a shopping spree tomorrow?"

When they returned to the villa, Cleve left them in the entry hall. "You young people probably want a nightcap, but if you'll excuse me, I'm going to bed."

"I'd better take off, too," Rand said. "My day started early."

"All right. I'll see you in the morning, then. Good night, my dear," Cleve said to Dani.

"Thank you for a wonderful time." On an impulse, she reached up and kissed the older man's cheek.

Cleve was so surprised and touched that he couldn't say anything. He patted her cheek and left hurriedly, but not before she saw the glisten of tears in his eyes.

"That was a very sweet thing you just did," Rand said gently.

"I . . . I hadn't planned to. It just happened."

"That's the very best way." Rand's voice deepened to a husky pitch.

She didn't pretend to misunderstand. The desire that was always present between them flared into the open, but Dani wasn't prepared for another encounter with Rand. She bent her head to avoid the blaze in his tawny eyes.

Suddenly her own eyes widened. "The necklace! I forgot to give it back to him."

"He wants you to keep it."

"How can I accept a gift like this?"

"With grace. It would give your grandfather a great deal of pleasure to see you wear it."

"And it would make me feel as though I'd sold out," she said angrily.

"Still determined to nurse your grudge to the bitter end?" Rand asked impatiently.

"I wouldn't expect you to understand!"

"I wish to God *you* did," he muttered.

"Spare me another of your lectures. I've had my quota for today." Dani was fumbling with the intricate safety catch without success. Finally she turned her back to Rand. "Unfasten this!" she ordered.

"I ought to make you sleep in it," he grated, but he did as she said. When the clasp was undone he bent his head to kiss the smooth nape of her neck. "Stubborn, misguided little Dani. When that chip falls off your shoulder, you're going to be a lot more comfortable."

Rand's warm mouth on her neck was making Dani's legs feel like rubber. Her anger faded as his big hands began to massage her shoulders gently, but she refused to weaken. Rand could convince her of anything with these tactics, but she mustn't permit it.

She twitched away and turned to face him. "I believe you mentioned something about being tired. Thank *you* for a lovely evening, also."

A slow smile lit his eyes. "Don't I get a kiss, too?"

"I think a handshake is safer," she answered warily.

He took her hand and pulled her closer. Dipping his dark head, he kissed the corner of her mouth. "I hope I'm around when you get tired of playing it safe."

Before she could react, he was gone. Dani was filled with frustration as she went into her bedroom with the emerald necklace clenched in her hand. She had been clutching it so tightly that it left marks on her palm. The impressions would fade, but would she ever be free of the mark Rand had put on her?

Chapter Six

Rand hadn't said what time he was taking Dani shopping, but she was up and dressed early. It was disappointing to find that neither he nor Cleve were anywhere around.

After looking in the den and on the terrace, Dani asked Marie where her grandfather was.

"He went to his office, Miss Zanetelle."

"I thought his office was here," Dani said blankly.

"Mr. Barringer does most of his work here," the maid explained. "But he has corporate headquarters downtown. Sometimes he goes there. Would you like the telephone number?"

"I don't want to bother him." Dani hesitated. "Were there— Did he leave a message for me?"

"There were no messages, Miss Zanetelle."

Dani wandered aimlessly onto the terrace. After feeling sorry for herself for a while, she began to get angry.

Rand was the one who'd suggested going shopping. If he'd changed his mind, the least he could do was let her know.

When the phone rang about eleven she dashed for it eagerly. The light went out of her eyes as she heard Keith's voice.

"I know you said your plans were up in the air, but I thought I'd take a chance that you're free today," he said. "How about lunch?"

For a moment Dani was tempted to accept. If Rand ever did get around to calling, it would show him she had better things to do than wait by the telephone. Then she remembered the endless hours in the dark restaurant.

"I'm sorry, Keith, not today."

"Come on, Dani," he coaxed. "I got up early just for you."

Her eyebrows rose. "Do you sleep this late every day?"

"Well, uh . . . I was out rather late last night."

"Mrs. Stanhope must be quite a swinger," Dani remarked.

"What do you mean?" he asked sharply.

"Weren't you supposed to take her someplace last night?"

"Yes, we . . . One of her cronies had a bridge party." He laughed lightly. "Those old ladies really have stamina. I couldn't get away until the early hours."

"It's a good thing you don't have to punch a time clock."

"Wouldn't that be gruesome?" His voice deepened. "No, I'm free as a bird and longing to see you."

"Not today," she repeated. "I . . . um . . . I'm waiting to hear from Grandfather."

Dani was glad she hadn't acted childishly when the phone rang again a short time later. It was Rand.

"I would have called sooner, but I got tied up in a meeting," he explained. "They're expecting me back in there, so I'll have to make this brief, honey."

Disappointment enveloped her like a cloak. "I understand."

"I'm sorry I can't make lunch today."

"It's all right," she mumbled.

"Will it be okay if I pick you up about three?"

Joy suddenly replaced Dani's depression. "That would be perfect! I thought you were calling to cancel our date."

"Would I stand up such a rich lady?" A cold finger touched her spine until he added, "That money must be burning a hole in your pocket."

"Oh...yes, I did want to buy a dress," she said. Rand mustn't know that shopping took second place to the pleasure of his company.

"I'll get away earlier if I can, but don't worry, we'll still have plenty of time."

The dress salon Rand took her to had such a rarefied atmosphere that Dani was glad at least one of them looked as though he belonged.

Rand wore a pale gray suit that was perfectly draped over his big frame. Although he must have dressed early that morning, his light blue shirt and coordinated tie were as fresh as if he'd just put them on.

An elegant brunette drifted across the white carpeting toward them. She directed a provocative smile toward Rand. "May I help you?"

"Miss Zanetelle would like to select a new wardrobe," he said.

When she reluctantly dragged her fascinated gaze from Rand's rugged face and turned it on Dani, the woman's expression seemed to say it was none too soon. "Of course, monsieur. If you'll be seated I'll bring some things to show mademoiselle.''

"I only want a dress, not a whole wardrobe,'' Dani protested as they sat down on a purple velvet love seat.

"Be a sport,'' he coaxed. "Blow the whole wad.''

Dani waited until the saleswoman had left. "This place looks terribly expensive. I don't know if I can afford more than one dress—if that.''

"Sure you can. Didn't you see all those thousand-franc notes?''

"It looked like Monopoly money,'' she said doubtfully. "How much do I have in dollars?''

"Enough. Trust me.''

Dani's smooth brow wrinkled. "I'd be terribly embarrassed if I bought more than I could pay for.''

"Your grandfather would be delighted to make up the difference,'' Rand said casually.

Her small chin set firmly. "We've been through all that.''

"Okay, let's do this. Give me your money and I'll tell you when you've reached your limit.''

It wasn't like Rand to give in so easily. "I don't believe you.''

"Is that a nice thing to say to a man who walked out on the president of a bank just so I could take you shopping?''

"Did Grandfather tell you to do that?'' she asked searchingly.

A look of annoyance crossed his strong face. "Do you see any strings attached to my arms and legs? I'm not a puppet, Dani. I'm here because I want to be, but you're making it hard for me to understand why.''

"I'm sorry,'' she said miserably. "But you're always trying to make me do something I don't want to do.''

"Without much success," he commented dryly.

"I'm in Monte Carlo," she pointed out.

"Do you regret it?" He watched her without expression.

Dani honestly couldn't answer that. Coming to Monaco had changed her life—but for better or worse? She was becoming accustomed to things she couldn't afford, and she was falling in love with a man who would never settle down with one woman.

That was the minus side, but there were pluses, too. Dani knew she would never meet another man like Rand. He made everything magic. The smallest things became fun when she shared them with him—buying postcards, discussing anything at all. He could read the telephone book aloud and make it sound interesting.

"Your silence speaks volumes," Rand remarked coldly. "Well, at least you're not running out on Cleve. He'll have this month, anyway."

"I'm not sorry I came," Dani said quietly. "And I'll always remember this month, too."

Rand's grim expression vanished. "We'll have to make it a memorable one," he said softly.

The saleslady reappeared with an armful of garments that she placed over one of the chairs facing them. "I'm sorry it took so long. I wanted to select only our most fashionable outfits."

The gowns she displayed were outstanding. Dani had never seen anything like them in the discount stores where she usually shopped. There were afternoon dresses and evening gowns, sportswear and hostess gowns. The fabrics were costly and the workmanship superb.

"Shall we start with evening attire?" the saleswoman asked. "I always think they're the most interesting."

Also the most expensive, Dani thought privately. The chiffon, lace and satin creations she held up for their inspection were obviously costly.

"Those really aren't what I had in mind. I saw a stunning little black dress on someone," Dani said tentatively.

"I brought some of those, too, but first you must see this divine little thing."

With a theatrical flourish she held up a glittering outfit that completely captivated Dani. Narrow black satin pants were topped by an overblouse covered in multicolored sequins. The design was so subtle that it took a while to notice it was actually a tiger's face.

"It's gorgeous!" Dani gasped.

"And so in right now," the woman observed.

"Try it on," Rand suggested.

"I don't have any place to wear a thing like that," Dani objected.

"There's a charity affair scheduled," Rand said. "The foundation always takes a table. And you never know what other occasion might turn up."

"It would be a terrible waste of money. I wouldn't have any use for it when I got home." Dani's protest was weak as she eyed the seductive garment.

"At least try it on," Rand urged. "That doesn't cost anything."

Dani didn't notice the almost imperceptible signal he gave the saleswoman. After showing Dani to a dressing room, she returned to Rand. He gave her crisp instructions.

Dani was sold when she gazed at her reflection in the full-length mirror. The image staring back at her was that of a totally assured woman of the world, one Rand would be proud to be seen with. The top was colorful without being garish, and the slim black pants made her look tall and willowy.

It was probably wildly expensive, but Dani knew she couldn't live without it. She decided to consider it a very expensive souvenir. After all, it wasn't really her money, she reminded herself.

Rand's reaction was the clincher. His eyes lit up like the spangled top. "Fantastic!" he exclaimed. "You're going to take it, aren't you?"

She smiled wryly. "You knew I would."

"A very wise choice, mademoiselle." The saleswoman held up a short cream-colored silk dress with a pleated skirt. "And for less formal occasions, you might want to consider this."

Dani shook her head. "I think my shopping spree is over."

"The gentleman told me you were very fortunate at the casino," the brunette said tactfully. "You won enough for a complete wardrobe."

"Really?" Dani looked at Rand.

He let the saleswoman answer for him. *"Absolument,"* she said. "Your winnings will cover all of this." She indicated the garments piled over the chair.

Dani wouldn't have believed Rand, but a salesperson would scarcely lie. It must be something about the rate of exchange, Dani decided. The intricacies of foreign money baffled her.

Once she accepted the fact that she could afford it, Dani selected dresses and sportswear with happy abandon as Rand watched indulgently.

"I won't have to buy anything for the rest of the year," she told him.

He smiled. "You're not like other women I've known. Some of them consider a day wasted if they don't go shopping."

Roxanne, no doubt! "Most people have to work for a living," Dani commented primly. "Even if I didn't, I'd find something more meaningful to do with my time."

"Good for you," he said approvingly. "The parasites of this world are a boring lot."

"That's why I don't intend to become one," she said grimly.

What a hypocrite he was, Dani thought indignantly. Roxanne was about as useful as a Bible to an atheist, but that didn't seem to turn Rand off.

He frowned. "I presume you're referring to your grandfather. Letting him take care of you scarcely qualifies you as a grasshopper."

"It doesn't make me an ant."

"Okay, how about a compromise? Have you ever considered getting a job in Monte Carlo?"

"And living with Grandfather, you mean."

"What's wrong with that?"

"Not a thing. I could have breakfast in bed before being chauffered to work in his limousine," she said sarcastically.

"Now you're being ridiculous!" Rand said impatiently. "You can be just as independent as you would be in New York."

"You don't honestly believe that!"

They had reached a familiar impasse. It was recessed when the saleslady appeared and handed Rand a sales book to sign.

"Thank you for your patronage," she said happily. "I'll have your purchases delivered first thing in the morning, Miss Zanetelle."

"What's that for?" Dani asked ominously, eyeing the charge slip. "Do I owe more money?"

The woman hesitated, glancing at Rand, who tried to hide his annoyance at her indiscretion. He answered for her. "It comes to fifty-three dollars and eighty-six cents. Would you like to write me a check now, or wait until we get home? I don't want you to violate your principles by accepting anything that might be construed as a gift."

Dani began to wonder if she'd been naive. Could her winnings really have paid for everything she'd bought? The woman's hesitation was highly suspect. But Rand's face was like a thundercloud. If she questioned him here, it would lead to an argument, and she didn't want to squabble in front of the saleswoman.

His anger dissipated quickly once they left the dress salon. It was one of his endearing traits that he never sulked. But he did take her grandfather's side in every conflict. It would be nice if Rand cared that much about her, Dani thought wistfully.

The next two weeks were like a fairy tale. The times alone with Rand were the high points, but Dani also enjoyed the occasions when her grandfather joined them. It would have been difficult not to. Cleve received the kind of deference reserved for someone very rich and important, although he never asked for it.

It was more than the VIP treatment she received when she was with him, though. Dani found herself liking her grandfather in spite of herself. There were long periods when she forgot why she shouldn't. It made her all the more resistant when Rand pleaded Cleve's case—which he did at every opportunity. It was the source of their only arguments for a while.

There was just one other thing that bothered Dani, but she was careful not to mention it. In spite of the attention Rand lavished on her, there were nights when she didn't see him, nor did he mention what he was doing. Dani knew she had no right to expect it, but she suffered from a vivid imagination. Was he with Roxanne? The beautiful blonde was still very much in the picture. Since Monte Carlo was a small town, they ran across her often. Roxanne always left her party to come over and say hello—and to sink one of her barbs.

They were at a restaurant one night when she appeared at their table. As usual, she kissed Rand warmly. "I was going to call you, darling. The most dreadful thing happened," she said breathlessly. "I broke the clasp on the gorgeous bracelet you gave me and I feel lost without it."

He looked back at her calmly. "That doesn't sound earth-shattering. Have it repaired and send me the bill."

She threw her arms around his neck. "I knew you'd say that! He's so generous," Roxanne told Dani complacently.

After she left Rand said, "She had a birthday party and I gave her a little gold bracelet. Roxanne always makes a big deal out of everything."

"People tend to do that when something means a lot to them," Dani remarked coolly.

He started to reply, then changed his mind. Dani let the matter drop, too, because she didn't really want to face the facts.

Roxanne forced the issue the next time they met, putting an end to Dani's self-deception. It was in a nightclub this time. Roxanne rushed over without her usual smile.

The girl's eyes were wide with distress as she said, "I have something terrible to confess, *chéri*! I lost the key to your apartment."

Dani drew back her breath sharply. It was a tacky thing to say to a man who was with another woman, but Roxanne had clearly done it on purpose. She was spelling out their relationship, as Dani continued to poach on her property.

There were lines around Rand's firm mouth as he glanced at Dani's face. "Well, don't worry about it."

"Can you ever forgive me, darling? I don't know *how* it happened!"

"I *said* don't worry about it," he grated.

"I promise to be more careful next time." She kissed his cheek and skipped away before he could answer.

Rand broke the quivering silence that descended after Roxanne's departure. "It isn't what you're thinking," he began.

"I wasn't thinking anything." Dani lifted her chin and looked out over the crowded room.

"Then you're unique," he said gently. "There is usually only one reason why a man gives a woman a key to his apartment. But in this—"

"Oh, I don't know," Dani interrupted brittlely. "I can think of several. Maybe she volunteered to wash your windows or do your laundry. Roxanne must be marvelous at ironing shirts."

"If you'll just listen to me for a minute . . ."

"I'm sure you have reasons for everything you do, but it isn't necessary to give them to me. You must be having enough trouble explaining to Roxanne why you have to spend so much time with me."

"I don't *have* to do anything," he said evenly.

"It's nice of you to keep up the fiction."

Dani's heart felt like a leaden lump in her breast. Although she'd told herself that Rand's attentiveness was part of his job, she'd hoped it wasn't true. Now she knew it was. A man who gave his key to one woman didn't willingly spend most of his time with another. It had been stupid to think he was really interested in her. Suddenly Dani couldn't go through with the pretense anymore.

"Would you mind taking me home?" she asked.

"Dani, honey, you're overreacting." He took her hand. "Let me tell you what happened."

His voice was like dark velvet. It infuriated her that he thought she could still be taken in.

Dani removed her hand. "Don't you understand?" she said as lightly as she could manage. "I'm giving you time off for good behavior."

His mouth straightened to a grim line. "I don't know why I even bothered. You always know all the answers."

"And you're always trying to convince me I don't!"

"Not anymore. I'm considerably over twenty-one and I don't have to answer to you or anyone else!"

"Not to me, anyway," Dani said bitterly. "Can we go now?"

They were both silent in the car driving home. When they reached the villa, Rand left the motor running while he walked her to the door. He left her there with a coldly formal good-night. The tires screeched as he gunned down the driveway in his hurry to leave.

Dani really expected to hear from him the next day. Rand never held a grudge—although this was the angriest she'd ever seen him. Her remark about good behavior had struck a nerve, and she was sorry about it.

During a long sleepless night, Dani had come to terms with her situation. Rand had tried very hard to make her happy, no matter what his reasons. He'd played straight with her, too. He hadn't pretended he loved her, only that he wanted her. Perhaps that was reprehensible, considering that he was sleeping with Roxanne, but he hadn't tried to hide his actions from either of them. Rand was just a very virile man who wanted no commitments. You took him the way he was—or not at all.

Dani's romantic dreams were shattered, but there was no reason to stop seeing Rand. He was a marvelous companion, and there were only about two weeks left of her visit. Rand had promised to take her along the Grande Corniche, and she was anxious to see the places he described. Especially since her leg was almost healed. Who knew when, if ever, she would get to Europe again? Roxanne could just practice patience, Dani decided grimly.

There was only one problem. Rand didn't call.

The first day, Dani thought that for once he was sulking. But when he didn't phone or come to the villa the second day, she had to face the possibility that he didn't intend to.

Dani questioned her grandfather, trying to sound casual. "I haven't seen Rand around lately. Is he out of town?"

Cleve was evasive. "No, he…um…he's rather heavily involved in this Amsterdam deal. I've tried to tell him not to work so hard, but he has a mind of his own."

Dani got the picture. Rand could be pushed only so far.

When Keith called later that afternoon, she accepted his invitation to dinner. Keith had been phoning almost every day. He had coaxed, pleaded and begged, but even when Rand hadn't made a date in advance, she'd kept herself free in case he called at the last minute. Now she knew he wasn't going to.

Keith was ecstatic at his good fortune. "I'd almost given up hope," he remarked as they drove away from the villa. "I thought perhaps I'd done something to offend you."

"I've just been busy with Grandfather," Dani replied evenly. "That's really why I came here, to see him."

"You had time for Rand," Keith observed bitterly. "People saw you all over town together."

"Grandfather asked him to take me a few places." Her voice was emotionless.

"You'd think he'd ask me," Keith complained. "At least he knows he can trust *me*. I wouldn't let my *grandmother* go out with that stud!"

"I'm sure we can find something more interesting to talk about," Dani said distantly.

"You're right, darling. Let's talk about us," he murmured soulfully.

She didn't consider that a great improvement. "I'd rather not, if you don't mind," she said firmly.

"They've turned you against me, haven't they?"

"For heaven's sake, Keith! Can't we have a conversation that doesn't revolve around your injustice at the hands of my grandfather and Rand?"

"I'm sorry, Dani," he said hastily. "I guess I go overboard sometimes. I promise it won't happen again."

She regretted snapping at him, but any mention of Rand rasped on her already frayed nerves. Still, she shouldn't take it out on Keith.

"It's all right. I understand," she said in a muted voice. "They're both very strong personalities."

He resisted the temptation to agree with her. "Where would you like to go for dinner?" Keith asked instead.

"You pick the place," she said indifferently.

"I don't think you cared much for my last choice." He smiled wryly.

Dani hadn't thought he was that perceptive. "The food was delicious, Keith. It was just so...dark," she finished lamely.

"I wish you'd said something. I want so much to please you, Dani, but I don't know how unless you tell me."

"It was lovely," she said uncomfortably. "I just meant there wasn't any view."

"Tonight we'll make up for it by going to the Vistaero," he announced. "It's a smashing place. You can see the Côte d'Azur on one side, and the Italian Riviera on the other."

"Not the Vistaero," she said faintly.

They settled on a restaurant that held no memories for Dani. It had the required view and excellent food. As the evening progressed, Dani's tension lifted. Keith turned out to be surprisingly good company once he stopped whining. He wasn't as witty or well informed as Rand and her grandfather, but he was amusing. And his obvious devotion was balm to her wounded ego. Keith let it be known that he really was in love with her, but he didn't belabor the point.

Dani had such a pleasant evening that she accepted a date for the following day—after finding out what he had planned. She didn't intend to suffer through another cocktail party with his jet-set friends. But Keith suggested an art exhibit that was generating a lot of interest.

Dani dressed for her date in a white linen suit with an emerald green silk shell underneath. It was one of the outfits she'd selected with Rand. She remembered his comments about how flattering it was with her green eyes and long auburn hair.

Keith was extremely complimentary. His eyes glowed the way Rand's had. Would everything always remind her of Rand, Dani wondered despairingly.

At least the showing took her mind off him. The Impressionist paintings required all Dani's concentration.

After that, Keith took her to tea at his mother's house. It had a starkly modern interior, which had obviously been furnished by a decorator—and looked it. Everything was done for effect, not livability. Dani couldn't help comparing it to her grandfather's villa, which was more elegant, yet at the same time comfortable.

Lulu looked older in the daylight. Her throat was slightly crepey, and there were lines around her mouth that no number of face lifts could completely erase, but she was as chic as she'd been the night at Cleve's house. Her hair was perfectly coiffed and her caftan was expensive.

After greeting Dani effusively, Lulu inspected her outfit with a knowledgeable eye. "What a stunning suit, *chérie*. Did you get it in New York?"

"No, at a shop on the Boulevard St-Martin."

Lulu nodded. "I thought it was the one I saw there. I wanted it passionately, but it was so terribly costly and I've spent my allowance for the month."

If this woman said it was expensive, Dani shuddered to think what her suit had cost. Once more Rand had put something over on her. She hadn't won enough to pay for all those clothes. Didn't he ever tell her the truth about *anything*?

The conversation shifted to other topics, not necessarily for the better. Lulu complained that she hadn't seen Dani since that first night.

"It's your own fault, Mother," Keith commented. "Weren't you going to give a luncheon for Dani?"

"You're right. I've been in such a whirl lately that it completely slipped my mind. That's no excuse, though."

"I appreciate the thought, but it isn't necessary," Dani said hastily.

"Oh, but it is! What will people think? It's the very worst manners not to entertain for a guest."

"Please don't bother. I won't be here much longer, anyway."

Lulu looked startled. "You're not leaving already? You just got here!"

"It's been almost two and a half weeks."

"Then we'll have to phone instead of sending out written invitations," Lulu said decisively. "Sunday is indecently soon, but I think I can pull it together."

"I can't make it on Sunday," Keith said.

"Of course you can. What's more important than dear little Dani?" When he looked at her meaningfully, Lulu said, "Oh, that's right, I forgot. Your...um...other commitment." She opened a leather engagement book. "Oh, dear, next week is a disaster."

"I'm sure you'll find time," Keith said.

Something in his voice made her look up quickly. As their eyes met, Lulu said, "You're right, of course. We'll have it on Monday. Save the date, Dani."

There was nothing else she could do. When they left, Lulu was happily writing down names.

That was on Friday afternoon. Dani spent the evening with Keith, and also the next day. On Saturday night she begged off, saying she had to spend it with her grandfather. Dani really did feel guilty about neglecting Cleve, although he hadn't complained.

They had dinner on the terrace again. Dani's eyes were shadowed as she looked out over the marina. She was going to miss this place. Even now that the breathless excitement of being with Rand was over, she could still appreciate Monte Carlo's charm. She would miss her grandfather, too, Dani admitted to herself.

"It's very lovely here. I'm glad I came," she said quietly.

Hope flared on his face. "Would you consider staying?"

Dani shook her head regretfully. Even if she could reconcile it with the years of prejudice against him, there was still Rand. In the days since he'd walked out of her life so abruptly, Dani had come to a realization. She was in love with Rand. It wasn't just a sexual attraction. She wanted to spend the rest of her life with him. How could she bear to stay when it was an unattainable dream?

"It's better if we leave things the way they were," she told Cleve gently.

"You know that's impossible. I can't lose you now! Will you at least come back for a visit?" he pleaded.

Dani gazed down at the lace tablecloth. "Maybe you'll come to New York to visit me instead."

Cleve's eyes narrowed as he stared at her bent head. After a long moment of speculation he said, "If that's what you'd prefer. But why are we talking about it now? Your visit is far from over."

After dinner, Cleve taught Dani to play chess. While she pondered the intricate moves, his enigmatic eyes never left her face. Anyone who'd ever had dealings with

Cleveland J. Barringer could have told Dani he was a wily opponent who didn't give up easily.

As they were saying good-night, Cleve remarked, "I hope you have plans for tomorrow, my dear. Unfortunately I won't be able to spend the day with you. A long-standing engagement," he explained apologetically.

Dani assured him she didn't mind. After she'd gone to her room, Cleve went into the den and closed the door. In spite of the late hour, he picked up the phone and dialed a number.

"I didn't expect you to be home on a Saturday night," he said when Rand answered.

"Why did you call, then?" The younger man's surly tone made Cleve smile unaccountably. "I was reading in bed," Rand muttered.

"Alone, I take it."

"Yes, if you must know. What do you want, Cleve?" Rand's voice suddenly took on a different note. "Is something the matter? Is it Dani?"

"Yes, it's Dani. Tonight at dinner she talked about going home."

"So what else is new?" Rand asked sardonically.

"I just thought you might want to see her before she leaves."

"She isn't leaving in the next couple of days, is she?" Rand sounded startled.

"We didn't get around to mentioning an actual date, but I gather time is running out." Cleve sighed heavily.

After a moment's silence, Rand said irritably, "I *told* you to see that she was amused. I suppose she's getting bored."

"I don't think that's it. Keith has been keeping her busy night and day."

"And you permitted it?" Rand's outrage sizzled across the telephone wires.

"What could I do?" Cleve sounded helpless, but he looked extremely pleased with himself.

"You could tell her that your nephew is a gigolo who supplements his allowance with gifts from the wealthy women he services!"

"You know I couldn't do that. Keith has undoubtedly filled her full of stories about how unfairly he's been treated. That you and I are in a conspiracy against him. Besides, as long as she's leaving so soon, anyway, I'd rather she didn't find out the truth," Cleve added craftily.

Rand swore savagely. "I'd like to take that little creep apart!"

"Well, none of this is your problem. Sorry to have disturbed you. I guess I just wanted to tell my troubles to someone. Go back to your book."

"Wait!" Rand called urgently. "I suppose I could talk to Dani again, although I don't think it will help." He sounded extremely frustrated, which was unusual for Rand.

"It couldn't hurt."

"I'll try and give her a ring tomorrow," Rand said casually.

"I'd really appreciate that. She doesn't have any plans, and I have something I can't get out of."

Cleve's patrician face was filled with amusement as he hung up. Even a wily young maverick like Rand could be tamed by the right filly.

Chapter Seven

Cleve offered Dani the car and chauffeur if she wanted to go anyplace that Sunday, but she decided to stay by the pool all afternoon. Until then she'd never made use of it.

After lunch, she put on a pink bikini and went out on the patio with a book, a small portable radio and a big straw hat with a rose on the brim. She turned the radio to soft music and stretched out on a chaise to enjoy the sunshine.

Dani looked regretfully at her creamy skin. She'd wanted to bring back a tan from the Riviera, but now it was too late. It would have faded rapidly anyway, she consoled herself. Would her memories of Rand be that cooperative?

She stood up swiftly and pinned her long hair on top of her head before sliding into the pool. Dani had no intention of spending the day feeling sorry for herself. After a vigorous couple of laps, she grasped the coping to rest for a while. She was enjoying the beautiful scenery in the distance when a splash startled her. Someone was swimming underwater toward her, like a shark closing in.

Rand surfaced just inches away. He blinked star-pointed lashes as he raked the thick dark hair off his forehead.

"What are you doing here?" Dani gasped. She couldn't have been more surprised if he *had* been a shark.

White teeth gleamed in his tanned face. "I decided to forgive you."

"What makes you think I forgive *you*?" she asked indignantly.

"For what?"

For making me more miserable than I've ever been in my life! she wanted to shout. "You know very well," she muttered instead.

"It seems to me *I'm* the injured party here. At least I don't condemn people without a trial."

"You weren't on trial. You have the right to do anything you like. I guess I was just annoyed at the way it came out. You'll have to admit it was a little tacky." Dani couldn't keep the resentment out of her voice.

"Extremely so."

Frustration engulfed her. "Then if you agree with me, why didn't you phone?"

"Because I don't appreciate being called a gigolo like—" He stopped abruptly. Reaching out, he cupped a hand around her neck, pulling her closer. "Did you miss me?" he murmured.

They were so close that their thighs touched and then parted as the water bobbed them back and forth. Rand scissored his legs around both of Dani's to keep her from floating away. The contact was even more intimate because only two scraps of cloth separated their bodies.

Even the cool water couldn't dispel the surge of heat from his powerful loins. It lit a smoldering fire in Dani that water wouldn't douse.

His fingertips trailed tantalizingly over the base of her throat. "You didn't answer my question."

She was having trouble remembering what it was. The water was moving her sensuously against Rand's body, in the center of his clasped legs. She wanted to put her arms around his neck and pull him even closer.

Dani moistened her lips nervously. "No, I... Keith was very nice to me."

Rand's expression hardened for an instant. Then he bent his head and nibbled on her earlobe. "It isn't difficult to be nice to you."

"You've certainly changed your tune since the other night," Dani said faintly.

He traced the curving top of her bikini bra, easing it down until it just covered her nipples. "It was hell staying away from you. I missed you even if you didn't miss me."

If he only knew! Dani couldn't keep it from him any longer. "I did miss you, Rand," she whispered. "Nothing was any fun without you."

Triumph flared in his eyes. "My dear little Dani!"

His mouth covered hers hungrily, drinking all the sweetness within. He probed with a deep masculine desire as Dani clung to him and the water lapped sensuously around them. She surrendered completely, allowing her love to express itself because she knew he would mistake it for mere passion.

As Rand dragged his mouth away to cover her face and neck with tingling kisses, Dani closed her eyes to savor the exquisite feeling. But when he freed one small firm breast and lifted her slightly so it was above the water, Dani's eyes flew open.

"Rand, you mustn't! The servants!"

"I don't care about them," he muttered. "I want to look at you and touch you."

Her protests stilled when he licked a drop of water from the underside of her breast. His tongue made a circle, lapping up each drop on her sensitive skin until Dani was trembling in his arms. When his lips sucked a final drop from the tip of her nipple, she moaned and dug her nails into his back.

Rand clasped her tightly and buried his face in her neck. "That must be what nectar tastes like," he murmured huskily. His fingers fumbled with the string ties on her briefs. "I want to taste every inch of your beautiful body."

Dani grabbed for his hand. "You have to stop, Rand! It isn't only the servants. Other villas look down on this one!"

"They can't see underwater."

He released her and ducked under the surface. While he held on to her ankles, Rand's mouth slid up the inside of her thigh. His teeth fastened on the edge of her bikini bottom and tugged it aside so he could reach his objective. A bolt of pure pleasure raced through Dani, like none she had ever experienced before. After the initial shock she tugged feebly on Rand's hair, but he held her ankles apart and continued his torment.

When he finally surfaced for a huge gulp of air, Dani flung her arms around his neck so he couldn't dive again. "No more, Rand," she gasped.

He kissed the corner of her mouth. "Don't fight it, sweetheart. We're going to make love. You know it's inevitable."

"Not here." It was the only objection she could offer.

"Would you like to go to my place?" His voice was as liquid as the water around them.

"Yes! Oh, yes," Dani breathed.

Rand helped her out of the pool and wrapped her in a big towel. His topaz eyes were brilliant as he stared down at her. "It's going to be so good, angel."

"I know," she whispered, but she couldn't look at him.

There was no question about how good it would be, yet Dani couldn't help wishing these moments would happen when they were alone in a private place. Where they could make love spontaneously, without time for little doubts to surface.

As though he read her mind, Rand said, "Before we go, I want to talk to you." He led her to a chair at an umbrella table and sat down facing her. "It's about Roxanne."

Dani's long lashes swept down. "You don't have to tell me anything."

"I know I don't. If I did, I wouldn't." He laughed. "Does that make sense?"

"Yes, but I'd rather not hear it if you don't mind."

Dani had made her decision. There was no turning back in spite of the pain that might lie ahead, so what was the use of spoiling what little time she was allotted?

"I do mind," he answered. "I didn't give Roxanne a key for the reason you think. She doesn't live with me. She doesn't even visit."

"Please, Rand." Dani looked up reproachfully.

"I'll admit I had a short fling with her some time back." He shrugged. "It isn't being ungentlemanly to say that many men have had a short fling with Roxanne. She's happy to supply the details. But it's been over with us for a long time. Roxanne simply refuses to accept the fact."

"The key?" Dani's question was almost too faint to be heard.

"She asked if she could give a surprise party for her mother at my apartment. I was going out of town, so I gave her the key. She never returned it. As a matter of fact, I forgot all about it. Until the other night," he added grimly.

A huge weight seemed to have lifted from Dani's shoulders. "Why didn't you tell me?"

"I tried to, but you wouldn't listen. And then I lost my temper. But you must admit you goaded me into it."

Dani looked at him repentantly. "Why do you put up with me?"

Rand's hand circled the base of her throat. "I can think of a couple of hundred reasons." As he bent his head to kiss her, Cleve came onto the patio.

"What a nice surprise, Rand," he said casually. "Have you been keeping Dani amused in my absence?"

Rand smiled mischievously. "You'll have to ask her."

Dani's color rose as she stammered, "Yes, we... uh... we went swimming."

"That's nice." Cleve turned to Rand. "Are you busy this evening? Charlotte Langlois asked us over to-night—you too, if you're free. I said I couldn't answer for you."

"Well, Dani and I had sort of made plans."

Cleve frowned. "I wish I'd known. Charlotte asked some people she'd especially like Dani to meet. But of course you didn't know."

"It's up to Dani." Rand's eyes sought hers.

She was torn in different directions. Dani knew what she *wanted* to do, but there were other considerations.

She admired the woman she'd met at the casino, and it was kind of her to entertain a virtual stranger. Cleve was looking forward to it, too.

Rand took pity on her. "I guess we can put our plans on hold." He gave Dani a melting smile. "I've been promising you a trip to Nice. Suppose we start early and make a day and night of it." The last was added with a special gleam in his eyes.

Dani was about to agree eagerly when she remembered Lulu's luncheon. She couldn't help groaning as she told them about it.

Rand's tender amusement fled, leaving his expression icy. "Whose bright idea was that?"

"I tried to talk her out of it, but she didn't pay any attention," Dani said apologetically.

"A perfect description of my sister Lulu," Cleve remarked dryly.

"I'm sure she's going to invite both of you," Dani said. "You'll come, won't you?" She was anxious for moral support.

It was obvious that Rand, at least, wasn't going to give it. "Lulu would sooner invite the Boston strangler to lunch," he snapped. "And I'd rather share it with him." It was evidence of his deep disappointment, because Rand's comments about Lulu and Keith were usually only lightly derogatory.

"You'll come, won't you, Grandfather?" she asked hopefully.

"I'd love to, my dear, but I'm severely allergic to my sister's luncheons," he said with a twinkle in his dark eyes.

"You're two of a kind," Dani said disgustedly.

"It's your own fault." Rand wasn't sympathetic. "You ought to learn to say no." When she raised a feathery eyebrow at him, he laughed. "At least when the possibilities of enjoying yourself are limited."

Dani's mouth curved in an irresistible smile. "I'll expect you to make it up to me tomorrow night." When she realized that might sound too revealing to her grandfather, she added, "My sacrifice should be worth a first-rate dinner."

Before Rand could confirm it, Cleve said, "You're meeting Stevens at the airport tomorrow night. He's bringing those contracts from Amsterdam, and he has to fly back as soon as we check them over."

Rand swore under his breath as he gazed somberly at Dani. "At this rate we might never get around to all the things we planned. Cleve says you're leaving soon."

"Well, I... Maybe I could stay a little longer," she said.

"That would be wonderful, my dear!" In an excess of joy, Cleve clasped Rand's shoulder.

The gesture wasn't lost on Dani. Was she being flimflammed again? Had Rand made love to her just to keep her here for her grandfather's sake? But when she remembered his tenderness, and the passion that couldn't be faked, Dani was impatient with herself.

The party at Charlotte Langlois's villa was a sheer delight. It almost made up for the loss of Dani's evening alone with Rand. Almost. She did get to meet a lot of fascinating people, though.

Dani had a feeling they were the kind of people Keith's friends were trying to be. Charlotte's guests were erudite without being superior, friendly without wanting any favors. They were all involved in some kind of work instead of frittering their time away in a boring attempt to keep occupied. Dani's eyes sparkled as she told Rand about the man who had explained the Common Market in terms she could understand.

"I intended to do that once I got your full attention," he teased.

"You never noticed I have a mind," she replied impatiently.

His laughter fled. "Don't ever say that, Dani. I want a great deal more from you than your body."

Her heart took a giant leap. Was there really hope? Before she could explore the possibility, their hostess joined them.

"I hope you didn't mind this last-minute invitation," Charlotte said.

"Not at all. Dani and I were wondering what to do with ourselves tonight." Rand's mouth curved wryly.

Charlotte's intelligent eyes regarded him understandingly. "They do say patience is a virtue," she murmured.

Rand chuckled. "The people who say that are usually eighty years old."

"I've been admiring your paintings," Dani told Charlotte hastily. "Are they your work?"

"Some of them."

Dani mentioned the Impressionist showing she'd been to, and the discussion turned to the different schools of art.

Dani and Rand drifted into separate groups after that. Sometime later he rejoined her and curved his hand around the back of her neck.

Bending his head, he murmured in her ear, "I think we've fulfilled our obligations to everyone. How about cutting out?"

Their eyes met in a glance that made Dani's pulse beat faster. "I'd like that. Just let me tell Grandfather."

He was sitting in a chair at the far end of the room while a cluster of people stood around him. As Dani and Rand walked toward the group she felt a prickle of apprehension. Cleve's face appeared drawn. He wasn't displaying his usual charm, either.

"I don't think Grandfather looks well," she said.

Rand frowned in concern. "He does look kind of rocky." When they reached the group, he put his hand on Cleve's shoulder. "How about it, Chief? Are you ready to leave?"

The older man's smile was forced. "Dani's enjoying herself. It's early yet."

"The party's over," Rand stated firmly.

Over Cleve's protests, they made their farewells and hurried him out.

"We know you don't feel well. What seems to be the trouble?" Rand asked in the car going home.

"Not a thing. You're making a big fuss about nothing," Cleve insisted.

"You don't have to be a big brave boy in front of us," Rand said impatiently. "I'm calling Dr. Leroux when we get home."

"Don't do that. It's just a little indigestion."

Dani knew the same symptoms could indicate something more serious. She held his hand tightly. "Please let Rand call the doctor. I'm worried about you."

There was a catch in her grandfather's voice as he said, "That makes me feel a hundred percent better."

"And *we'll* feel better after you've seen the doctor," Rand said grimly.

"He'll tell me what I already know. That a man my age shouldn't eat chili dogs with onions on them."

"Where would you be served something like that?" Rand asked in surprise.

"I walked past a little hot dog stand and they smelled so good." Cleve looked slightly shamefaced. "The second one was a mistake, though."

"That's putting it mildly!" Rand exclaimed. "Your stomach's only accustomed to the finest French cuisine."

"It's going to welcome some American antacid tablets," Cleve answered ruefully.

There was no question of leaving him alone. After Cleve had gone to his room, Rand said good-night to Dani in the entry.

He took her in his arms and rested his cheek on her temple. "I'd stay, but it would only frustrate both of us."

"I know," she murmured, inhaling the heady masculine aroma of his skin.

He brushed his lips lightly across hers. "Tuesday seems like a million years away."

"To me, too." The tip of her tongue traced the closed line of his lips.

He captured her tongue in his mouth and curled his hand around her breast. A spreading warmth started in the pit of Dani's stomach as his thumb made slow circles over her sensitive nipple. When she moved against him, clasping her arms around his neck, he gripped her hips tightly and held them against his thrusting loins.

After a long moment, Rand dragged his mouth away with a groan. "Oh, God, this is just what I was trying to avoid. In a minute I'm going to take you right here on the floor, and I don't want it to be that way, sweetheart." He lifted her chin and looked deeply into her eyes. "I want to make love to you, not just have sex."

"Oh, Rand." It was all Dani could say, but it was enough.

He kissed the tip of her nose. "If you need me for anything at all, don't hesitate to call."

Concern for her grandfather made Dani's passion recede. "You don't think it's anything more than indigestion, do you?"

"I hope not."

That frightened her. "I'm worried, Rand. I think we should have called the doctor."

He looked at her searchingly. "You'd care if it were serious, wouldn't you?"

"Of course I would!" she exclaimed. "He's my grandfather! What kind of person do you think I am?"

"A very wonderful one." He folded her in his arms and kissed the top of her head.

After Rand left, Dani undressed and got into bed with a book. She was too keyed up to sleep, but she couldn't concentrate on reading, either.

Did Rand really want more from her than sex, as he'd said twice that night? That would mean he loved her! Enough to marry her, though? That was like asking for the moon. She would settle for his love. It was more than she'd ever dared to hope for. Maybe in time... but there wasn't much of that left.

For the first time, Dani considered staying in Monaco. Wouldn't she be out of her mind to leave now when there was so much at stake? It would also make her grandfather very happy.

Dani's dreamy expression faded as she remembered how bad Cleve had looked. He was such a handsome, dynamic man that he seemed ageless, but with that gray tinge to his skin he'd looked every one of his years.

Was it really just indigestion? Dani's apprehension grew. What if he needed something and couldn't reach the bell? After a few moments of indecision, she got up and put on a robe.

Dani opened her grandfather's bedroom door noise-lessly, but Cleve wasn't asleep. He was reading in bed and he looked a great deal better than when they'd brought him home. In the soft light of the bedside lamp, his color was normal and his face was free of pain.

"Did you want something, child?" Cleve looked up questioningly.

"I just wanted to be sure you were all right. Rand and I were worried about you."

"I'm sure he told you I'm much too mean to die." Cleve smiled to cover his emotion.

Dani felt the same constraint. She wanted to tell him not to talk about dying, but they both had trouble expressing their feelings. "You wouldn't run out on me when we're just getting to know each other," she said lightly.

"I've had a full life, but you've given meaning to it, Dani," he said quietly. "I know how hard it was for you to come here, and I'll always be grateful."

"Nobody would consider it a hardship to accept a trip to the Riviera," she joked.

"You did," he answered somberly. "You don't want anything from me."

"That should be refreshing." Dani tried to get back on a light note.

"Money has its advantages and its drawbacks," he admitted. "You learn to accept the fact."

"I never realized that before," she said slowly. "I always thought it was an unalloyed blessing."

Cleve's mouth curved wryly. "I take it this visit has been an eye-opener."

"It's been a revelation," she agreed. "I never knew how important money was to some people."

"Unfortunately, not to you," he said dryly.

She gazed at him steadily. "Would you want it to be?"

"No, you're everything I could have wished for." He looked at her lovely face almost clinically. "I always wanted a daughter, but it wasn't meant to be. Maybe you're God's reward for some of my disappointments in life."

"They must have been minor." Dani glanced around the baronial bedroom that was larger than the living room in many houses.

"If you're judging by material things. But we agreed that money isn't everything. If you strip away the fancy trappings, I'm a childless old man."

"You aren't old," Dani protested. "Certainly not by today's standards."

He smiled. "You're very kind, my dear. But you can't dispute the fact that I'm alone."

"Why didn't you ever marry again?" she asked curiously.

"In retrospect, I should have. But I channeled all my energies into business. And my son took a lot of time." His eyes were shadowed.

"No one ever told me how my father died," Dani said tentatively.

"He was killed in an automobile accident."

"That must have been horrible for you!"

Cleve sighed. "His life was so wasted."

"I know it hurts to talk about him, but he was my father. Couldn't you tell me something about him?"

Cleve hesitated. "He was very handsome and very charming."

"But what was he like? Was he compassionate? Did he have a sense of humor? Was he someone you could lean on?"

They both knew who she was describing. "Danny wasn't anything like Rand," Cleve said gently.

"I didn't mean . . ." Her voice trailed off.

"There aren't many men like Rand. I don't know what I would have done without him."

"I'm glad he was there when you needed him," Dani said impulsively.

"That's very generous," Cleve said softly. "Can I hope you've changed your mind a little since you came here?"

Dani stared down at her fingernails. "You're different from what I expected."

"But?" He sensed the reservation in her answer.

She lifted her head and looked straight at him. "You've never explained why you broke up my mother's marriage."

A veil dropped behind Cleve's eyes, although he continued to look back at her. "My only excuse is that I made a terrible mistake."

It didn't seem enough to compensate for the ruin of her mother's life. And it didn't jibe with the kind of man her grandfather appeared to be. Maybe he had changed through the years. It had all happened such a long time ago.

Dani suddenly realized this was no time for such a discussion. Cleve's face looked white and strained again. "You'd better get some sleep," she said.

Dani went back to her own room with the same unanswered questions buzzing around in her head. One of the largest concerned her father. It was frustrating the way the conversation always veered away from him. Would she ever find out what he'd been like?

Cleve seemed fully recovered the next morning. Dani found him in the den with Rand, hard at work.

After exchanging a special glance with Rand, Dani asked about her grandfather's health. "Shouldn't you be taking it easy today?"

"I'm a new man." He grinned like a small boy. "And a wiser one."

"Don't trust him," Rand warned. "He might have given up hot dogs, but he's probably switched to tacos."

"At least warn us when you're going on an eating binge so we won't get into such a flap," Dani scolded.

"He likes the attention," Rand said.

"How else can I get a beautiful young girl to sit by my bed?" Cleve asked.

Rand laughed. "You're older than I thought, Chief."

"Since you two seem so chipper this morning, how about coming to Aunt Lulu's luncheon with me?" Dani asked hopefully.

Cleve smiled broadly. "You wouldn't ask that of a sick man, would you?"

She raised an eyebrow. "I thought you were all better."

"The pain comes and goes."

When Dani looked at Rand, he shook his head hastily. "I caught what Cleve had."

"It's the first time I ever heard of indigestion being catching, but I get the message," she remarked, giving them up as a lost cause.

The chauffeur drove Dani to Lulu's villa. As she smoothed the pleated skirt of her silk print, Dani was grateful that at least she was dressed in style. It would probably be the only thing she had in common with her great-aunt's friends.

Her prediction proved to be correct. Lulu had assembled an unexpectedly large number of people at such short notice, all of them brittlely sophisticated. Since it was a luncheon on a week day, Dani was surprised at the number of men present.

They were all ages, not merely older men who might be retired. The things they had in common were expensive clothes, glib tongues and an almost fanatical preoccupation with fitness. There wasn't a paunch or a sagging chin on any of them.

Dani commented on it in a delicate way to the older man she was chatting with. "The gyms in Monte Carlo must be very busy."

"The plastic surgeons are busier," he answered dryly.

"I was referring to the men," she explained.

"So was I."

Dani was startled. She knew that movie stars and many people in the public eye had cosmetic surgery, but why would these men go through that? Her grandfather kept trim by exercising, and the lines in his face gave him character.

"It's the pursuit of youth and women." The man gave a little laugh. "Not necessarily in that order."

"Women find older men interesting," she protested.

"But they don't want to sleep with them."

Dani couldn't help finding that distasteful. The man looked to be in his late forties, but she had a feeling his true age was ten years more than that. He ought to be playing with his grandchildren instead of being obsessed with his sex life.

"There's always marriage as an option," she said coolly.

He laughed. "You're a naive little thing, aren't you?"

"For believing in getting married and growing old gracefully with one person?"

"You certainly don't take after your father," he said derisively.

Dani stiffened. "You knew him?"

"Everyone knew Danny Barringer. He was a smashing chap."

"What was he like?" When the man looked at her in surprise she said, "I never met him."

"That's strange!" There was curiosity in his eyes. "Which one was your mother—number one, two or three?"

"My father was married three times?"

"You didn't know that, either? Yes, Danny boy wore a path to the altar. Let's see if I can remember all their names. There was Bobbi and Sylvia, and what was the other one's name?" His brow wrinkled and then cleared. "Of course! Margo Benson. How could I forget? She was a real looker. Married to the Duke of Chisholm and living in London, last I heard."

Dani was no longer listening. It was a shock to find out her father had been married three times after his brief marriage to her mother. Cleve had ruined his son's life, too, she thought bitterly. Danny had gone through his shortened life looking for the happiness he'd had and lost. A terrible thought occurred to her. Maybe his death hadn't been an accident, after all.

"My father must have been a very unhappy man," she said soberly.

"You've got to be joking! Good old Danny was the life of every party. Terrible shame the way he wrapped himself around that tree, but that's the way he would have wanted to go. There's only one way that would have pleased him more.'' The man smiled suggestively.

A shiver of distaste ran up Dani's spine. She was about to walk away when Keith joined them and put his arm around her shoulders.

"What do you think of my girl, Willard?" he asked. "Isn't she gorgeous?"

"Simply smashing." It seemed to be his favorite adjective. "You really hit the jackpot this time."

"I know." Keith smiled fatuously at Dani. "I can't believe my good fortune."

"Are congratulations in order?" the older man asked.

"No, they're not!" Dani snapped. "You'll have to excuse us." She dragged Keith over to a corner of the room. "I wish you'd stop giving people the impression that there's something going on between us!"

"There is for me." He put his hands on her shoulders and gazed at her with such hunger that Dani's anger softened.

"We've talked about this, Keith. I told you it was too soon."

"I don't have much time to convince you." His hands moved caressingly. "I can't just let you walk out of my life, darling. You mean too much to me."

"I'm really sorry, Keith." She didn't know what else to say.

His hands tightened almost painfully. "I won't give you up, Dani! I've waited all my life for something like this—someone like you to come along, I mean."

"People are staring at us," Dani murmured as Lulu bore down on them.

"You two look very *intime* over here in the corner," Lulu said archly. "Is something going on that I should know about?"

"No, nothing," Dani said hastily.

"I heard a rumor about wedding bells," the older woman persevered. "Is there going to be an announcement? Wouldn't that be a delicious surprise for the guests!"

"That's a marvelous idea!" Keith exclaimed. "We don't have to set a date, baby doll. Just let me tell everyone we're engaged."

"It's out of the question!" They had Dani pinned in a corner, and she was beginning to feel desperate. Keith and his mother were like juggernauts rolling over her.

Relief came from a strange diversion. A murmur swept the room, like the rustle of dry leaves. It even penetrated Lulu and Keith's absorption. They turned to see what was happening.

Blanche Stanhope was standing in the door of the living room, her face masklike. As she started toward them, a path opened in the crowded room. Even the people who continued their conversations watched expectantly.

The woman's eyes glittered with some strong emotion as she reached their little group. "I knew my invitation must have been lost in the mail, so I decided not to stand on ceremony."

"Well, I... There wasn't time to send invitations, so I...I just telephoned." Lulu's face flushed unbecomingly. "You...uh... I couldn't reach you."

"How strange that you didn't have Keith ask me." Blanche's thin lips curled in something that was supposed to be a smile. "He asks me for everything else."

Keith's face was white as he glanced at Dani's expression. "Let me get you some champagne, Blanche." He took her arm, but she pulled it free.

"I wouldn't dream of taking you away from your... What did you call her? Cousin?" Her eyes raked Dani from head to toe. "You must be very rich, darling."

It was such a tasteless remark that Dani's mouth actually dropped open.

"She *is* my cousin," Keith said urgently. "Please don't make a scene, Blanche."

"I already have," she answered mockingly, looking around at the avidly listening guests.

They hurriedly went back to their own conversations, but it was obvious that she was right.

There was no longer any doubt that Keith had some kind of relationship with the woman. Dani felt a shiver of distaste ripple up her spine. Had he actually made love to her? It seemed to be the national pastime among these people. No wonder none of them worked. They didn't have time!

Their decadence made Dani feel like going home and scrubbing her skin clean. She decided the first part was in order, anyway.

"If you'll excuse me, Aunt Lulu, I have to leave now," Dani said firmly.

"You can't leave yet! Everything will... Oh, dear... I just wish..."

Dani left her in midbabble. She saw Keith start forward, and Blanche put a jeweled hand on his arm. Dani had reached the limousine when Keith caught up to her.

"You can't leave like this! I can explain," he said.

"I'm not interested," Dani replied curtly.

"I know how it looks, but at least listen to my side of it, darling. Blanche came here today expressly to make trouble."

"I figured that out for myself. Goodbye, Keith."

"Wait!" He put a hand on the door handle, preventing her from getting in the car. "All right, she's in love with me. But that isn't my fault, is it?" He looked at her boyishly.

"She just got the idea all by herself? You had nothing to do with it?"

"I told you about taking her out to please Mother. That's how it all started. I just considered her a good deed. How could I think of her any other way?"

"Evidently you did," Dani said distastefully.

"No! What happened was, one night Blanche had too much to drink. She began to talk about her marriage. I'd always assumed it had been happy, but apparently her husband was a brute. She began to cry."

"Blanche?"

"I was surprised, too. It's kind of terrible to see such a strong person go to pieces. She said no man had ever really loved her, that nobody gave a damn. Well, what could I do? I put my arms around her and told her *I* cared. I meant as a *person*, a friend. But she didn't take it that way," he said helplessly.

"Why didn't you set her straight?"

"She was so pathetically grateful that I couldn't bring myself to do it."

"You don't seem to have gotten around to it since then, either," Dani observed grimly.

"God knows I've tried!" he groaned. "But she won't let me alone. You saw how she showed up uninvited today. And you undoubtedly heard all the jokes people are making. I just don't know what to do."

His explanation made Dani feel better. She didn't like to think Keith was that depraved.

"You have to stop being such a wimp," she said impatiently. "If you don't clear things up, your life won't be your own."

"You're right, of course. That's exactly what I'm going to do." His rather weak face firmed as he opened the car door. "I won't ask you to come back inside because this is bound to be unpleasant, and I don't want you involved. I'll make it all up to you tonight, darling."

"Not tonight," Dani said. She'd had enough of Keith for one day. "And not tomorrow, either," she added hastily.

He didn't put up as much of an argument as she expected. Keith seemed anxious to get back inside. He probably wanted to get the whole mess over with, Dani decided.

She couldn't help feeling sorry for him, even though he'd brought it on himself. But Dani had her own problems. The things she'd learned about her father were deeply depressing. No wonder Rand and her grandfather never wanted to talk about him.

The fragile rapport that had started to build between Dani and her grandfather was shattered by the day's revelations. Cleve had destroyed both her parents. No amount of charm could blind her to that anymore. His remorse was after the fact.

Dani could hear Rand's voice when she entered the villa, but for once she didn't want to see him. She was starting for her room when he came out of the den.

"I thought I heard you come in. How was your luncheon?" He grinned impishly.

"About what I expected."

Rand's smile faded as he noticed her set expression. "Is anything wrong, Dani?"

"No." She turned toward the hall again, but he stopped her.

"Something happened, and I want to know what it is."

"Nothing happened," she insisted. When he continued to block her way, Dani said tautly, "I just discovered a few facts about my father that you and Grandfather conveniently forgot to mention."

An array of emotions crossed Rand's strong face. "I'm sorry you had to find out this way, honey, but it's really for the best," he said gently. "I told Cleve that."

"I can see why he didn't agree. It was hard enough to forgive him for what he did to my mother, but any man who would destroy his own son is simply beyond redemption."

"What are you talking about?" Rand asked incredulously.

"My father never got over loving my mother, did he?" Dani demanded. "He went from one woman to another, trying to find someone like her. Grandfather could have lifted his ban, but she hadn't gotten any more socially acceptable. So he sat back and let his son waste his life. Did my father commit suicide?" she asked suddenly.

"My God! Who told you these things?"

"That doesn't matter."

Rand stared at her, struggling to control himself. Finally he said, "I need to discuss this with Cleve. Somebody has to have a talk with you."

"Not tonight," she pleaded.

Dani was emotionally drained by the day's events. She went to her room, wanting only to be alone for a while. But even through the closed door she could hear raised voices coming from the den.

Chapter Eight

Dani spent a troubled evening after the unpleasant luncheon at Lulu's. Neither Rand nor her grandfather made any attempt to talk to her. It was what she'd requested, but it didn't make the problem go away.

Her budding romance with Rand was another casualty of that fateful luncheon. If he'd really cared, he would have offered her comfort instead of trying to tell her none of what she'd heard was true. As usual, Rand was working for her grandfather.

Dani sensed before she opened her eyes the next morning that there was some reason why she didn't want to wake up. Full consciousness brought back all the misery she was trying to avoid. She groaned and turned over on her stomach.

When she heard the door open, Dani said, "I don't want any breakfast."

Rand's deep voice answered, "That's not why I'm here."

She turned over quickly and ran her fingers through her tousled auburn mane. "I thought you were Marie. What are you doing in my bedroom?"

"We have to talk, Dani." He sat down on the edge of the bed.

She carefully moved her legs and pulled the covers up to her chin. "It can wait until I get dressed."

"We've waited too long already," he answered somberly.

"Then a few more minutes won't matter. I know what a good salesman you are, Rand, but it's not going to work. Even you can't whitewash Grandfather convincingly this time."

"I don't know what you were told yesterday, but it was either a pack of lies or you misinterpreted what you heard."

"I could have predicted you'd say that!"

"Where did you get the wild idea that Danny committed suicide?"

"You wouldn't admit it to me if he had," she said bitingly.

"Your father was responsible for his own death, if you want to call that suicide," Rand said grimly. "He took a curve too fast and lost control of the car. He was a criminally reckless driver."

"Because he didn't care that much about living," she challenged.

Rand's eyes glittered with anger. "Danny was reckless because he thought rules didn't apply to him. He lived a carefree life without any responsibility."

"How can you say that? He must have been a wonderful person! Grandfather himself told me my father was handsome and charming. And that man yesterday said everyone loved him."

A muscle jerked in Rand's strong jaw as he struggled to keep his promise to Cleve. "Then how can you reconcile that with a suicidal intent?"

"Well, I... Maybe he wasn't as happy as he appeared."

"I can assure you he was. What else did you hear that turned you against Cleve?"

"It wasn't what I heard, it's what I read between the lines."

"You think Danny was a three-time loser because he kept searching for someone like your mother?"

"They loved each other," she insisted.

"And Cleve broke them up, thereby ruining both their lives?"

"Yes!"

"Has it ever occurred to you that they both gave up rather easily?" Rand asked softly.

"Who knows what lies Grandfather concocted?" she said bitterly.

He examined her beautiful, impassioned face. "If I loved someone, I don't think anything or anyone could keep me from her."

"You're older," Dani protested. "They were just kids."

"That's a cop-out, and you know it," Rand said impatiently. "Love doesn't have anything to do with age."

"My father was an only child of a very strong-willed man. Grandfather probably dominated him."

"Even after he grew up? Do you think Cleve approved of Danny's frequent trips to the altar? His fondest dream was to see his son settle down and start a family."

"He should have thought of that before he broke up his first marriage."

Rand made a sound of disgust. "I suppose it's easier to blame Cleve than your mother or father."

"Don't you dare talk about my mother! I told you why she accepted the situation."

In an excess of frustration Rand gripped her shoulders and jerked Dani toward him. His eyes were a topaz blaze as he glared down at her. "Okay, now tell me why Danny did. If Cleve made up terrible things about the woman he loved, why didn't he go to her and ask for an explanation instead of meekly trotting back to college?"

"Are you saying that he didn't love her?" Dani demanded.

Rand's grip loosened and the fire went out of his eyes. He chose his words carefully. "I'm only asking you to keep an open mind. The whole affair was a tragedy, but your grandfather wasn't the evil genius who orchestrated it. There were misunderstandings all around. He was as much the loser as either Danny or Elizabeth."

"It only turned out that way," she said, but the conviction was gone from her voice.

For the first time, Dani began to question her father's behavior. Why *had* he allowed his marriage to be destroyed so easily? Wasn't it important enough to make even a submissive son stand up to a dominant father? But if she accepted Rand's contention that Cleve wasn't to blame, it meant her father hadn't loved her mother. Dani couldn't accept that. It was becoming clear that he hadn't loved her *enough*, though. She stared at Rand in confusion.

There was compassion on his strong face as he watched uncertainty undermine her confidence. "Danny was very immature at the time. If they'd met at a later date, un-

ler different circumstances, perhaps there would have
been a happier ending." Rand knew that wasn't true, but
it was the least he could do for her.

"It's so sad that they never had a second chance at
happiness," she whispered.

"That's why you have to go through life trying not to
hurt anyone," he said gently. "Your grandfather certainly didn't intend to."

Dani wanted with all her heart to believe him. Maybe
Rand would say anything to convince her, but Dani suddenly realized she'd stopped hating Cleve weeks ago. His
gentleness and sensitivity had won her over. If he'd tried
to pressure her, using his money as a lever, it would have
been different. But he had accepted her decision in every
instance and been movingly grateful for the smallest show
of affection. That wasn't the behavior of a tyrant.

"Think about it for a while, honey," Rand said, understanding the emotions that warred inside her.

"I will," she murmured.

"I'll let you get dressed." He stood up, looking at his
watch. "Will an hour give you enough time? I have to go
to the office first."

She looked at him blankly. "Enough time for what?"

"We're going to Nice today. Had you forgotten?"

Dani had. "I guess with everything that happened..."

"Would you prefer not to go, Dani?" he asked quietly.

It would be foolish to pass up a trip she'd looked forward to. That wouldn't solve anything. Maybe she'd
never know the truth about what happened long ago. Or
maybe there wasn't one simple answer. Everyone might
have thought he was doing the right thing. Was she com-
petent to judge?

"I'd like to go if you'd still like to take me," Dani answered.

Rand smiled warmly. "I can't think of anything I'd enjoy more."

She tried to put it all behind her as she dressed quickly in white linen pants and a yellow silk blouse. The past had shadowed her life long enough. The future was the important thing now. Dani's spirits rose as she contemplated the day ahead with Rand.

The Grande Corniche wound through spectacular scenery. They drove through lush green hills covered with majestic trees, then the road would curve and they could see the Mediterranean glittering far below. It was a changing spectacle.

Their first stop was Eze, a medieval village perched twelve hundred feet above sea level. It was like nothing Dani could have imagined. The cluster of stone buildings seemed untouched by the passage of time. She wouldn't have been surprised to see strolling minstrels and men and women in period dress.

No cars were permitted inside, so they walked up from the parking lot over a path that had known only cart wheels. The cobbled stones were worn smooth, but they were uneven.

"Now you know why we had to wait until your leg was better," Rand remarked. "Tell me if it starts to bother you, though. Everything is uphill from here on."

"It's completely healed, and I don't want to miss a thing!"

The narrow streets were bisected by others, equally steep and winding. It was like a stone maze, with buildings instead of hedges forming the barriers. There were small shops at intervals along the street, dark little warens with crooked windows and uneven floors. Dani refused to bypass a single one.

"At this rate, we're going to spend the entire day in Eze," Rand said, laughing.

"I don't care—it's fascinating! Oh, Rand, look! He's making jewelry."

They entered through a narrow doorway and walked over to a low counter where a man was fashioning gold wires into lovely ornaments. It was painstaking work.

He finished twisting a delicate strand before glancing up with a smile. "Can I help you?"

"No, we just wanted to watch," Dani said. "Will it bother you?"

"Not at all," he assured her.

While she stood over him in fascination, Rand prowled around looking at the finished products displayed in glass cases.

He pointed to a small ring with an intricate design. "Isn't that a double love knot?"

The man came over to take it out of the case and hand it to Rand. "You are correct, monsieur."

"We have to have this." The special smile Rand gave Dani made her heart beat faster.

As she held out her right hand, the man slanted a look at Rand. "In France we wear this on the left hand, mademoiselle," he remarked.

Dani's long lashes shaded her eyes. The man meant well. He was just reading more into the gift than Rand intended. "I'm an American," she said brightly.

Rand slipped the ring on her finger without comment. She was looking down at it, so she didn't see the expression on his face.

"It's beautiful," she said softly. "Thank you."

He smiled. "It seemed appropriate."

"Another souvenir?" she murmured.

Rand's eyes were unreadable. "Something to add to your collection."

They left the shop and strolled through the crooked streets, stopping to watch other craftsmen at work. Some were making hand-dipped candles, others were tooling leather or filling little net bags with fragrant potpourri.

"The rose petals come from Grasse," Rand told her. "It's one of the major producers of essential perfume oils in the world."

A little later they passed a small bakery. "Look at those yummy lemon tarts," Dani said. "Let's get some."

"Didn't your mother ever tell you that eating lemon tarts at eleven o'clock in the morning will spoil your lunch?"

"Often. That's the advantage of being an adult."

"It isn't the only one," he said mischievously, putting his arm around her shoulder and leading her into the bakeshop. "Unfortunately, we can't take advantage of the others right now."

Dani stifled a sigh. It seemed to be the story of her life.

"I really enjoyed Eze," she said when they were in the car, continuing on their way. "Where to next?"

"I thought you might enjoy seeing the Rothschild estate."

"Is it open to the public?"

He nodded. "No one lives there now. The house is a museum, and the grounds have been preserved, too."

Visiting the elegant Rothschild mansion was like entering a different period of history. It was filled with costly Aubusson and Gobelin tapestries, an exquisite porcelain collection, priceless paintings and much, much more. Dani had trouble taking everything in as they wandered through the spacious rooms.

"Did they actually live here?" she asked. "I can't imagine anyone sitting on that delicate French furniture."

"Some of it is priceless," Rand agreed. "There are pieces that belonged to Marie Antoinette. Madame de Rothschild was a great collector with eclectic tastes. She liked anything beautiful, regardless of origin or period."

Dani nodded. "I saw some Impressionist paintings mixed in with the Fragonards and Bouchers."

After touring the vast house, they walked in the gardens that stretched for acres. Winding gravel paths led through flower beds and along stone walls before disappearing into towering shrubbery. Dani and Rand finally sat down on a bench in front of a massive reflecting pool clogged with water lilies.

"Everything is done on such a huge scale," she marveled.

"It isn't exactly your standard backyard with a barbecue," he agreed.

"The grounds are daunting enough, but can you conceive of keeping that house clean? It boggles the mind!"

"I don't imagine Madame de Rothschild worried about it," Rand observed dryly.

Dani grinned. "You never can tell. Maybe that's why she moved out—the help kept quitting."

"It's a possibility," he said, chuckling.

Her eyes grew pensive. "I wonder what it would be like to live in a place like this."

"This one isn't for sale, but I'm sure Cleve would buy you something suitably grand."

Dani frowned. "Don't be ridiculous!"

"You might as well get used to being rich."

"I'm not!" she answered sharply.

"You will be someday."

"I don't want Grandfather to leave his money to me."

"That isn't very sensible, Dani."

"Maybe not, but since I've been here I've seen what money does to people, and I don't like it."

"Do you really think money is to blame?" Rand's expression hardened. "Some people are just naturally lazy, or shiftless, or conniving. They'd be that way, anyhow."

"Perhaps." Dani hesitated. "But if you were very wealthy, you wouldn't really know whether people liked you for yourself, or what you could do for them."

He cupped her chin in his palm and gazed at her tenderly. "That's something you'll never have to worry about, little one."

Rand's touch had the usual effect, but the subject was too important to Dani for her to let herself be sidetracked.

She looked at him searchingly. "Did Grandfather tell you he was leaving his fortune to me?"

"Who else would he leave it to?"

That didn't answer her question. "There's charity," she said tentatively.

"Part of his estate will go there, certainly. But the bulk of it will come to you."

So Rand did know the terms of her grandfather's will. "You're talking about his money, I presume. Surely the business will go to you."

"No."

Dani couldn't read anything in Rand's controlled face. "You're so close to him," she said. "It seems logical."

His firm mouth curved. "You're closer."

"I don't know anything about business," she protested.

"I'd stay on as CEO if you wanted me to," he said casually.

It wouldn't be the same as being the undisputed boss, though. Could a man like Rand, given his former expectations, accept that fact with the unconcern he appeared to be showing? Or was he biding his time like a patient tiger, sure of his ultimate goal? Dani didn't want to think that way, but she was afraid not to.

He stood up and pulled her to her feet. "I don't know about you, but my lemon tart has worn off. Let's have lunch."

He drove to an elegant restaurant where the food was outstanding. Dani couldn't fully appreciate it, however. She kept stealing glances at Rand's rugged face, hoping to find some answers there. The only thing that showed was that he was enjoying his lunch hugely.

The Maeght Foundation just outside Saint-Paul was their next stop after the restaurant.

"We started in a medieval village, made a visit to the nineteenth century and now we're up to the present," Dani commented, gazing up at the two white concrete arcs on the roof of the museum.

The grounds in front of the modern building were studded with abstract sculpture that looked as though it had grown there, especially the gigantic bronze flowers scattered among the trees.

Inside was the largest collection of modern masters Dani had ever seen. She wandered happily among the Matisses, Chagalls and all the others, while Rand watched her with an indulgent smile. It was dusk when they left. They'd lingered over a late lunch and spent hours in the museum.

"I know I promised to take you to Nice," Rand said, "but I think we should save it for another time."

"I agree." Dani nodded. "I don't believe I could absorb another thing. It's been a wonderful day, Rand!"

"And it isn't over yet." He put his arm around her and kissed the top of her head.

Dani's heart gave a sudden leap, but he was so casual. What did he have planned? She decided to wait and take things as they happened.

"I wonder if I should call Cleve before we start back." Rand frowned thoughtfully.

"Didn't he feel well this morning?" She gave him a worried look.

"He's fine. It's just that we've been out of touch all day, and I usually check in."

"Call him," she urged.

Dani stood by the phone, waiting for reassurance. It was strange. That morning she could have sworn she didn't care what happened to her grandfather. But Dani realized she did. A tenuous bond had formed between them in spite of her long-standing prejudices. She wanted to believe Rand's defense of him. It would hurt deeply if Rand was wrong—especially if he knew it.

Dani refused to let ugly doubts rear their heads. The day had been too perfect.

Rand was scowling as he listened to Cleve's voice. "How could he say a thing like that?"

"What's the matter?" Dani asked anxiously.

"Nothing. Just business." He glanced at her without really seeing her. "Why didn't you read him the terms of the contract?" he asked Cleve. After listening for a moment, Rand smacked his forehead with the heel of his hand. "That's right! I took it home with me to double check for loopholes. Well, no harm done. We're on our way back now. I'll call Singapore as soon as I get to my apartment."

"Are you sure everything's all right?" Dani asked after he hung up.

"Yes, just a business matter," he repeated. "It's a good thing I called, though."

Rand was preoccupied on the return ride. He tried not to show it, but it was evident that his thoughts were elsewhere. Well, so much for romance, Dani thought sardonically. It couldn't hold a candle to high finance.

When the lights of Monte Carlo appeared in the distance, Rand said, "Do you want to come with me while I make a phone call, or would you rather I dropped you off at home? Are you tired, honey?"

Dani *was* tired. It had been a long, eventful day. But she didn't want it to end, even though she had a feeling Rand wouldn't mind terribly.

"I'm not a bit tired," she said brightly. "I'll go with you."

"Great!" He patted her hand. "I'll get this over with as soon as possible, and then we'll go out to dinner."

When they reached his apartment, Rand was withdrawn once more, although he made her comfortable before going to telephone.

"Stretch out on the couch." He lit the lamps and handed her a magazine. "I'll try to make it speedy."

Dani kicked off her shoes and settled back gratefully on the soft down cushions. She was just starting to flip through the magazine when Rand returned.

"I'm really sorry, honey. It's going to take longer than I anticipated. The man I need is out, but they expect him back momentarily. I have to wait for him to call me back."

Dani smiled. "I *thought* that was the shortest phone call on record."

"Would you like me to have Cleve send the car for you?"

"Are you trying to get rid of me?" She hoped the question sounded joking.

"You know better than that." He stroked her cheek with caressing fingertips. "I just don't want you to be bored."

"I'm not. I have a magazine to read."

"Can I get you anything? A drink? Or how about a snack?"

"I'm still full from lunch. Go look at your contracts—or whatever it is that turns you on."

"A provocative statement if I ever heard one." He sat down on the couch next to Dani and traced the shape of her mouth with a long forefinger. "You know what turns me on."

"Another million-dollar deal," she said lightly, trying to keep the bitterness from showing.

"Since that's an incorrect answer, you'll have to pay a forfeit." His warm mouth trailed a path from her ear down her neck to the hollow in her throat.

"What's the forfeit?" Dani murmured faintly.

"I thought you'd never ask."

His mouth followed his fingers as they unbuttoned her blouse. When his lips reached the shadowed cleft between her breasts, she cupped his chin in her palm to stop him before he did any more damage. The tiny embers smoldering in the pit of her stomach threatened to burst into flames at any moment, and Dani knew she couldn't bear it if the phone interrupted his slow excursion when she'd reached the point of no return.

"I want to see the rule book before I pay up," she said breathlessly.

"I make my own rules when I want something badly enough." His brilliant topaz eyes held hers as he framed her face in his hands and rubbed his thumbs slowly over her cheekbones.

"Isn't that cheating?"

He smiled like a giant cat. "Only when you don't admit it."

The phone rang, as Dani had known it would. It wasn't the call Rand was waiting for, however. When he came back to tell her, she pretended great interest in her magazine. Maybe he could take these fragmented moments of intimacy, but she couldn't!

"Go do your work while I finish this article," she instructed firmly.

He laughed as he dropped a kiss on the tip of her nose. "Okay, but don't think this gets you off the hook."

Dani gave up the pretense of reading after Rand left the room. She was wound as tightly as a steel coil, although he clearly wasn't. How could Rand switch from an ardent lover to a joking companion with no trouble at all? It would be nice to think he was simply better at concealing his emotions, yet Dani knew that was wishful thinking. Rand was a very virile man. Women were important to him, but they weren't his top priority.

The phone rang again, and this time the murmur of Rand's voice went on and on. It wasn't the short call he'd promised.

Eventually he returned to the living room with a look of satisfaction on his face. "I'll just give Cleve a quick report and then I'm all yours." He disappeared before she could answer.

Dani put on her shoes and got up slowly. A desolate feeling replaced her former anticipation. Rand's eagerness to call her grandfather told Dani exactly where she stood on the descending list of importance. Rand could put passion on hold because he had a greater passion. He would get around to her, but only when it was convenient.

She'd always known that, so why did it hurt so much? It didn't change the way she felt about him. Nothing could. Which left her with a choice. She could either accept the crumbs of affection he was willing to throw her way, or try to forget about him. Neither option was very palatable.

Dani's eyes were troubled as she got out her compact and started to repair her makeup.

Rand was in high spirits when he returned. "There, that didn't take long, did it? Cleve sends his love."

"That's nice." Dani concentrated on putting the compact back in her purse.

Rand came up behind her and swept her long hair away to kiss the nape of her neck. "I told him we might be late," he murmured.

She kept her head bent. "What did he say?"

Something in her tone alerted Rand. He turned her to face him. "Is something wrong, Dani?"

"No." She stared at the third button on his shirt.

He tipped her chin up to look searchingly at her. "Tell me what it is, sweetheart."

"It's nothing," she insisted. Talking about it wouldn't solve anything.

"Have you changed your mind?" Rand asked quietly.

"I . . . I don't know what you mean."

"I think you do, Dani. You know I intend to make love to you. Are you having second thoughts?"

"That sounds so . . ." Dani's long lashes swept down.

Why didn't he just take her in his arms and kiss her? Rand's sensuous mouth could make her forget everything. When he held her so tightly that she was aware of every whipcord muscle in his powerful body, nothing else was important. The decision would be taken out of her hands.

Rand didn't comply. "We have to talk about it, darling."

"What would you do if I said I...I was having doubts?"

"I'd take you home."

She couldn't read anything from his impenetrable expression. "You don't really care one way or the other, do you?" she sighed.

"You must know better than that."

"No," she said sadly. "You wouldn't give up that easily if it mattered to you."

"Listen to me, Dani. I want you more than I've ever wanted a woman. Right now it's difficult to keep from picking you up and carrying you into the bedroom. I want to lie next to you and feel your body come to life in my arms. I can think of a hundred different ways to make love to you."

The enflaming word pictures he was painting made her heart beat like a tom-tom. "I won't stop you," she whispered faintly.

"No, darling. I could make your body respond to me, but it wouldn't be fair. You have to make the decision without coercion."

"I do want you, Rand." Her soft mouth trembled.

Dani's surrender was total. No arguments her mind could raise were as strong as her need for this man she loved so desperately. She swayed toward him, but he didn't take her in his arms.

"You did earlier, but when I came back a few minutes ago I sensed a change. What happened while I was gone, Dani?"

"I felt— What difference does it make?" she pleaded. "We want each other. Isn't that enough?"

"No. If there's something bothering you, I have to know about it."

She could tell he was prepared to question her until he got the answer. Her head drooped on her slender neck. "I just wanted to be more than a casual diversion for you," she mumbled.

He stared at her incredulously. "What are you talking about?"

"I didn't seem to matter. After your long-distance call you couldn't wait to get back to Grandfather, not me."

"Because if I didn't, I knew he'd phone here." Rand folded her in his arms at last, resting his cheek on her shining hair. "I didn't want anything or anybody to interrupt us."

Dani lifted her face to look up at him. Was that really the reason? Had she made her own misery? The blaze in his tawny eyes was reassuring.

"Dear heart, I've waited so long for this moment." His lips gently brushed her eyelids. "We're going to shut out the world and make a special one of our own. You're going to belong to me completely."

He didn't know it, but she already did in every way but one. And that one made Dani tremble with anticipation. She put her arms around his neck. "Oh, Rand, I thought it would never happen."

He lifted her in his arms, chuckling softly. "I'm about to make a believer out of you."

She buried her face in his neck as Rand carried her into the bedroom, whispering things that made her cheeks burn.

He put her down on the wide bed and stretched out beside her. "I've dreamed about this, night after night." He pulled her against him and feathered tiny kisses over her face. "I'd reach for you in my sleep and wake up aching when you weren't here."

"I wanted to be." She tangled her fingers in his thick hair, holding his head still so her mouth could capture his.

Rand's arms tightened around her slender body as he parted her lips. His tongue entered with a male dominance that took her breath away. Dani curved her body into his, wanting to be joined in every way.

Rand's loins pulsed at the intimate contact. He wound his legs around both of hers, making her aware of his mounting passion. When he pulled her blouse out of her slacks and replaced it with his palm on her lower back, Dani's desire equalled Rand's. As his questing fingers reached the curves below she moved against him with a tiny sound of pleasure.

"My sweet, passionate, Dani." Rand turned her on her back and stared down at her with glowing eyes. "I want to make you so happy."

"You do," she murmured, reaching up to unbutton his shirt.

He sat up to shrug it off impatiently, then leaned over Dani to kiss the hollow in her throat. As his mouth burrowed under her blouse to glide along her collarbone, he slowly unfastened the little pearl buttons down her front. As each button gave way he widened the opening until her breasts were exposed.

Rand bent his dark head to kiss each one. His mouth felt sensuously warm and wet through the filmy lace bra. It was a tantalizing feeling. Dani twisted restlessly. Her whole body throbbed with an aching need. It accelerated when he unclasped her bra and ran his fingertips across her breasts.

"You're so incredibly lovely!" His eyes scorched a trail over her creamy, rose-tipped skin.

After he lifted her slightly and removed the encumbering garments, Dani put her arms around his torso. She clutched him tightly, burying her bare breasts in the curling dark hair on his chest.

"I want to see all of you," he muttered against her throat. "Every exquisite inch."

His mouth returned to hers while he unzipped her slacks and slid them down. Dani raised her hips to help him, reaching out trembling fingers to his belt buckle. She couldn't wait to feel Rand's firm, muscled body impressing its masculinity on her yielding flesh. She wanted to melt into him, to merge with him completely.

But after Rand had flung his clothes aside, he didn't remove the last of hers immediately. Kneeling over her, he stroked her body from collarbone to thigh, lingering along the way. The slow exploration was almost unbearably erotic.

"You're driving me out of my mind," Dani moaned.

"I want to make it good for you, sweetheart."

Dani gasped as he lifted her leg and kissed the soft skin of her inner thigh. White-hot flames seared her as he worked his way upward. By the time his fingertips slipped inside the elastic waistband of her panties, Dani was a fluid mass of desire.

After he slid the little scrap of lace down her legs she held out her arms to him. When he returned to her, she arched her body into his. The burning contact sent a shock through both of them.

"Now, darling?" His tawny eyes seemed lit by inner flames.

"Oh, yes! Now!"

His deep possession made Dani's taut body arch in ecstasy. Rand's thrusting force filled the aching void inside her, promising rapturous release. She was driven wild by throbbing excitement that came in mounting waves, tossing her higher and higher. When the crest was reached, Dani paused on the brink for one unforgettable second before experiencing the ultimate satisfaction.

She clung tightly to Rand as the waves receded slowly, diminishing in intensity, but not in pleasure. The warm bond between them was still strong.

They were both too contented to move for a long time. Finally Rand traced the pure line of Dani's profile with his eyes still closed. "Have I told you how beautiful you are?"

"Not in the past few minutes."

He smiled lazily. "I was a little busy."

"That sounds like you were working." She pouted.

He opened his eyes, then, to gaze at her tenderly. "No, darling. You're pure pleasure."

"You too." She wriggled in remembered delight.

"We'll have to talk about extending it."

Dani was afraid to move a muscle. Was Rand making a commitment? "How long?" she asked breathlessly.

He chuckled. "Could you give me fifteen minutes?"

Dani stifled a sigh. She should have known it was too good to be true. But it didn't matter at that moment. She had reached undreamed-of heights in Rand's arms. Even if she couldn't have his love, the passion they'd shared almost made up for it. And Rand must feel *something* for her. He'd been such a tender lover.

Dani's eyes were dreamy as she remembered the molten excitement his hands and mouth had brought. She traced the tapering line of his broad chest down to his flat stomach. The muscles were relaxed now instead of rigid.

As her hand dipped lower, Rand cupped her breast and bent his head to kiss it.

"Fifteen minutes goes by fast, doesn't it?" he murmured.

It was a long time later before either felt like moving. Dani was almost asleep in Rand's arms.

Suddenly he said, "We didn't have any dinner."

"We were a little busy." She laughed, echoing his words.

"True." He kissed the tip of her nose before reaching for his shorts. "Stay here. I'll see what's in the refrigerator."

"I'll come with you." When she would have gotten dressed he stopped her. "You're insatiable," Dani said as Rand's arms closed around her.

He nibbled on her ear. "Aren't you glad?"

"After I fix us something to eat, I'll show you just how glad," she whispered.

"I could be talked out of dinner." His voice was husky.

"No, you'd be thinking about it," she teased. "I demand full attention."

"You're going to get it, beautiful lady," he promised.

Rand's robe was impossibly large, so Dani settled for one of his T-shirts. It drooped on her shoulders and came halfway down her thighs, but at least it didn't trip her.

Rand laughed as she bent over to see what was in the refrigerator. "You're the sexiest-looking cook I've ever had." He lifted the hem of her shirt to caress her bare bottom.

She grinned at him over her shoulder. "It's the uniforms you provide."

"Don't you believe it," he answered in a smoky voice.

Rand's refrigerator showed that he didn't eat home much. There was very little other than the staples, so they settled for scrambled eggs and toast. While Dani prepared the eggs, Rand set the table with silver and napkins.

They talked and laughed, completely relaxed with each other. All the sexual tension was gone. It was replaced by the warm aftermath of sated passion. They could have been a happily married couple sharing the everyday things of life.

The thought brought a pang. If only it were a reality. They were so good together. Or was she just kidding herself? Rand could make any woman feel she was special. Did Roxanne feel that way? Did they also putter around in the kitchen after making love? Dani looked at Rand's splendid, half-naked body moving unselfconsciously around the room. She decided not to dwell on the thought.

Dani glanced at the clock as they finished eating. "It's terribly late. You'd better take me home."

"I suppose so," he agreed regretfully. He got up to kneel by her chair and put his arms around her waist. "I wish you could stay all night. I'd like to find you in my arms when I wake up in the morning."

"I'd like that, too," she said wistfully.

He caressed her bare thigh lingeringly. "I don't suppose it's possible. We couldn't do that to Cleve."

"No." She sighed.

With a sudden movement Rand stripped off her T-shirt and lifted her into his arms. "We'll observe the conventions for his sake, but he'll have to do without you a little longer."

Chapter Nine

Dani slept late the next morning. It had been almost dawn when Rand finally brought her home.

She awoke with a smile on her face. Her eyes grew dreamy as she remembered the events of the night before. Rand hadn't been able to get enough of her—nor she of him. Their lovemaking had intensified with each mind-spinning occurrence. She jumped out of bed when the memories became too moving to dwell on.

After her shower, Dani dressed with great care. She and Rand hadn't gotten around to making any plans for the day, but whatever they did, she wanted to look her best for him.

She chose a white cotton dress that Rand had urged her to buy at the fancy salon. It had tiny tucks down the front, and the dropped waist and skirt were banded with what the saleswoman had called moon and stars embroidery. It seemed appropriate since she had certainly reached heaven with Rand the night before. The square neckline and elbow-length sleeves were trimmed with the same delicate lace.

After applying a touch of makeup and brushing her long hair until it gleamed, Dani went out to greet Rand. The sparkle in her green eyes dimmed a trifle when he wasn't in the den or on the patio. Her grandfather wasn't around, either.

Dani questioned the maid who told her, "Mr. Stryker hasn't been here this morning, and Mr. Barringer went to his office."

"I see." Dani bit her lip. "Were there any messages for me?"

"No, Miss Zanetelle."

Could Rand have slept late, too? It didn't seem likely, knowing him, but it was possible. A secret smile tilted Dani's full mouth. He'd had a very strenuous night.

She wasn't really surprised when no one answered at his apartment. It was like Rand to go to work no matter how little sleep he'd gotten. Dani dialed the office number with anticipation. She needed to hear his voice.

"Mr. Stryker isn't in the office," a receptionist informed her.

It was a terrible letdown. "When will he be back?"

"I really couldn't say. Would you like to leave a message?"

"No...no, thank you," Dani said slowly.

A quiver of apprehension went through her. Why hadn't Rand tried to get in touch with her? He could barely part with her the night before. Wouldn't it seem logical that he'd want to reestablish their bond the next day, if only on the telephone? *She* had.

Dani wandered onto the patio, trying to tell herself she was being foolish. Rand had probably expected her to sleep late. He didn't want to wake her. Then why hadn't he left a message? Maybe he was tied up in a meeting. But the receptionist said he wasn't in the office. Well, maybe he had a business appointment.

Dani answered all her questions with excuses because she didn't want to face the chilling fact that perhaps he'd gotten all he wanted from her. She didn't have wide experience, but she'd heard that sometimes men lost interest after they'd fulfilled their objective.

Then she remembered Rand's tenderness. Passion came easily to men, but tenderness was reserved for the woman they cared about. It was a comforting thought. Dani reminded herself of it every time another ugly doubt surfaced.

But as the afternoon wore on, she found it difficult to sustain her illusions. Why didn't he call? Was she really just another warm body in his bed?

When the phone finally rang in the late afternoon Dani raced for it. Her eagerness died when it was Keith's voice that greeted her instead of Rand's.

"You're really hard to reach," he complained.

"I've been home all day." She tried to keep her disappointment from showing.

"Not yesterday, though. I called on and off all day. Uncle Cleve said you went out with Rand."

"Then why did you keep calling?"

"I didn't think you'd be gone that long." Keith sounded annoyed. "Doesn't God's gift to women have to work anymore, or were you his assignment?"

That struck too close to home. "I'm sorry you feel someone has to be paid to take me out," she said coldly.

"Baby doll, I'm sorry! You know that's not what I meant. I'm just jealous. Uncle Cleve keeps pushing Rand on you," he said resentfully.

"What makes you think that?" Dani asked carefully.

"He'd do anything to keep you away from me."

"You're being paranoid again, Keith."

"I'll bet he doesn't jump for joy when you tell him you're going out with me."

"Grandfather doesn't tell me what to do, or whom to go out with." That part was true. He had been very careful not to be possessive. Dani's next statements were not true. "Rand offered to drive me along the Grande Corniche, and I accepted because I wanted to see all those places. That's why we were gone so long."

"I would have taken you sight-seeing if you'd asked me."

"Your idea of a point of interest is a new item on a menu," she answered impatiently.

"That's not fair, Dani! I'd do anything to please you, if I just knew what it was."

She was immediately sorry for her burst of temper. Keith had tried to be accommodating. He couldn't help it that their tastes were so different. She was really blaming him for not being Rand, which wasn't his fault, either.

"I enjoyed the things we did together," she said gently. "I just meant it's better to go sight-seeing with someone who doesn't mind doing it."

"I love sight-seeing!" he said eagerly. "Where would you like to go?"

"I really can't think of anyplace."

"How would you like to drive to Beaulieu for dinner? It's a beautiful ride, and I know a smashing place for dinner. With a view," he added hastily. "This place is right on the water."

Dani was about to refuse automatically. There was only one person she wanted to be with. But Rand didn't care about being with her. This long, frustrating day had proved it. What was she going to do—sit around and examine the cracks in her broken heart? Dani's small jaw set firmly as she made up her mind. She was through playing the starry-eyed romantic.

"I'd love to go with you, Keith," Dani said more curtly than she'd intended.

Fortunately he was too ecstatic to notice. "Wonderful! I'll pick you up in an hour."

The phone rang again almost as soon as she put it down, and Dani's heart leaped. She waited to pick it up until she was sure her voice would be steady. Rand must never know what agony she'd gone through. She even decided to be a little cool at first to make him pay. Maybe she'd threaten to keep her date with Keith. With all her good intentions, Dani's voice was warmly breathless when she answered.

Cleve's cultured tones put an end to her joy. "I'm sorry I missed seeing you this morning, my dear. You were still asleep when I left."

"Yes, we...uh...I got in rather late." Why did she bring that up? Dani berated herself.

Cleve didn't comment, however. "Did you have a good time?" he asked pleasantly.

"It was very nice," she answered tonelessly. "I especially enjoyed Eze."

"I rather imagined you would, and the Rothschild estate, as well."

"Did you tell Rand to take me?" Dani demanded.

"I thought the two of you made those plans together."

It occurred to Dani that her grandfather seldom answered her questions directly, but there was nothing to be gained by making an issue of it. "Yes, I suppose we did. I'd forgotten."

"Well, I'm glad you had a good day. I called to say I won't be home this evening. I feel bad about leaving you alone, but it's a matter of some urgency. I'd send Rand in my place, but he—"

"Don't worry about me," she cut in swiftly. "I won't be around, anyway. I'm having dinner with Keith."

Dani didn't want to hear Rand's excuses secondhand. Had he put his foot down with Cleve, telling him he'd played the attentive escort long enough? She wondered bitterly what her grandfather would say if he knew just how much attention Rand had devoted to his work.

Dani tried her best to enjoy the beautiful scenery on the drive to Beaulieu. She also attempted to appear interested in Keith.

"Did you manage to set Mrs. Stanhope straight?" she asked.

"We had a talk. See that spit of land jutting out? That's Cap Ferrat. I'll have to take you there. It's quite posh."

The change of subject seemed too pat. Was Keith still involved with that dreadful woman? "It must have been a relief to get her off your back," Dani remarked casually.

"Yes." He stared ahead at the road.

"The scene she made at your mother's luncheon was embarrassing," Dani persisted.

Keith crushed her fingers in a tight grip. "I'd give anything if you hadn't seen that!"

"I didn't mean embarrassing for me. You were her target. I just got the fallout." Dani wrinkled her nose in distaste. "How could anyone throw such a tantrum in front of a roomful of people?"

"She'd had several martinis, I believe. Blanche has a bit of a drinking problem."

"Plus a few others! She must have pulled out all the stops during your little talk."

"It wasn't pleasant." Keith's face was grim in the gathering darkness. His expression changed as he lifted Dani's hand to his lips. "Why are we talking about Blanche when we should be talking about you—us?"

She tried to head him off. "There's nothing to talk about. I'm not as flamboyant as your friends."

"You're adorable," he protested. "Every man in Monaco would like to be in my shoes right now."

Not *every* man, Dani reflected miserably. "Oh, sure, I'm a regular femme fatale. Men can't seem to stay away from me." The words didn't come out as lightly as she'd meant them to.

"That's the way it's been for me," Keith said meaningfully. "You don't know how I suffered when you were out with Rand, knowing he has Uncle Cleve's blessing."

"I wish you'd stop saying that! Grandfather doesn't run my life, and there's nothing between Rand and me, anyway. I don't even expect to see him again before I go home."

Keith stiffened like a deer hearing a twig snap. "When are you leaving?"

"Soon. I'm going to speak to Grandfather tomorrow."

Cleve would be unhappy, but it couldn't be helped. The situation had been different when she'd promised to stay longer. Even the mention of Rand's name was painful now. It would be unbearable to see him—although the only chance of that would be accidentally. Rand had made his intentions clear.

"I won't give up," Keith stated. "I'll follow you to New York, if necessary."

Dani sighed. "Please, Keith, not now. Let's talk about something else. Tell me about . . . oh . . . the film festival in Cannes. Have you been to it?"

He followed her lead reluctantly. For the rest of the drive they discussed movies, famous people and other casual subjects.

The restaurant Keith had selected was delightful. Dani was beginning to think it was impossible to get a bad meal on the Riviera. They lingered over the delicious food and wine for a long time. After dinner, Keith suggested going to a disco.

"I haven't danced since my accident," Dani remarked.

"Does your leg still bother you?"

"No, it's completely healed, thank goodness!"

"Then there's no problem." Keith covered her hand on the white tablecloth. "That's one way I can get to hold you in my arms."

The thought didn't thrill her, but Dani loved to dance. It was one of the things she'd missed during her long convalescence. If she expected to go back to work soon, this was a good chance to get back in practice.

The disco was dark and noisy like discos all over the world. Dani loved it. She moved in time to the music, letting the beat take over without having to think about it, or anything else.

"You're really good," Keith commented admiringly.

She laughed happily for the first time. "I hope so. I get paid for teaching this sort of thing."

"I'd pay them to play something slow," he complained.

Eventually he got his wish. A slow number had the added benefit of thinning out the crowded dance floor.

"This is better." Keith drew her into his arms with a look of satisfaction.

He was a couple of inches shorter than Rand, and his shoulder felt padded. She could always feel solid bone and muscle under Rand's jackets. Dani didn't want to make the comparison, but it was inevitable. She'd become intimately acquainted with every muscle and tendon in Rand's lithe body only the night before. Her nails curled into Keith's jacket as she tried to obliterate the memory.

He held her closer when he felt the convulsive movement. "You do feel something for me, don't you, darling?"

"I'm very fond of you, Keith." She attempted a smile. "We're family."

"You know that's not what I meant! Tell me there's hope for me, Dani. Give me some little crumb of encouragement. I'm so crazy about you."

She could only feel sorry for him. Dani knew what it was like to love hopelessly. It made her compassionate.

"I'm not ready to get married, Keith, but if I were, you'd be in the running," she said gently.

He crushed her tightly against him, his eyes blazing with triumph. "You don't know what that means to me! I'll never give up now."

She had only meant to let him down easily, not encourage him. Keith didn't know that Rand had spoiled her for all other men.

Keith's hands were moving caressingly over her back. "I want to make you so happy, darling."

The words were like a ghostly refrain. Dani could almost see Rand's dark, intense face poised over hers, his husky voice saying the same thing as he filled her with delirious joy.

"I know I could if you'd let me," Keith was purring in her ear. He drew her hips close and moved against her sensuously.

When Dani jerked away with an incoherent sound of protest, he was instantly apologetic.

"I wasn't making a pass, my beloved. I just got carried away." He looked alarmed. "Say you forgive me."

"It's all right, Keith. Maybe we'd better sit down."

They left soon after that. Keith was still uneasy. When they got to the car, he put his hands on Dani's shoulders and gazed at her earnestly.

"I lost my head in there for a minute because I'm so mad about you. But I want you to know I *respect* you, darling," he said urgently.

"I told you, I understand."

"I want to love and cherish you." He kissed her chastely on the forehead. When she didn't pull away, Keith kissed her tentatively on the lips.

His mouth was soft and wet instead of firm and warm, but Dani forced herself to endure it. This was the way it was going to be from now on, so she might as well get used to it. She couldn't go through life flinching from every show of affection. As a test of willpower, Dani put her arms around Keith's neck. His clasp tightened, but he was careful not to touch her other than that.

The ride home was uneventful. Keith seemed willing to settle for the ground he'd gained, for which Dani was grateful. It wasn't until they entered Cleve's driveway that tension returned. Rand's bright red Ferrari was parked in front of the villa.

Keith scowled. "What's he doing here?"

"I don't know," Dani answered faintly.

"I thought you said you weren't going to see him again."

"He didn't come to see me," she replied tonelessly.

"I'll bet! What else would he be doing here at this hour?"

"Rand and Grandfather are probably closeted in the den, going over one of their endless deals."

Keith's rather weak jaw set stubbornly. "I think I'll come in and say hello."

Dani shrugged. "You can if you like. I'm going to bed."

He looked at her uncertainly. "Well, in that case maybe I won't bother."

"That's up to you," she said indifferently.

Keith walked her to the door. At the entrance, he turned Dani to face him. "This has been the most wonderful night of my life." His voice was thick with emotion.

"I'm glad," she murmured, scarcely hearing him.

Dani's entire consciousness was centered on the dynamic man inside. She longed for him with every fiber of her being, but Dani was praying that she could get to her room without seeing Rand.

"We got close tonight. I could feel it," Keith was saying. He took her in his arms and bent his head.

Dani put her arms around his neck automatically. It was a reflex action. She wasn't even conscious of doing it. When Keith's eager mouth covered hers, she stiffened—just as the front door opened.

Rand stood like an avenging god on the threshold. His face was rigid. Fury and incredulity deepened the tired lines that were already present. His fiery eyes bored into Dani like a laser beam, rendering her speechless.

The tense confrontation wasn't lost on Keith. He smiled victoriously. "You're working rather late, old chap. Too bad. Dani and I were having a ball, weren't we, darling? You know what they say, all work and no play makes Jack a dull boy."

"You'll never have to worry," Rand said ominously.

"Good of you to say so," Keith answered smugly.

The short exchange between the two men gave Dani a chance to pull herself together. She turned and held out her hand. "Good night, Keith. Thank you for a lovely evening."

He took her hand in both of his. "It was more than I could have hoped for," he replied, with a sidelong glance at Rand.

Dani could sense the tightly suppressed violence in Rand's taut body. She slipped by him and started for the hall. The door slammed shut and he grabbed her arm, whirling her around.

"Where do you think you're going?" he thundered.

"To my room."

"Just like that? Without any explanation?"

Even in a towering rage, Rand could make her bones melt. Dani wanted to touch his grimly compressed mouth and feel it soften under her fingers. She wanted to feel it on her lips, on her body. Would his eyes lose that terrible glare if she followed her impulse? Would he make love to her again? Perhaps. He had a healthy male appetite. He was also extremely casual in his affairs.

The painful knowledge made Dani fling her head back. "I wasn't aware that I owed you any explanations."

"Then you damned well better think again!" He jerked her toward him. "What the hell were you doing with Keith?"

"Don't swear at me," she ordered.

"I'll do a lot worse than that if I don't get some answers. How could you let that little toad kiss you?"

"It was quite pleasant," she lied.

"Oh, really?" Rand's tiger eyes glittered. "As pleasant as last night?"

Dani glanced apprehensively at the door to the den. There was a light on inside. "Will you please lower your voice?" she murmured.

"No, I will not. But you're right, this conversation needs privacy."

Keeping a tight grip on her arm, Rand dragged Dani down the hall to her room. When they were inside with the door closed, he swung her around to face him.

"Okay, now tell me how Keith's kisses stack up against mine. Was he as adept at pleasing you? Did you make that sweet little sound that you made with me?"

Dani couldn't bear to have Rand talk about their love-making as though it had been only a physical gratification. Maybe it was for him, but it had been so much more for her.

"Please don't," she whispered, averting her face.

He jerked her chin up. "Don't remind you that you were in my bed last night?"

Dani's cheeks flamed, but she stared back at him steadily. "I didn't think you remembered."

His punishing grip on her chin loosened. "How could I ever forget?"

"Very easily, evidently. Even after a social event, the polite thing is to phone and say you had a nice time."

"Is that what this is all about?" he asked incredu-
ously. "You went out with Keith because you were an-
ry that I didn't telephone?"

He made it sound like a simple oversight! Dani's an-
,er rose when she remembered the tortured hours spent
vaiting to hear from him.

"I realize I can't compete with one of your million-
lollar deals," she said coldly.

"Dani, honey, you know that's not true, but I do have
o work. Cleve called at eight o'clock this morning to say
had to go to Paris. Didn't he tell you?"

She remembered how he'd tried. Why hadn't she lis-
ened to him? A great load dropped from Dani's shoul-
lers. Poor Rand. He looked so tired. He couldn't have
.otten more than a few hours' sleep.

Rand was frowning. "It isn't like Cleve to forget to
.ive a message."

"Well, uh, something came up."

Rand's frown deepened. "That still doesn't explain
vhy you went out with Keith."

"It was just a dinner date. I don't know why you're so
ingry."

"Was I supposed to be delighted to find him kissing
ou?"

"It was just a friendly kiss." She was secretly thrilled
hat Rand was jealous.

"There's nothing friendly about Keith," he said
.rimly.

"You and Grandfather are too hard on him," she
.rotested.

"You do know how Cleve feels about him, then?"

"Yes, but I don't know why. Keith might not be a
vorld beater like you two, but he's really very sweet."

"I wish to God Cleve would do his own dirty work instead of always leaving it to me," Rand muttered angrily.

Dani tensed. "What do you mean?"

"Your grandfather doesn't want you to have anything to do with Keith. It's as simple as that."

"Did he phone you in Paris after I told him I was having dinner with Keith? Is that why you came home?" Dani demanded.

"Where did you get an idea like that?" Rand asked impatiently.

Rand was another one who didn't answer awkward questions directly, Dani thought grimly. "It must be very difficult tending to business and playing nursemaid to me, too," she commented acidly.

There was a white line around his mouth. "I won't dignify that by an answer."

"Very convenient. I'm just supposed to accept your word for everything?"

"Why would either of us try to deceive you?"

"To get me to do what you want. You're both very good at that," she said somberly.

"Do you regret it, Dani?" Rand's expression softened, and his hand curved around the back of her neck.

As his long fingers massaged her tense muscles, Dani felt a familiar warmth rising. He could convince her of anything with those tactics, but it wouldn't necessarily be the truth. She needed to think clearly because her whole life was at stake.

"Would you do anything differently?" he asked softly.

"I don't know," she answered slowly. Dani couldn't regret the night with Rand, yet if she'd never come to Monaco she wouldn't know what she'd missed.

"I'm sorry to hear that." His tender expression hardned.

Dani pleaded for understanding. "You and Grandfaher are a closed corporation. I always have the feeling ou're keeping something from me."

The mask that dropped behind Rand's eyes convinced er of it. "Why would you think that?"

"It's hard not to. I can almost feel the intrigue in the ir."

"Don't you think you're being a little dramatic?"

"No, I don't! There are so many things neither of you vill talk about."

"Like what?"

"My father, for instance. Grandfather never even nentions his name. Is that normal?"

Rand's face was guarded. "It's a painful subject."

"He was an only child! I should think Grandfather vould *enjoy* talking about him. It isn't as though his leath was recent. I wouldn't even have known my father vas married three more times if a stranger hadn't told ne."

"Is that the sort of thing you want to know?"

"It doesn't make me wildly happy, but I'm not a child. can take it."

"That's what I told Cleve," Rand muttered almost ander his breath.

"You admit there are other skeletons in the closet, hen!" She had a sudden inspiration. "Is that why you vant to keep me away from Keith? Because he might shed some light on them?"

A muscle twitched in Rand's clenched jaw. "Keith is an oily little rat. That's reason enough for staying away rom him."

"I once told Keith he was paranoid about you and Grandfather. Now I'm beginning to wonder if it's not the other way around."

"Do yourself a favor, Dani. Don't have anything to do with him."

"Why? Give me a reason," she challenged.

"He's the most immoral man I've ever run across— and I'm not talking about sex. Keith would do anything to anybody for personal gain."

"Generalities again. Give me an example."

"You wouldn't like it," he said curtly.

"Can't you ever tell me the truth about anything?" she asked in frustration.

Anger flared in Rand's tawny eyes. "I've never done anything else. Okay, you insist on the truth? I'll give it to you. For one thing, your precious boyfriend is a fortune hunter."

Dani stared at him blankly. Then the import of his words sank in. "Are you saying Keith is interested in me because he thinks I have money?"

"You're an heiress—that's good enough for him."

Rage engulfed her. "You mean I'd have to be rich for a man to fall in love with me?"

"You know that's not what I mean. And we're not talking about a man, we're talking about Keith. He'd romance a female porcupine if she made it worth his while. Why do you think he hangs around that—" Rand stopped abruptly.

Dani was too furious to notice. "It's nice to know your true opinion of me. Was that the reason *you* treated me to that night of bliss? Because I'm an heiress?"

His face turned white. "I ought to break your beautiful neck," he grated.

"Evading the question, as usual?" she taunted. Dani knew her accusation was reprehensible, but she was too sick at heart to stop herself. They were all using her in one way or another.

Rand's fingers tangled in her hair, jerking her head back. "I made love to you because I wanted you more than I've ever wanted any woman." He looked her over insolently. "Luckily I got you out of my system—because, unlike your boyfriend, all your money couldn't pay me to repeat the experience."

Dani lashed out wildly because she was drowning in pain. "I'm beginning to wonder about this fixation you have with Keith. Could it be that you're afraid of him?"

He stared at her as though she'd dropped from outer space. "What could I possibly have to fear from that little wimp?"

"You've done a job on Keith with Grandfather, but suppose he had a change of heart and drew up a new will? What if Grandfather designated Keith to run the business instead of you?"

"That dumb jerk couldn't run a lemonade stand without help from a small boy," Rand said contemptuously. "And the only way he's going to inherit anything sizable is if he marries you. But just in case he has grandiose ideas, you can tell him for me that he'll never get his grubby hands on the business. I won't let him tear down everything Cleve's spent a lifetime building."

Dani gazed into his coldly determined eyes, feeling her heart break in a million pieces. "That's all you really care about, isn't it?" she whispered.

A wealth of emotions coursed over his lean face before it hardened into an impenetrable mask. "You've always suspected as much, haven't you?" Before she could answer he reached for the doorknob. "I'll have to hand it to you, Dani. Nobody can put anything over on you."

She stared at the closed door for a long time after Rand left, still seeing his dark, mocking face. That wasn't the memory she wanted to take away with her. How had things escalated to this point? How could she have said such terrible things to him? Was Rand just retaliating out of the same anger and hurt, or did he really mean the things *he'd* said? It didn't matter. Nothing could repair the damage they'd done to their relationship. They couldn't even be friends now.

Dani got undressed, feeling greater despair than she'd felt on a remote mountaintop when she didn't know if she was going to live or die. She would live, but there wouldn't be any joy in her life without Rand.

She was getting into bed when there was a knock on the door. Dani stiffened. Had he forgotten some insults? It was Cleve instead of Rand, however.

"I know it's late," he apologized, "but I haven't seen you in a couple of days. Are you too tired to visit for a few minutes?"

Dani didn't know how to refuse. She couldn't very well tell him she was emotionally drained. "No, I'm not too tired. Please sit down." She led the way to the sitting area.

He smiled warmly at her. "I feel as though I've been neglecting you."

"There's no reason to."

"You're very kind, my dear, but if I couldn't be with you the least I could have done was leave Rand to take my place. He did tell you I was the culprit who sent him to Paris?"

It wasn't hard to deduce that her grandfather had heard them arguing. "It didn't matter. Keith filled the gap admirably," she said, watching him covertly.

Cleve's pleasant expression didn't change, leading Dani to suspect that he was a first-rate poker player. "I'm glad you weren't alone."

Suddenly Dani felt as though she were stifling. The civilized pretense, the evasions and half-truths were becoming unbearable.

"I was going to talk to you about something tomorrow," she said abruptly. "But as long as you're here now we might as well get it settled. It's time for me to go home."

Cleve's eyes turned as wary as Rand's. "I thought you'd decided to stay a little longer."

"I changed my mind." She tried to smile. "That's supposed to be a woman's prerogative."

He didn't return her smile. "Did something happen to upset you, Dani?"

"No, I just want— I've stayed longer than I expected. If I don't get back to work soon, they won't hold my job." Dani braced herself. Why had she brought that up? Now her grandfather would renew his offer to support her.

He didn't, however. "When did you plan on leaving?"

"As soon as possible. Tomorrow?" she asked hopefully.

"That might be a bit of a problem. The airlines are booked rather heavily at this time of year."

"Well, the earliest flight, then."

"Can I persuade you to stay just one more week?" he coaxed. "You never did get aboard the yacht. We could take a short cruise."

She shook her head. "I'm really sorry."

Although he seemed to accept her decision, Dani knew Cleve's keen mind was searching for alternatives.

"Of course I'm disappointed, but I quite understand, my dear," he said smoothly. "There's just one thing left to do, then. We'll have to give you a gala going-away party."

It was the last thing Dani was in the mood for. "There won't be time. I'm sure I can get a plane reservation in a couple of days at most."

"Let's see, this is Wednesday night. We could have the party on Sunday and you could leave on Monday. That's really only four days more, since you can't count Monday." He smiled charmingly. "Couldn't you manage to put up with me that much longer?"

"You know it isn't that," she said miserably. "You've been very good to me."

"Then indulge an old man, Dani. I think we'll have the party on the *Sea Siren*. At least you'll get to see it, if nothing else." He seemed to take it for granted that the matter was settled.

Dani didn't know how she was going to get through four more days there. She had a feeling that with his influence, Cleve could have gotten her on a plane the next day, but there was nothing she could do about it. Being short of money in a foreign country where she didn't speak the language put her pretty much at his mercy.

After he left a few minutes later, Dani got into bed wearily. Once more she'd been cleverly maneuvered into something against her will, but at least the end was in sight.

Chapter Ten

Dani managed to get through the next four days somehow. She spent the evenings with Cleve and the days with Keith. Surprisingly, the days were more relaxed.

Although her grandfather was more stimulating to be with, Dani felt wary around him. For one thing, he never mentioned Rand. Obviously he knew about their argument, but he didn't try to patch it up. That was suspicious in itself.

Even though Cleve never interfered openly in her affairs, Dani had no doubt that he was the power behind the scene. It made her very nervous. She was always afraid he would find some pretext for bringing Rand and her together.

Keith, on the other hand, held no surprises. His proposals were a little repetitious, but his single-minded devotion was balm to her bruised spirit. If Keith was only interested in her money as Rand alleged, he was remarkably good at hiding the fact. He certainly acted like a man in love.

Just out of curiosity, Dani decided to find out if Rand was right. She and Keith were sitting by the pool, and he had just proposed again.

"I don't know if you're a good prospect," she answered jokingly. "You never seem to work. How do I know you can support me?"

His eyes lit up at the small sign of encouragement. "You'd live like a little queen, my love!"

Dani raised an eyebrow. "One of the deposed nobility who run a restaurant for a living?"

"You'd never have to work if you were my wife," he declared.

"Don't you think one of us should?"

"Are you serious, Dani? Are you really considering it?" he asked eagerly.

She was a little ashamed of herself, but the urge to know for sure overcame guilt. "I'm fond of you, Keith, but I can't pretend to be in love with you," she began.

"It's enough to start with, darling!"

"Yes, but under the circumstances I'd really have to know something about your finances." She watched him from under her thick lashes. "I don't intend to take anything from Grandfather."

"Of course not! I wouldn't expect you to. I wouldn't take a penny from him, either."

"But Rand said—" Dani could have bitten her tongue.

"I'm sure he told you plenty," Keith remarked sardonically. "What did he say?"

"It isn't important," she mumbled.

"It is to me. If he's blackening my name, I have a right to know."

"He didn't do that," Dani protested. "I just got the idea that Grandfather gave you an, uh, allowance every month."

Keith's expression was ugly. "I might have known he'd tell you that. He'd say anything to discredit me."

It was useless to try to convince him that Rand hadn't actually told her anything. "It isn't true?"

He made an effort to control his anger. "Uncle Cleve administers a trust fund my father set up for me. He sends me a dividend check every month—if you call that an allowance."

"I must have misunderstood," Dani murmured.

"No, you didn't. Rand wants you to think I'm a sponging weakling! Someday I'm going to get even with him," Keith snarled.

Dani could have told him to forget it. Rand was too clever for both of them. He had a deadly combination of charm and brains. He'd bragged about always telling her the truth, but she was just finding out how he could twist words to mean whatever he wanted them to.

That night at dinner Dani questioned her grandfather about Keith.

"Did you know his father?" she asked, trying to sound only casually interested.

Cleve's smile was faintly mocking. "I knew all Lulu's husbands. But none of them was Keith's father."

"I know he's adopted. I meant the one whose name he took."

"Yes, I knew him."

"Was he wealthy?" It sounded rather crass, but Dani couldn't think of any other way to put the question.

"No." Cleve didn't amplify the statement.

Dani frowned. Keith's explanation of the trust fund had sounded truthful, coupled with his indignation that she thought he took an allowance from his uncle. Then Dani realized her grandfather used a different yardstick. By his standards, very few people would be considered rich.

His dark eyes were regarding her enigmatically. "Is there some reason for your interest?"

"No, I was just making conversation. Shall we play chess?" she asked hurriedly.

The only thing Dani was looking forward to about her going-away party was the chance to wear the beautiful outfit she'd purchased with Rand. There would be music and dancing aboard the yacht.

She wondered if Rand would be there. It might seem rather strange if he weren't, but everyone would just assume he was out of town. If he did show up, would he at least be civil? Rand's manners were usually exquisite, but he hated hypocrisy. That's why he probably didn't plan to put in an appearance.

Dani tried to be glad. It would be difficult to act normally if he were there, but she'd like to have seen him one last time, if only to erase the memory of their angry quarrel. Cold civility wouldn't be much of an improvement, though. Her eyes were shadowed as she dressed for the party.

The *Sea Siren* was lit up like a cruise ship—and looked almost as large. Multicolored bulbs were strung along the railings, and every salon and stateroom was a blaze of light. It was a splendid sight from the beach.

A fleet of small tenders was moored to the dock, waiting to ferry the guests. As Dani and her grandfather boarded the yacht, music greeted them, and respectful young officers in gleaming white uniforms stood ready to help them onto the polished teakwood deck.

"I feel like royalty!" Dani exclaimed.

Cleve nodded approvingly. "You look like a princess, my dear."

The eyes of every man present discreetly admired Dani in her sparkling top and black satin pants. She was an enchanting sight with her long hair pulled back in a mass of auburn curls. Excitement made her cheeks pink and her eyes sparkle like jewels. It would have been difficult not to be stimulated by such an exotic setting.

"Shall I show you around before the guests begin arriving?" Cleve suggested.

"I'd like that," Dani agreed eagerly.

The main salon was an impressive room with wide windows on both sides. It was furnished sumptuously. There was even a grand piano in one corner, and priceless oil paintings adorned the walls. The large dining salon had the chairs pushed back for the party so guests could walk around the big mahogany table that was completely covered with delicacies.

The buffet was a visual delight, as well as a gastronomic one. Crystal bowls of black caviar nestled in beds of shaved ice, flanked on one side by pale pink smoked salmon, and on the other by the little red lobsters called langoustes. There were also silver chafing dishes and trays of hors d'oeuvres, each one looking like a miniature work of art.

"Don't tell me Henri did all this!" Dani gasped.

Cleve chuckled. "No, he draws the line at working outside his own kitchen. I think you'll find we have an adequate chef, however. Would you like a sample?"

As he reached for an hors d'oeuvre, Dani tapped his fingers. "You have to wait until the guests arrive. You'll leave a gap in the tray. That's as bad as using the linen towels in the powder room. Didn't your mother ever tell you not to do that?''

Cleve laughed as he put his arm around her and kissed her cheek. "Thanks for reminding me. It's been a long time since anyone's corrected me.''

"That's because you're so rich.''

"It doesn't seem to impress *you*." When her smile faded, Cleve said quickly, "Now we'll go below and see the staterooms.''

The master suite had a king-size bed, a couch piled with pillows and various chests and end tables.

"I thought everything was built in on a ship,'' Dani remarked.

"It is on commercial ships, but we're fortunate in having enough space to spread out a little more,'' he said deprecatingly.

"It's like a home.'' She looked admiringly at the big dressing room and full bathroom that adjoined the bedroom. There were large windows, too, that opened onto a private section of the deck.

"The *Sea Siren* is an ocean-going yacht. If you'd stayed longer, we could have taken a cruise,'' Cleve said delicately.

Dani pretended she hadn't heard the last part. "Are the other staterooms this fabulous?''

Before they could complete the tour, a crewman came to tell them the guests were arriving.

Cleve had invited a mixture of people from various age groups. They were all sophisticated, charming and beautifully dressed. Dani was thankful for her own elegant outfit, even if she never got to wear it again.

It was a very glamorous party. Unobtrusive waiters circulated with trays of hors d'oeuvres and champagne cocktails. They also took orders for other drinks, or guests could visit one of several bars set up in different locations. A small orchestra played for those who wanted to dance on the broad aft deck.

Most of the younger couples gravitated there, but Dani stayed by her grandfather's side. He was taking such obvious pride in introducing her around. She smilingly resisted his halfhearted urging that she join in the dancing.

"You're monopolizing the most beautiful girl here," Keith complained. He and Lulu were among the guests.

"Age has its privilege." Cleve smiled at Dani. "Besides," he said softly, "this is our last evening together."

Dani had a lump in her throat. "You're coming to New York to visit me, remember?"

"I can't imagine how you can leave Monte Carlo in the middle of the season," Lulu said disapprovingly. Her attention was distracted by a newcomer. "Look, there's Roxanne. Doesn't she look stunning?"

Dani had been having a better time than she'd thought possible. Until Roxanne arrived. Dani held her breath, waiting for Rand to appear behind her. But Roxanne was alone.

She came directly over to them. "*Maman* sends her regrets. She's desolate about missing your beautiful party, but the poor dear has *la grippe*."

Lulu was more interested in Roxanne's dress, a daringly low-cut black lace with a hemline above her shapely knees. "What a stunning frock! I haven't seen anything like it."

"I got it in Paris this week."

"I wish I'd known you were going to Paris," Lulu lamented. "I'd have asked you to bring me some face cream from Bernadine's. No one in Monte Carlo carries it. You could also have picked up my pearls at the jewelers.''

"I was only there for a day," Roxanne protested.

"How can anyone go to Paris for a day?" Lulu demanded.

Roxanne shrugged. "It's better than nothing."

Dani's suspicions were aroused when the girl said she'd been in Paris that week. As soon as she mentioned being there only a day, Dani knew Rand had taken her. It must have been very annoying for both of them when Cleve called him home so unexpectedly, she thought bitterly. Dani's heart was like a cold little lump in her breast. Rand had gone directly from her arms to Roxanne's. He was beneath contempt!

The evening was completely spoiled for her after that. She only went through the motions of enjoying herself.

It was ten-thirty when Rand arrived. Dani was standing with a group of people in the main salon. She looked up with the feeling of being stared at, and their eyes met. The conversation went on around her, but it was unintelligible through the sudden thundering of her heart.

Rand wore a dark suit and conventional tie instead of dinner clothes like the other men. His lean face was austere. Had Cleve insisted he put in an appearance, Dani wondered miserably. Her mouth felt dry as he started toward her. This didn't promise to be much better than the last time. Still, she couldn't move away.

Neither said anything for a long moment after he reached her. Then Dani rallied. "If you're looking for Roxanne, I believe she's dancing."

His mouth became a trifle grimmer. "I wasn't looking for Roxanne."

"Oh." After a tiny silence she said, "Would you like a drink?"

"No." He continued to stare at her, as though memorizing her features.

Dani couldn't go on playing the polite hostess. "Why did you come, Rand?" she whispered.

A little muscle jerked in his jawline. "To say goodbye."

Her long lashes swept down to hide the glitter of tears in her eyes. "That was nice," she murmured.

"I don't feel nice," he replied savagely.

He didn't look it, either. Rand resembled an angry tiger being prodded to jump through a hoop. Cleve should have left well enough alone, Dani reflected sadly.

"I couldn't let you go without apologizing for my behavior the other night," he said moodily.

"It's all right. I said some things I'm sorry for, too."

He raked his fingers through his thick hair. "I don't know what the devil happened!"

She sighed. "We both lost our tempers."

"That's not a good enough reason for letting it end like this." He touched a shining auburn curl. "We had something wonderful together."

"Please, Rand," she said in a tortured whisper.

Dani couldn't bear to be reminded of what they'd shared. Not now when she knew it was only a casual night of sex for him. It wasn't even that satisfying. The very next day he'd taken Roxanne to Paris.

As she turned away, Rand put his hand on her arm. 'Dance with me."

He ignored her refusal, pulling her toward the dance floor. His grip was so strong that she couldn't break it without making a scene. Dani had to accompany him, but it was under protest.

Yet the moment Rand took her in his arms, all the reasons for remaining aloof were swept away in a tidal wave of longing. Her body was independent of her mind. It remembered every taut muscle in his powerful frame and hungered to feel each one again. With a tiny sound of contentment she closed her eyes and nestled against him.

Rand held her in a close embrace, resting his cheek on her hair. They swayed in time to the music without moving from one spot. She was rocked in the cradle of his arms, as she'd dreamed of being every lonely night since they were together last.

It was an intolerable intrusion when someone tapped Rand on the shoulder and said, "May I cut in?"

"No, you may not!" Rand snapped.

"You can't keep this beautiful lady all to yourself," the other man objected.

"Watch me!" As another determined partner bore down on them, Rand took Dani's hand and led her off the floor. "Come on," he muttered. "Let's get out of here."

He guided her toward the gangway leading to the staterooms, ignoring the protests that followed them. When they reached the master cabin, he drew her inside and locked the door.

"I'm the hostess. I can't leave the party," Dani protested weakly.

Rand reached for her without bothering to answer. His mouth covered hers so urgently that it canceled out any argument. Dani couldn't have made one, anyway. How could she deny her aching need for this man?

He dragged his mouth away and hugged her convulsively. "God, how I've missed you!"

She touched his cheek with a kind of wonder. "I thought I'd never see you again."

"I couldn't stay away." He feathered frantic kisses over her face. "I was scheduled to go to Paris this morning, but I booked a midnight flight instead. I told myself t was because I couldn't get away any sooner, but I knew hat wasn't the reason. I had to see you just once more."

Her dazed happiness started to fade when Rand mentioned Paris. Every instinct begged her not to spoil this ast wonderful moment with him, to let this be the memory that would stay with her. But Dani had to know.

"Did you take Roxanne to Paris with you?" she whispered.

He looked puzzled. "I don't know what you mean."

"Last Wednesday when you left so unexpectedly. Did you have an...an arrangement with Roxanne?"

He looked at her incredulously. "That was the day after our night together. Do you honestly believe I would have any interest in another woman?"

"She told Lulu she'd gone to Paris just for the day. That's all you were there so I thought maybe..." Dani's sooty lashes swept down to veil her misery.

Sudden comprehension erased the lines on his forehead. "Is that why you went out with Keith?" He framed her face in his palms and lifted it to his. "Dear heart, we have to talk."

He led her to the bed and pushed her gently down on t, taking a seat beside her. "If Roxanne was in Paris the same time I was, this is the first I've heard of it. She has a boyfriend who takes her on little jaunts now and then. That isn't important. What matters is the fact that you'd think I was capable of something like that."

Dani didn't think it would make Rand feel any better f she told him that wasn't the reason she went out with Keith. He would still be hurt by her lack of trust.

"Don't you know how I feel about you, angel?" He stroked her neck, burning a path of fire down its length. "How could a man want anyone else after you?"

"She's so beautiful, and so... available."

Rand's slow smile raised Dani's blood pressure. "She doesn't have hair the color of autumn leaves, or eyes like emerald stars."

After gently urging Dani onto her back he leaned over her, his tawny eyes lit with a familiar glow. When his mouth brushed hers and his hand caressed her bare midriff under the spangled top, she felt excitement start to build.

"No other woman has skin as soft as yours, or a body that can drive a man out of his mind," Rand murmured huskily.

The sensuous feeling of his fingertips stroking her stomach made Dani shiver with pleasure. She opened her arms and Rand gathered her close, pressing her into the mattress with the strength of his powerful body. His mouth was almost savagely possessive, as though he wanted to put his mark on her.

Dani surrendered willingly. She ran her fingers through his thick hair, traced the width of his shoulders, the straining muscles in his back. Her movements were frantic in her need to experience him.

"How can I let you go?" he groaned against her throat.

She smoothed his ruffled hair gently. "You're the one who's always leaving *me*."

"Only when I've had to, and I always come back." He lifted his head to look searchingly at her. "Will you come back, Dani?"

"I can't," she said softly.

"You mean it's all over?" A nerve pulsed in his temple. "There's nothing I can do to change your mind?"

Dani took pity on him. "I can't come back because I'm not leaving."

His face blazed with incredulous joy. "You're really staying?"

She smiled tenderly. "At least until you make love to me a hundred different ways."

"Would you like to start now?" His voice throbbed with desire.

"Not here." She laughed as he reached for her.

"You're right. We'll go to my place." He drew her to her feet, looking deeply into her eyes. "I want to make love to you in our bed."

"I can't leave yet," Dani said reluctantly. "Grandfather's giving this party for me."

"I'll close the bar," Rand growled. "That will get rid of everyone."

She bubbled with laughter. "You'd do it, too."

"Like right now!"

As he took her hand and started toward the door, Dani held back. "You know we can't do that, Rand. Besides, you have to go to Paris."

"To hell with Paris! I'm not leaving you again."

She was torn between desire and duty. "Were you going to be gone long?"

"Just a couple of days, but it doesn't matter because I'm not going." He wrapped his arms around her and rubbed his cheek against her soft curls. "You mean more to me than any business deal, sweetheart. I'm not taking a chance on anything else going wrong between us."

"Nothing will," she promised.

It took a while, but Dani eventually convinced him. She didn't want him to go, either, yet it was the right thing to do. People were depending on him. The knowledge that Rand was willing to give up an important trip to be with her was the significant thing.

"You go ahead," she said after he finally gave in. "I have to fix my hair first."

He wound a shining strand around his finger and tugged her head back so he could kiss the hollow in her throat. "If you'll let me stay, I'll take the pins out and brush it for you when we get home."

"We settled all that. Go!" she ordered.

He sighed, consulting his watch. "Well, if you insist, I guess I'd better. I'm cutting it pretty close as it is."

After he left, Dani made rapid repairs to her hair and makeup. She had been gone from the party much too long already. Her movements slowed for an instant and her mouth curved in an enchanting smile as she remembered the worthwhile way the time had been spent.

When she entered the main salon, Dani was surprised to see Rand was still there. He was talking to her grandfather.

Rand had been stopped frequently by people who greeted him as he made his way through the crowded room. He had avoided more than brief responses, but he couldn't brush Cleve off.

"Someone told me you were here," the older man said. "I thought you weren't coming."

"I decided to stop by."

Rand was slightly self-conscious after the turbulent scene he'd made when Cleve had told him about the going-away party. He'd been adamant in his refusal to attend. Rand was sure Cleve knew the reason, but neither had mentioned it.

"Have you seen Dani?" Cleve asked.

"Yes, I saw her."

"Doesn't she look beautiful?" Cleve asked softly.

"Very lovely." Rand had to keep himself tightly in check to avoid babbling like a lovesick schoolboy. This wasn't the time to discuss his earthshaking plans for the future.

"I'm so proud of her," Cleve said wistfully.

"You have a right to be." Rand glanced at his watch and frowned. "I have to go or I'll miss the helicopter."

"You *are* going to Paris, then?" Cleve looked at him searchingly.

"Didn't we spend the past two days getting those figures together?" Rand demanded.

"Yes. I just thought perhaps..." The older man sighed. "Well, have a nice trip."

"If I ever get out of here," Rand muttered.

As he reached the door, Roxanne rushed up to him. "Are you leaving?"

"I'm *trying* to!"

"Oh, good! Will you give me a lift? I have another date and I'm scandalously late."

"Sorry, but I'm on my way to the airport."

"This is right on your way."

"I can't help you, Roxanne," Rand said firmly.

She put her hand on his arm and looked up coaxingly. "Don't be difficult, darling. Surely you can do me this itty bitty favor?"

Rand knew how tenacious she could be. It would be less time-consuming to give in than to argue about it. He put his arm around Roxanne's shoulders and hurried her out the door. "All right, but we're leaving right this minute. No protracted goodbyes."

Dani had watched Rand's conversation with her grandfather. His handsome face wore the absorbed look she knew so well. She smiled fondly. How different it was

from the expression he'd worn just a few moments be
fore.

Her smile faded when he left Cleve and was joined a
the door by Roxanne. Dani was too far away to hear wha
they said, but she witnessed the urgent exchange be
tween them, saw Rand put his arm around the girl an
hurry her out.

Dani felt the familiar demons of jealousy starting to
tear at her vital parts. Was she being set up again? Every
time the doors of paradise swung open, she found Rox
anne there ahead of her!

But then she thought about her tender reunion with
Rand in the cabin. No man could be that good an actor
He'd been consumed with the same hunger for her tha
she felt for him. It was more than a sexual attraction.
There was something very special between them. What
ever had just taken place between him and Roxanne
couldn't mean anything.

"Where have you been?" Keith's petulant voice dis
tracted her. "I've been looking all over for you."

"I've been around," Dani answered vaguely. She gave
him a brilliant smile. "Isn't it a wonderful party?"

He gazed at her soulfully. "It would be if it were given
for a different reason."

Lulu joined them before Dani could mention her
change of plans. "Everyone's having a smashing time,"
the older woman remarked.

"Everyone except Rand." Satisfaction was written on
Keith's face. "I saw him leave a minute ago. Maybe he
was embarrassed at not wearing a dinner jacket." He
snickered.

"Nothing embarrasses that man!" Lulu snapped.
"He's a total nonconformist."

"He *is* different, isn't he?" Dani said softly.

Lulu lifted her eyebrows. "You're being kind, my dear. Imagine wearing a business suit to a gala event like this."

"I believe he was catching a midnight flight for Paris," Dani remarked.

"Oh. Well, I suppose that would explain it," Lulu said unwillingly.

Keith had noticed Dani's expression change the minute Rand's name was mentioned. He adopted an elaborately casual manner. "That might explain why Rand left early, but why do you suppose Roxanne went with him? She usually closes up the party."

"Did Roxanne leave?" Lulu asked. "I wanted to find out about that shop in Paris."

Keith's laugh had a lascivious sound. "Give her time to get there first and then you can call her at the hotel tonight."

"You mean she and Rand are still...?" Lulu shrugged. "Honestly! I don't know what she sees in that man."

"Oh, come now, Mother! Don't be so naive." Under cover of laughter, Keith watched Dani's reaction.

"Well, I'll have to admit he *is* a sexy devil," Lulu said grudgingly.

Dani refused to let their nasty gossip upset her. She knew what they were saying wasn't true. That's all that mattered.

"If you'll excuse me, I have to speak to Grandfather about something," she said serenely.

Dani needed to get away from Keith and Lulu, but it wasn't just an excuse. She did want to tell her grandfather about her decision to stay. It could have waited until later, but Dani knew how much it would please him. She wanted the whole world to be as happy as she was at that moment.

Cleve was standing with a group of people. He wel
comed her with the special smile reserved for her alone
"Are you having a good time, my dear?"

"A fabulous time!" she replied. After a few words t
the others, Dani murmured to her grandfather, "Can
speak to you alone for a minute?"

He immediately led her away from the group. "Wha
is it, child?" he asked when they were alone.

Dani laughed self-consciously. "I said it's a woman'
prerogative to change her mind, but I'm about to abus
the privilege. It's a little embarrassing after you gave m
this gorgeous going-away party, but I'd like to sta
longer, if you don't mind."

"Mind? You must know how very welcome you are."
Cleve struggled to contain his deep emotion.

Dani knew he was holding himself in check for fear o
doing or saying the wrong thing. It made her feel con
strained, too. They still found it difficult to express thei
true feelings.

"Well...I thought I should tell you so you wouldn'
get up early to take me to the airport."

"That was very thoughtful of you," Cleve said gravely

Their formality suddenly struck her as absurd. "Wh
am I kidding? That wasn't the reason at all!" She threv
her arms around his neck. "I hoped you'd be pleased."

His arms closed around her and he stroked her hair
"Thank you for making an old man happy."

Dani blinked away happy tears. "I told you to stop
calling yourself old," she scolded. "You aren't in th
least."

He smiled fondly at her. "Having you here has mad
me feel young again."

"If I stay long enough you might regress enough t
marry Roxanne's mother," Dani teased.

Cleve laughed, shaking his head. "Your wedding is the only one I want to go to."

Her face was radiant as she considered the possibility. "I'll see what I can do about it," she murmured.

Dani was glad that other people joined them at that point. She was sure Cleve knew her reasons for staying, but it was too soon to talk about marriage. She was still getting used to the fact that Rand had come back to her. If only he hadn't had to leave, Dani thought wistfully. Who knew what might have happened?

It was a frustrating night for Rand, too. He had an instinctive feeling that he shouldn't have left Dani, yet common sense told him nothing could happen in a couple of days except they'd miss each other terribly. This time he'd make sure to call her often, and in the future he'd take her with him. Rand's face was soft with wonder as he realized he'd found the woman he wanted to spend the rest of his life with.

After he dropped Roxanne at her destination, Rand drove like a race driver to the airport. His relief that the helicopter hadn't taken off was short-lived. It was having mechanical problems. Rand strode impatiently up and down the tarmac. It was only a short flight to Nice, but he was cutting it dangerously close.

When the helicopter was finally pronounced serviceable, Rand knew he had only minutes to spare. As it happened, he was being optimistic. The giant jetliner was taxiing down the runway as he dashed up to the gate at the Nice airport.

After swearing pungently, Rand went to the reservation desk. "I just missed my flight to Paris. When's the next one?"

"Not until six-thirty tomorrow morning," the man informed him.

Rand's jaw set a little more firmly. "How about one of the other airlines? Can you check for me?"

The clerk shook his head. "There isn't another plane until morning, monsieur. Would you like me to book you on our early flight?"

Rand considered the idea and rejected it immediately. He wasn't going to sit around an airport all night. The thought of going all the way back to Monaco only to turn around a few hours later and fly back to Nice wasn't an acceptable alternative, either. He frowned, looking for a solution.

"I'm afraid that's the best I can do for you," the man remarked. "You can wait in our lounge, if you like. It's quite comfortable."

Rand sighed. "No, I need a decent night's sleep. I haven't gotten much of that lately. I'll just have to reschedule later in the day."

"That's probably wise, monsieur. Would you like to reserve your flight now?"

Rand tried to juggle times in his mind. The meeting in Paris with the corporate board was at nine o'clock. That would have to be moved up in any case—unless Broderick could hold the fort till he got there. He was a good man. They were grooming him for bigger things. Broderick had all the facts and figures, so there was no reason why he couldn't start the meeting without him.

Suddenly Rand's expression cleared as an idea took hold. Why couldn't Broderick handle the whole thing on his own? He would have to stand alone sooner or later. Perhaps this missed flight was a blessing in disguise. Rand had been deeply reluctant to leave Dani, uneasy ven. Maybe this was a sign that he shouldn't have, he decided.

"Can I make a reservation for you?" the clerk repeated.

Rand's smile lit up his whole face. "No, I have some unfinished business to clear up first."

He glanced at the wall clock as he started for the helicopter. The party might still be going on when he reached Monte Carlo.

But on the flight back, Rand changed his mind about returning to the yacht. This was Cleve's night with Dani. He deserved to have her all to himself this evening, at least. There wouldn't be many more opportunities.

Rand's topaz eyes gleamed in the darkness as he reviewed his plans for the following night.

Chapter Eleven

The party lasted well into the early hours. After the last guests departed, Dani and Cleve had a final drink together and discussed little things that had happened during the evening, although Dani neglected to tell him the most exciting one. She didn't realize it, but the happiness on her face told him all he needed to know.

There was a warm family feeling between them that delighted them both. Dani's wariness had completely disappeared. She was ashamed of her former reserve. There was no point in perpetuating past mistakes. Her grandfather's love was indisputable, and she found herself returning it. The future looked dazzling.

It was very late by the time she finally got to bed, but Dani couldn't sleep. The party had been stimulating in itself, but it was thoughts of Rand that sent excitement fizzing through her veins like the champagne that had flowed so freely all evening.

She pictured him in Paris, sound asleep in his hotel room. Did Rand wear pajamas? Somehow Dani doubted it. She knew what his lithe body looked like, down to the most intimate detail of the tiny birthmark on his hip. When she thought about him sprawled out in bed, sleep was out of the question. Finally Dani gave it up as a bad job. She got up and put on a long white eyelet robe rimmed with ruffles.

The house was silent as she walked through it and noiselessly opened the door to the patio. A few sleepy birds in the surrounding trees protested her intrusion, but other than that everything was quiet. The air had a fresh, clean scent perfumed by flowers. A subtle paling in the sky indicated a new day was dawning, which struck a chord with Dani. Her own life was just beginning.

She strolled around the pool and wandered in the gardens until the shrubbery began to take on the colors of day instead of night. When she finally became drowsy, Dani was reluctant to go back to her room. She chose a padded chaise on the patio instead. Curling up on the comfortable cushion, she closed her eyes and drifted off to sleep. Rand's voice entered her subconscious much later, but it didn't wake her at first.

In spite of the lateness of the hour the previous evening, Cleve was in his office by nine o'clock. He was working at his desk when Rand arrived.

"What are you doing here?" Cleve exclaimed. "I thought you went to Paris."

"I missed my plane." Rand explained the circumstances briefly.

Cleve frowned. "Shouldn't you be on another one? What's going to happen to the Gambrousse deal?"

"Broderick can handle it. I spoke to him on the phone this morning."

Their voices drifted out the open window as they discussed business.

Dani merely stirred at first, then her eyes opened slowly. For a few moments she thought Rand's voice was an echo of the wonderful dream she'd been having. He couldn't be here. He was in Paris, miles away.

But as Cleve's voice joined Rand's and their words started to register, Dani knew she wasn't dreaming. They were talking about stock options and incentives. Her mouth curved in an indulgent smile. That was real enough.

Mounting excitement chased away all traces of sleep. Rand had come back to her! They wouldn't be separated for endless days—and nights. Dani reached for her slippers, trying to decide whether to go in the den in her robe or get dressed first. She was wild to see him, but she wanted to look her best. As she was wavering, Dani heard her name mentioned. She paused for a moment.

"Dani will be pleased you're back," Cleve was saying.

"I hope so."

Rand's voice was noncommittal. He suspected that Cleve knew how things stood between Dani and himself, but until things were settled, Rand didn't like to say anything. There had been so many glitches.

"I think you can be fairly sure of it." Cleve smiled broadly. "It wasn't my scintillating company that put the sparkle in her eyes last night."

"I imagine the party had something to do with it. That was quite an extravaganza you put on."

Rand would just as leave have changed the subject, but Cleve persisted. "Dani didn't really start to enjoy it until you showed up."

"I'm glad if I contributed to her enjoyment," Rand answered lightly.

"Did she tell you she's staying on?"

"Yes, it was mentioned."

"But not by you. Why didn't you tell me before you left last night? I was afraid the situation was hopeless."

"I thought Dani should be the one to give you the news. I didn't want to jump the gun. She's been known to change her mind," Rand added dryly.

"Not this time," Cleve said confidently. "You're a wonder worker! I knew I could count on you."

"I can't say I shared your confidence. Your grand-daughter is a difficult lady to convince," Rand said softly.

Dani was transfixed to the spot, unable to move although their revealing words were battering her like physical blows. In those few terrible moments the bottom dropped out of her world. She cringed as Cleve's chuckle drifted out to the patio.

"A little romance works miracles," he remarked jovially.

"I'm afraid it's gone beyond that," Rand said carefully.

"I know."

There was no longer any pretense between them. "You don't mind?" Rand asked quietly.

Cleve looked at the man he'd always wished was his son. Having him for a grandson was the next best thing. Pride and affection shone on his face as he said, "I'm sure you know the answer to that."

Dani could scarcely trust her ears. The depth of her grandfather's depravity wasn't to be believed! He didn't even care that Rand had made love to her as long as it served to keep her in Monte Carlo. This was the man

Rand had accused her of judging too harshly? Well, naturally, by *his* standards! There wasn't a scrap of morality or ethics between the two of them.

"I hoped you'd feel that way," Rand was saying.

"I couldn't be more delighted, my boy," Cleve answered warmly. There was laughter in his voice as he said, "This deserves a promotion, but the only job higher than yours is mine, and you'll just have to wait for that."

"No problem—I'm a patient man." Rand sounded as though he were grinning.

"I might consider giving you a bonus," Cleve said.

They were both very pleased with themselves, Dani thought bitterly. Like con men exulting over a successful scam. Which was exactly what they'd pulled off. She wasn't a bit surprised at Rand's response to Cleve's offer.

"After what I've been through this past month, I ought to take you up on it." He laughed.

Dani couldn't bear to hear any more. She felt used and cheapened. As she stood up, the intensity of her emotions made her slightly dizzy. When she grasped the back of the chaise to steady herself, it moved with a grating sound.

Rand glanced over and saw her through the open window. His whole face lit up. "Dani, darling! I didn't know you were out there."

"Obviously," she said bitterly.

He came onto the terrace through the French doors. "Cleve told me what a late night it was. You should still be in bed."

"That's what you were counting on, wasn't it?" she asked tautly.

"It presented a very enticing picture." His topaz eyes glittered in the sunlight as he walked toward her. "I planned on coming in later to wake you up."

"After you made your report to Grandfather?"

Rand didn't seem to notice her rigid pose. "I've already done that."

"I know. I heard you."

"Aren't you going to ask me what I'm doing back from Paris?"

"That doesn't take much imagination. I've been known to change my mind," she said tonelessly.

Rand frowned. "Is something wrong, Dani?"

"How can you ask a thing like that? Don't you realize I heard every word you and Grandfather said?"

"I didn't mean to tell him about us, honey, but Cleve's no fool. He already guessed."

"I'm not surprised—considering it was his idea in the first place."

Rand grinned. "I wouldn't doubt it. He's a devious old bird."

"How could you do it, Rand?" Tears stung Dani's eyes.

He looked puzzled. "Do what?"

"Isn't there *anything* you won't do for money?"

Rand's eyes narrowed. "I have a feeling we're talking at cross-purposes. What does money have to do with it?"

"You must have known there'd be a bonus involved when you agreed to make love to me."

His face paled. "I can't believe you said that!"

"I wish it weren't true." Her slender shoulders drooped.

"It isn't!" He gripped her arms tightly. "Don't you know what you mean to me?"

"Yes." She sighed. "I've always known, but I didn'
want to admit it. Grandfather gave you an assignmen
and you fulfilled it."

He stared at her incredulously. "You really think he'
instruct me to make love to you—or that I'd accept it a
part of my job?"

Dani's lashes fluttered down. She couldn't look at him
remembering the incredible night in his arms. "What els
can I think when you indicated this was one of the wors
months of your life?"

"I meant because you almost drove me crazy!" H
lifted her chin and gazed at her tenderly. "When we ar
gued and I didn't see you for days, life wasn't worth liv
ing."

It was such a temptation to believe him, to pretend sh
hadn't heard Rand and her grandfather congratulatin
each other on their deception. Dani closed her eyes for
second to blot out Rand's compelling face, but his su
perb body still drew an answering response from hers, i
spite of everything.

"It was torture having to leave you last night after we'
made up. I wanted to carry you home and make love t
you for a week." His husky voice invited her to share th
memory.

Dani opened her eyes. "Instead of that you took Rox
anne home."

"Not Roxanne again!" he exclaimed. "I thought w
settled all that last night."

She backed out of his grasp. "You're very persuasive
and you have an answer for everything."

The light went out of his eyes as he watched her mov
away. "But you don't believe a thing I say. You neve
did."

"Unfortunately I did. I was even willing to overlook grandfather's past sins. He's as good an actor as you are. He played the poor lonely man to perfection."

Rand's face was austere. "Don't make him suffer for ur differences. He loves you, Dani."

"I wish you were that loyal to me," she said wistfully. "And I wish you were right about Grandfather. He wants keep me here because I'm the last of the Barringer ne—the only one whose life he hasn't messed up so far. m a possession to him, nothing more."

"You aren't too good at recognizing love," Rand said utly.

"That's pretty evident."

Frustration filled his strong face. "I've given up trying convince you of anything where we're concerned, but ou mustn't take it out on Cleve. You're his family!"

"You expect me to think that means anything? Look : the way he's treated poor Keith."

"Damned well, considering!"

"According to *you*. You've never been fair to Keith."

"It's difficult to judge him too harshly," Rand said rdonically.

"What right do you have to judge him at all?"

His jawline tightened. "What is this blind spot you ave where Keith is concerned?"

"I could ask you the same thing, except I already know e answer. You'd go to any lengths to discredit him."

"He's already done that himself. Anyone with a grain f sense could see through that phony."

Dani reacted angrily to the criticism. "At least he dn't make love to me in the line of duty!"

Rand's smile resembled a shark's. "Maybe the poor imp is saving himself for marriage."

"You could be right," she flared.

"Have you set the date yet?"

"No, but we'll get around to it." She would have said
anything to wipe the confident smile off Rand's smug
face.

She was successful. His eyes narrowed. "You intend to
marry him?"

"Just as soon as possible." Dani was appalled to hear
the words come out of her mouth. Had she really said
that?

"I suppose next you'll tell me you're in love with him."

"I don't have to answer to you, but for your infor
mation I . . . I'm very fond of Keith."

"Is that enough to get you through the nights?" He
snaked a long arm around her waist and jerked her
against him. "Will you be able to respond to him the way
you responded to me?" Rand's face was so close that
Dani could feel his warm breath on her lips. "Will you
tremble in his arms and call out his name when he brings
you pleasure?"

Rand's hands caressed her through the thin robe, kin
dling memories of the intimate moments he was describ
ing. It was an effort to remember this was Rand's most
potent weapon against her. He used it when argument
failed. She mustn't let him do it to her again.

Dani summoned up hidden strength to pull herself out
of his arms. She forced herself to look squarely at him.
"There's more to marriage than sex. But to answer your
question—yes, I expect our personal life to be quite
wonderful."

A nerve throbbed in his broad forehead. "Don't be a
little idiot," he said savagely. "I won't let you ruin your
life in a childish fit of pique."

He was the one who'd ruined her life. It didn't matter
to Rand personally whether she married Keith or not. His

how of anger was only frustration at losing. Rand wasn't
sed to that. Dani struck back out of pain and hopeless-
ess. At least she would show him he couldn't manipu-
ate her anymore.

She lifted her chin. "You can't stop me."

"Maybe not, but Cleve sure as hell can!"

"He wouldn't dare! Not after what he did to my
other."

Rand glared down at her, clenching and unclenching
is fists. "I thought you were smarter than your mother,
ut I was mistaken."

"That makes two of us! Stay out of my life, Rand.
nd tell Grandfather to do the same."

"You're determined to go through with this insan-
y?"

"Yes!" She glared back at him.

"Well, don't come running to either of us when your
rince turns into a toad." He swung around abruptly and
trode toward the house, fury in every line of his lean
ody.

"I wouldn't come running to you if the whole world
ollapsed!" she shouted at his retreating back.

Rand turned for just an instant to smile mirthlessly at
er. "Marry Keith and you'll think it did."

Dani stormed off to her room furiously. Before allow-
g herself second thoughts, she dialed Keith's number.
Underneath her anger was the realization that she was
aking a terrible mistake, but Dani wouldn't let herself
dmit it. All that mattered was showing Rand she didn't
are about him or his opinion. He must never know how
eeply he'd hurt her.

The phone rang for a long time before Keith an-
wered. He sounded sulky when he finally did. "Yeah.
Vho is it?"

"It's Dani."

"Oh...uh...good morning, darling." He tried t smother a yawn. "This is a nice surprise."

"I want to talk to you, Keith," she said urgently.

"What time is it?"

"I don't know," Dani answered impatiently. "Wha difference does it make?"

He evidently looked at the clock. "My God, it's th middle of the night! Why aren't you still asleep?"

"I've been up for hours," she said tautly.

He groaned. "You must not have had as much cham pagne as I did. Perhaps I'd better call you back, kitten.'

Dani gritted her teeth. "No, I want to talk to you *now* Keith."

He sighed. "Well, okay, but I warn you, I'm not to coherent until I've had my first cup of coffee. Maybe thi morning a little pick-me-up, too. Frankly, darling, I'm trifle hung over, so if it could wait until—"

"Do you still want to marry me?" Dani interrupte grimly.

There was a small silence, as though he wasn't sur he'd heard correctly. His next words proved it. "Wha did you say?"

"I asked if you want to marry me."

"This is so... I can hardly believe..." He was prac tically stuttering.

"Well, do you or don't you?" she asked curtly.

"Of course I want to marry you! This is the happies moment of my life, baby doll!"

"Okay, come over and we'll make plans."

"Now?"

"Right now," she said firmly. "The sooner the bet ter."

"Certainly, my love. Anything you say." Keith still sounded slightly dazed. "I'll be there as soon as I shower and dress."

Dani did the same, trying not to let panic overtake her. She was committed now. There was no turning back. She tried to tell herself it wasn't such a bad decision. At least Keith loved her. She couldn't spend the rest of her life pining for a man who never had and never would. But to stay in Monaco where she would inevitably run into Rand? To see him with one woman after another? Dani squared her slender shoulders. Why should she run away and hide? He was the one who should be ashamed to face *her*.

She dressed automatically, taking out the first thing she touched in the closet. It wasn't until she was fully dressed that Dani noticed it was the white cotton-and-lace dress she'd worn when Keith took her to Beaulieu. That was the same night she'd had the first searing argument with Rand.

A look of pain crossed her face. She started to change, then decided against it. For a while everything would remind her of Rand. She couldn't afford to give in to memories.

When she looked in the mirror to brush her hair, Dani saw how pale she was. Bright lipstick and a little blusher remedied the condition, but nothing could put the sparkle back in her eyes. She only hoped Keith wouldn't notice.

He didn't seem to. Keith was almost delirious with joy when he arrived a few minutes later. If he still had a hangover it wasn't slowing him down. The first thing he did was grab Dani and kiss her long and passionately.

After an instinctive recoil, she submitted passively, fighting to stem the revulsion that made it hard to breathe. How could she stand a lifetime of this?

Keith was too excited to notice her reaction. The first lengthy embrace was followed by a series of small wet kisses all over her face. They were punctuated by happy exclamations.

"I feel like I'm dreaming, darling! I still can't believe it's true! Tell me you're really mine."

"We have to talk, Keith," Dani said slowly.

His hands bit into her shoulders. "This isn't some kind of joke, is it?" he asked sharply. "You wouldn't play a dirty trick like that, letting me think you cared and then pulling the rug out from under me?"

It sounded terribly reminiscent. No, she couldn't do a rotten thing like that. Only Rand was capable of such tactics.

"I just meant we have to decide some things," Dani said quietly.

His punishing grip relaxed. "Don't scare me like that, baby! I think I just aged ten years."

"Do you suppose I could stay with your mother until we...until the wedding?"

Keith frowned. "Why would you want to move out of here?"

"It's personal."

"You haven't had an argument with Uncle Cleve, have you?"

"No, we haven't argued." Her voice was toneless.

She hadn't even told her grandfather she was leaving yet. But it was impossible to accept his hospitality under the circumstances. Dani only hoped it wouldn't provoke a confrontation with him, too. She didn't intend to indulge in recriminations. What was the use? All she wanted was to get away.

Keith recovered his calm. "Sure you can stay with Mother. I know she'll be delighted to help Uncle Cleve with the wedding, too, so you don't have to bother your pretty little head about it."

"I'd like a small ceremony," Dani said faintly.

"This is a big event, baby face," Keith protested. "All of Monte Carlo will expect to be invited."

That was exactly the kind of spectacle she wanted to avoid. "We'll talk about it later. You'd better alert your mother while I go and pack."

"You want to leave now?"

"Yes."

He looked uneasy. "How did Uncle Cleve take it when you told him we were getting married?"

"I haven't told him yet."

Keith's uneasiness changed to alarm. Then his face relaxed. "You wanted me with you when you broke the good news. That's sweet."

Well, why not, Dani thought fatalistically. Maybe it was the best way. It would give her an excuse to have Keith along when she said goodbye. Her grandfather could scarcely bring up their personal traumas with a third party present.

Cleve was standing at the window with his back to the room. He turned at the sound of their voices and looked at Dani. From his expression, she knew Cleve had heard her argument with Rand and anticipated the result. His face was drawn.

"Dani and I have something to tell you, Uncle Cleve." There was a glint of triumph in Keith's eyes as he put his arm around Dani's shoulders and drew her against his side. "We're getting married, and we'd like your blessing."

Cleve's face hardened into the one his adversaries knew only too well. "You're not asking me, then, you're telling me."

"Well, uh, I wouldn't put it that way." Keith's smile faded. "We just hope you'll be as happy as we are."

Cleve indicated two chairs before sitting down behind his desk. "This is a rather sudden decision, isn't it?"

"I've been asking Dani to marry me since the night I met her. It was love at first sight for me, and I guess I finally wore her down." Keith smiled fatuously at her.

"You decided this today?" Cleve's grave question was directed at Dani.

"Yes." She stared down at her locked fingers.

"I don't think you're in any condition at the moment to make such an important decision, child."

"I'm not a child, and I know what I'm doing!" she declared passionately.

"Do you? I don't think so." Her grandfather's face was impassive.

"Come on, Uncle Cleve, that's not fair," Keith protested. "We love each other."

"Love has been known to fly out the window when the bill collector comes to the door," Cleve remarked ironically. "What do you propose to live on?"

"Well, I thought you'd continue my...uh...income."

"Since you consider it inadequate to support your single life-style, I fail to see how it would stretch to support a wife. I understand you supplement your present income with outside activities." Cleve's eyes held disgust in their depths. "That source of revenue would be cut off once you're married."

Keith's face turned an ugly, mottled red. "Rand's been telling you lies about me again," he muttered.

"You needn't concern yourself with our finances," Dani broke in impatiently. "We don't intend to take a penny from you."

Cleve's gaze held Keith's. "Is that the way you feel, too?"

"Well, I wouldn't say... That is, Dani's a little naive about money."

She looked at him indignantly. "How can you say that? I told you I wasn't going to accept anything from Grandfather, and you said you felt the same way!"

"I'm glad to hear that, Keith, because if you marry Dani, you'll never get another cent from me." Cleve's voice was like steel. "And don't plan on waiting until I die, because I'll cut her out of my will the day she marries you."

Dani sprang to her feet. "That's a perfect example of your checkbook mentality! Do you think we care about your threats? Tell him, Keith!"

His eyes wavered away from hers. "Well, if Uncle Cleve feels that strongly about it..." At her strangled exclamation, Keith said placatingly, "I'm only thinking of you, darling. It wouldn't be fair to ask you to give up a fortune."

Dani stared at him as though he'd turned into a snake. "Rand was right," she whispered. "It was only the money you were interested in."

"You know that's not true, kitten. I'm crazy about you. Maybe if you reasoned with Uncle Cleve..." He sidled toward the door. "I'll leave you alone to talk to him."

Cleve broke the heavy silence after Keith left. "I'm sorry, my dear." He sighed deeply. "I'd have given anything to spare you this."

Her body was rigid. "Now I know how you got m
father to leave my mother—by threatening to cut off th
money. It must give you a lot of pleasure to play God
Why didn't you wait until *after* I married Keith so his
tory could repeat itself?"

Cleve's face was white, but he didn't flinch from he
furious words. "I had to do what was best for you."

"You don't care about me! You just like to move peo
ple around like pawns in a chess game," she said wildly
too hurt and humiliated to be fair. "You knew what Keith
would do, just as you knew what your son would do. You
use your money as a drug to make people weak. That'
what you planned for me too—a gradual dependenc
until I was as malleable as all your other clay dolls. Onl
this time it didn't work. I'm leaving here and I don't eve
want to see you again!"

Tears blinded Dani as she ran out of the room an
down the hall. She didn't see Rand until he put out a
arm to stop her.

"I want to talk to you," he said curtly.

Her eyes were too blurred to see the deep lines in hi
face. The autocratic tone was all that registered. Sh
jerked her arm away. "Go talk to your co-conspirator
The two of you can have another good laugh at my ex
pense!"

Rand frowned as he watched her run down the hall
His face was ravaged as he went into the den an
slammed the door. "What the hell happened here?" h
demanded of Cleve.

Dani had pulled her suitcase out of the closet and wa
flinging clothes into it when she stopped suddenly. Wha
was Rand doing back here? He and her grandfather wer
a dangerous combination. What devious plot were the
hatching to trap her again? This time she was going to b
forewarned.

Dani walked silently down the hall and deliberately
ood outside the den door listening. She suffered
rough Cleve's description of the scene that had taken
ace.

"Well, at least now she knows we weren't waging a
ndetta against Keith," Rand said when he finished.
She found out for herself what a worthless skunk he is."

"It was the *way* she found out. It was terribly painful
r her, but there was nothing else I could do," Cleve said
lplessly.

"She'll understand when she calms down."

"No, I've lost her." There was suffering in the older
an's voice. "She won't ever let me see her again."

"Because you saved her from a fortune hunter?" Rand
ked incredulously. "How can she hold that against
u?"

"It's more than that. Dani thinks I broke up her
other's marriage in the same way."

"And you didn't tell her the truth?" Rand sounded
traged.

Dani stiffened outside the door. Was she finally going
hear it?

"I couldn't. She'd been hurt too much already."

Rand swore violently. "Everybody has except your
n! She has to be told that her father wasn't much bet-
r than Keith. No, dammit, he was worse! Keith ro-
ances older women who know the score. Danny
duced and then ran out on an innocent girl without
eling a twinge of conscience."

"If you had a son like that, would you want to tell his
ughter about him?"

"You don't have any choice. Dani thinks you're a
onster, and her parents were tragic victims. The only
ay she'll change her mind is if she finds out that Danny
d when he told you he and Elizabeth *both* wanted the
nnulment."

"Elizabeth never believed me," Cleve said somberly.

"Because you didn't make Danny tell her himself, lik
a man! He went back to college and let you make his ex
planations. Of course Elizabeth didn't believe you. Sh
didn't *want* to believe you!"

Dani was transfixed outside the door. So *that* was th
true story! Her poor naive mother had wasted her whol
life idealizing a man who had betrayed her. At least sh
never knew. But her misplaced loyalty had cut her of
from someone who was worthy of her love. Dani woul
never have known her grandfather, either, if it hadn'
been for a twist of fate.

Rand was having trouble controlling his frustration
"You know if Dani walks out that door it's forever. Hov
can you let her go when you love her so much?"

"You love her just as much," Cleve answered quietly
"What have *you* done to keep her here?"

Dani's heart started to pound so hard that it was al
most audible. It couldn't be true! Her grandfather mus
be mistaken. She held her breath as she waited for Rand'
answer.

"All the wrong things." He groaned. "Dani's con
vinced I've pulled every dirty trick to get her to stay fo
your sake."

"Have you told her you love her?"

"She wouldn't believe that, either."

"You don't know that."

"It wouldn't do any good. Dani's attracted to me, bu
she doesn't love me. I can't settle for that, Cleve. I wan
to marry her!" There was anguish in Rand's voice.

"I suggest you tell *her* instead of me," the older ma
said gravely.

"She'd laugh in my face!"

"You've never been a coward, Rand."

"Don't you think I'd ask her if there was even a ghos
of a chance? You just don't know what you're talkin

about!'' The thick carpet muffled his footsteps as he stalked to the door.

Dani had been listening in a kind of trance. Rand collided with her when he charged out of the room.

He put his hands on her arms to steady her. ''Sorry,'' he muttered. It was almost a growl.

As she stared up at him in a daze, his hands tightened. He searched her face for a long moment, as though committing it to memory, then released her and started down the hall.

''Rand, wait!'' she called, but he didn't stop or turn around.

Dani was torn in two different directions. She had wronged both men, but the injury to her grandfather was the most grievous. She went into the den, scarcely knowing how to begin.

''Why didn't you let me make my own decision?'' she blurted out. ''Couldn't you see I wanted to love you?''

Cleve's pain deepened, but he returned her gaze steadily. ''Keith would only have brought you misery, Dani.''

''I'm not talking about *him*.'' She dismissed Keith impatiently. ''I meant my father! How could you let me go on sanctifying him and blaming you for everything but the Second World War?''

Cleve's face was a study in conflicting emotions. ''How did— You overheard us.''

''A good thing, too,'' she said impatiently. ''But I shouldn't have to listen at doors.''

''I couldn't blacken my own son's reputation,'' Cleve said slowly. ''Your mother told you he was a wonderful man. You deserved to go on thinking that, to love him like the father he never was.''

''I didn't love him. I never knew him. You're the one I love!'' Dani threw her arms around her grandfather's neck.

He clasped her tightly, too choked up to speak. For a long minute they just clung to each other. Cleve's voice was hoarse with emotion when he finally said, "Thank you, child. You've just made me the happiest man in the whole world."

Dani's tremulous laughter eased the tense moment. "That's what Keith said when I told him I'd marry him. At least I can believe you."

Cleve smiled tenderly. "You can make someone else this happy."

Dani's eyes were like stars. "I never knew!"

"Why don't you go and tell him?"

"Would you mind terribly? I . . . I might be gone for a while."

Cleve's eyes glinted with laughter. "I'll have the chauffeur bring the car around."

Rand took so long to answer the door that Dani was afraid he wasn't home. Frustration built inside her. Why did everything always conspire to keep them apart?

As she was about to give up, the door opened. Rand had a highball in one hand. His shirt was unbuttoned almost to the waist and his hair was ruffled, as though he'd raked his fingers through it repeatedly. He was a far cry from his usual, unrumpled perfection, but to Dani he looked like a knight in shining armor.

"I thought maybe you weren't home," she said, breaking the silence that had developed between them.

"I wasn't going to answer the door," he replied curtly.

"Oh. May I come in?" she asked when he didn't invite her.

He grudgingly opened the door wider. "I suppose you've come to say goodbye. It wasn't necessary."

"No, it wasn't, because I'm not leaving."

Something flared in his eyes, then was quickly extinguished. "Don't tell me you and Keith made up."

"Why would I want to marry a fortune hunter?"

Rand's face became a little less grim. "I'm glad you saw the light. Maybe now you'll stop kicking Cleve around like a football."

"I would have sooner if you'd told me the kind of man my father was. How was I supposed to know?"

"Thank God Cleve came to his senses," Rand said with satisfaction.

"He didn't tell me. I listened at the door," Dani said complacently. "I heard everything you said."

Rand looked at her warily. "Everything?"

"There were a lot of things you didn't tell me," she remarked conversationally.

"Nothing important." He jammed his hands in his pockets and turned to look out the window.

Dani walked slowly toward him. "You mean you've changed your mind?"

"We've said everything we had to say to each other. Go back to the villa, Dani."

"Not until you tell me you don't want me anymore."

His rigid control snapped as he turned around and gazed at her longingly. "What man wouldn't want you?" he asked hoarsely.

She smiled beguilingly. "A lot of men. There's Winston Churchill, and Charlie Chaplin, and Socrates."

Rand's tension slowly drained away as he looked deeply into her eyes. "They're all dead and I'm alive."

Dani discovered just how alive when he reached out for her compulsively. He held her so tightly that she could almost feel the lifeblood pulsing through his hard body. The kisses he rained over her face and neck were frantic in their hunger.

"Do you know what it's like to want someone so much you ache from it?" he muttered with his lips against her temple.

"Not until I met you," she whispered.

"I said it wasn't enough, but it will have to be," he groaned. "Maybe in time you'll grow to love me, sweetheart."

Dani cradled his face in her palms, looking at him tenderly. "I couldn't love you any more than I already do."

His tawny eyes lit with joy. "I know I can satisfy you, angel, but you mean it isn't just . . ."

"That, too," she murmured as she eased her hands inside his shirt and raked her nails lightly through the crisp dark hair on his chest.

He swung her into his arms and carried her into the bedroom, gazing deeply into her eyes. When he put her on her feet, Dani's legs felt weak.

"You look like a bride," he said huskily, touching the delicate lace around her hips.

"That's what I've dreamed of being." She put her arms around his neck. "Your bride."

While his mouth covered hers, Rand slid her zipper down and unhooked her bra. His hands stroked her bare back sensuously, leaving a tingling excitement in their wake. They slipped inside the waistband of her panties and cupped her bottom to lift her slightly into the juncture of his taut loins.

Rand's unmistakable passion lit a torch that ignited Dani. Her hands moved restlessly over his broad shoulders and up the column of his neck to clutch at his thick hair.

Rand groaned and plunged his tongue into her mouth as he slipped her dress off. His hands followed it as it fell to the floor, caressing her breasts, her waist, her hips. She started to tremble as he bent his head to kiss each aching nipple. When he removed her panties and placed her on the bed, Dani held out her arms in a mute invitation.

He knelt over her, stroking her thighs as he gazed at her with almost primitive desire. "I didn't know anyone could be this perfect," he muttered. He kissed the flat plane of her stomach, then dipped his tongue into her navel. His mouth drifted lower, driving Dani to a fever pitch.

"Please, Rand, I need you so," she begged.

Her soft entreaty snapped his restraint. He flung off his clothes and returned to cover her body with his.

Dani cried out with joy at the piercing wonder of him. Rand was the center of her world, the driving force that created spiral after spiral of mounting rapture. It climaxed in a burst of heat that warmed and soothed her whole body. She relaxed slowly in his arms as the throbbing died to a muted pleasure.

They were both too contented to move for a long time. Then they kissed tenderly and whispered all the things they'd never said before. It was a sweet time of sharing.

Finally Rand said, "How would you like to borrow the *Sea Siren* for our honeymoon?"

"That whole big ship just for the two of us?"

He feathered his fingertips lightly over her breasts. "Do you have someone you want to invite along?"

Dani smiled seductively. "Not if you think you can keep me amused."

"A hundred different ways, my love." Rand's eyes started to smolder as he fitted her body more closely to his.

Silhouette Special Edition

COMING NEXT MONTH

FOR NOW, FOREVER—Nora Roberts
Anna Whitfield couldn't have been less suited to become
Daniel MacGregor's heir-producing, child-rearing wife if she'd tried.
So why was the empire-builder moving heaven and earth to prove she was
his perfect mate?

SHADOW ON THE SUN—Maggi Charles
Although researcher Pamela Merrill and plantation owner Miguel Rivero
had barely met, their blazing passion rivaled the tropical sun. Yet Miguel's
tangled past shrouded their future in shadows.

ROSE IN BLOOM—Andrea Edwards
A place for everything and everything in its place: that was Rose Landen's
motto. Until devil-may-care Rick Weiller nonchalantly scrambled her
orderly existence with his soul-stirring kisses!

THE EXECUTIVES—Monica Barrie
When Ryan's seductive tactics distracted her from a crucial buy out, Talia
learned the hard way that mixing ruthless business and heady pleasure
often spelled romantic disaster.

GOLDEN FIRESTORM—Anne Lacey
Wynne knew that Indian activist Hawk Saddler was fiercely proud—
probably too proud to accept her and her "half-breed" children. Still, she
dared to dream their fiery attraction would burn away his doubts.

OBJECT OF DESIRE—Jennifer West
To American aristocrat David Winthrop, Angelina Zarsuela was wild,
exotic and utterly desirable. Though her dubious ancestry endangered his
blueblood ambitions, he had to have her...no matter what the cost.

AVAILABLE NOW:

FORGIVE AND FORGET
Tracy Sinclair

HONEYMOON FOR ONE
Carole Halston

A MATCH FOR ALWAYS
Maralys Wills

ONE MAN'S LOVE
Lisa Jackson

SOMETHING WORTH KEEPING
Kathleen Eagle

BETWEEN THE RAINDROPS
Mary Lynn Baxter